STUART GIBBS

spy school
AT SEA

A spy school **NOVEL**

Simon & Schuster Books for Young Readers

New York   London   Toronto   Sydney   New Delhi

SIMON & SCHUSTER BOOKS FOR YOUNG READERS

An imprint of Simon & Schuster Children's Publishing Division

1230 Avenue of the Americas, New York, New York 10020

This book is a work of fiction. Any references to historical events, real people, or real places are used fictitiously. Other names, characters, places, and events are products of the author's imagination, and any resemblance to actual events or places or persons, living or dead, is entirely coincidental.

Text © 2021 by Stuart Gibbs

Cover illustration and book design by Lucy Ruth Cummins © 2021 by Simon & Schuster, Inc.

All rights reserved, including the right of reproduction in whole or in part in any form.

SIMON & SCHUSTER BOOKS FOR YOUNG READERS and related marks are trademarks of Simon & Schuster, Inc.

For information about special discounts for bulk purchases, please contact Simon & Schuster Special Sales at 1-866-506-1949 or business@simonandschuster.com.

The Simon & Schuster Speakers Bureau can bring authors to your live event. For more information or to book an event, contact the Simon & Schuster Speakers Bureau at 1-866-248-3049 or visit our website at www.simonspeakers.com.

Also available in a Simon & Schuster Books for Young Readers hardcover edition

The text for this book was set in Adobe Garamond Pro.

Map art by Ryan Thompson

Manufactured in the United States of America

0722 OFF

First Simon & Schuster Books for Young Readers paperback edition September 2022

10 9 8 7 6 5 4 3 2 1

Library of Congress Control Number 2021938202

ISBN 9781534479432 (hardcover)

ISBN 9781534479449 (pbk)

ISBN 9781534479456 (ebook)

For Lennlee Keep and David Levinson.
Thanks for being my friends for all these years.

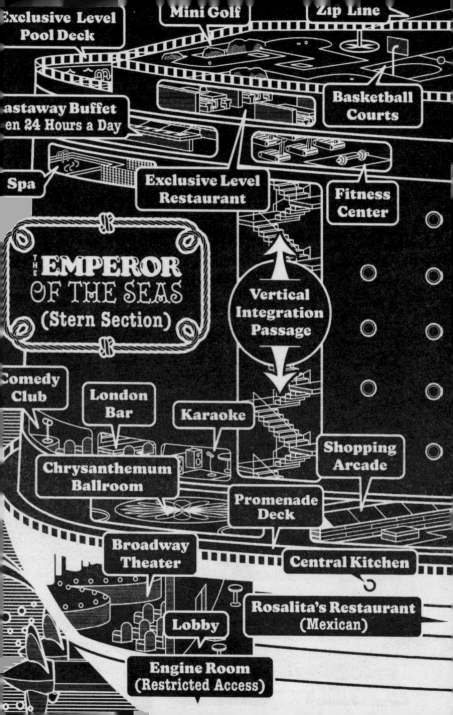

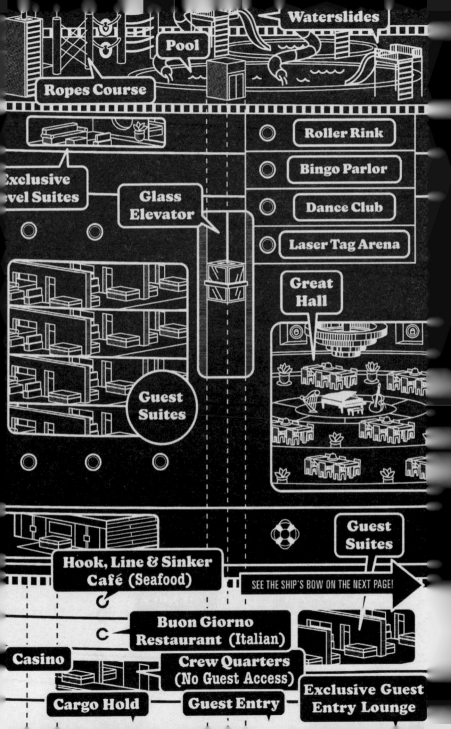

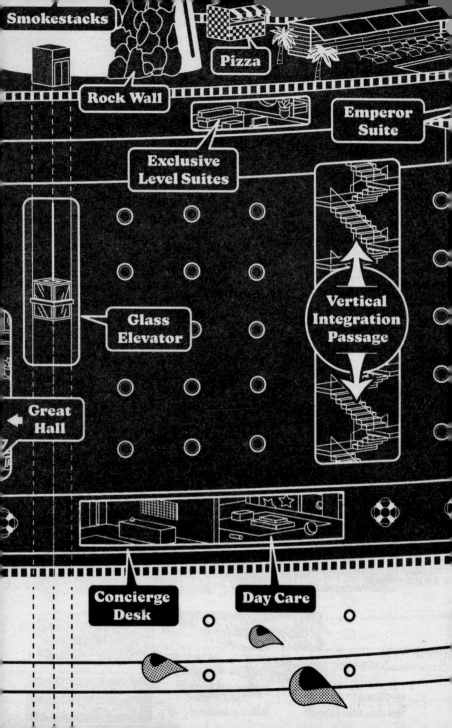

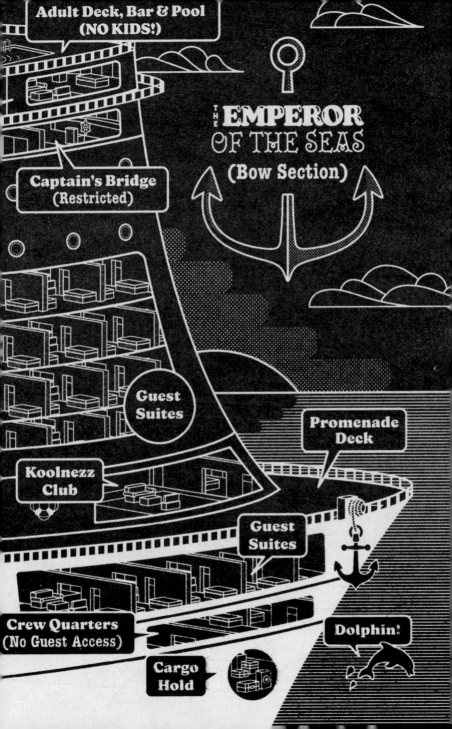

Contents

1: DEBRIEFING   3

2: PREPARATION   20

3: EMBARKATION   30

4: ILLEGAL ENTRY   48

5: REUNION   60

6: COUNTERFEIT PIRACY   78

7: CONFRONTATION   97

8: SURVIVAL AT SEA   108

9: HALLUCINATION   118

10: CONFRONTATION   127

11: REHABILITATION   134

12: REUNION   144

13: DISILLUSIONMENT   155

14: MUSICAL THEATER   163

15: EVASIVE ACTION   177

16: RECOVERY   187

17: ORDERS   195

18: INVESTIGATION   200

19: HOT PURSUIT   211

20: EVACUATION   221

21: INTERROGATION   231

22: APPREHENSION   243

23: WATER SPORTS   253

24: EMERGENCY PLANNING   267

25: VOLUNTEERING   277

26: EXPLANATION   285

27: MUTINY   298

28: COOL UNDER PRESSURE   314

29: WRAP-UP   327

spy school
AT SEA

May 14

To: Principal ███████████
From: ████████████████, CIA Deputy Director of Operations
Re: Operation Deadly Manatee

Dear ████████████████,

As you are aware, in the course of defeating the evil consortium
██████████████████ last month, agent-in-training ████████████
██████████ uncovered evidence that your former student ████████
██████████ may have recently visited Nicaragua. Our field agents have
now confirmed this to be true and have a lead as to his whereabouts.
Since we suspect that ████████████████ is up to no good, as
usual, tracking him down is a priority for the Agency. Therefore, we are
immediately launching Operation Deadly Manatee.

However, there are elements of this mission that will necessitate
activating some of your agents-in-training yet again: ██████████
██████████████████████, and ██████████████.
I would like to meet with them in your office, along with Agents
██████████████ and ████████████████ at your earliest
convenience tomorrow.

I know that this is a busy time at the academy and that it is generally
frowned upon to release students for active missions. But this order
comes straight from the top. Director ████████████████ has been
very impressed with the performance of these agents-in-training, which
is certainly a testament to your institution. (And letting them participate
in this mission might help Director ████████████████ forget that
you've had a few students defect to work for the bad guys lately.)

I will see you in your office promptly at 1500 hours.

Sincerely,

████████████████

P.S. If you do feel obligated to provide an assortment of cheeses again,
please make sure that they have all been properly refrigerated this
time. The last time I came to your office, I consumed a bit of rancid Brie,
which made me terribly ill and ultimately compromised Operation Feisty
Gerbil.

DEBRIEFING

Office of the Principal
Nathan Hale Building
The Academy of Espionage
Washington, DC
May 15
1500 hours

The principal was acting stranger than usual.

In my sixteen months at the CIA's Academy of Espionage, I had seen the principal display many aspects of his personality, none of which were good. He had been angry, bitter, paranoid, churlish, jealous, contemptuous, ornery, disdainful, mercurial, obnoxious, flummoxed, confused, passive-aggressive, and just plain mean. But the day I was assigned to Operation Deadly Manatee, his behavior was the most unsettling of all.

He was trying to be nice.

With most people, of course, this would have been a good thing. But with the principal it felt wrong, as though he was fighting every natural instinct he had. Watching him try to be nice was like watching a tiger try to eat a salad.

"Benjamin!" he exclaimed upon opening the door to his office, with what was obviously forced enthusiasm. "Such a pleasure to see you!"

"Er . . . thanks," I said warily.

"Please come in. Make yourself comfortable. Everyone else will be here soon." The principal waved me into his office and attempted to smile. It was evident that the man hadn't smiled very much and wasn't quite sure how to do it. Instead of appearing friendly and welcoming, he looked like someone suffering from a bad case of indigestion.

I cautiously stepped into his office—or rather, what remained of it. Nine months earlier, I had accidentally blown up the principal's office with a mortar round. (Which explained some of the principal's general ill temper toward me, but not all of it.) Budget issues and red tape had kept the repairs from proceeding quickly, forcing the principal to temporarily relocate his office to a broom closet, which he had been extremely peeved about. When I had been notified to report to his original office, I expected to find that it had been restored to its previous condition.

This was not the case. In fact, almost no work had been done on the office at all. The entire exterior wall was still missing. A haphazard attempt had been made to reinforce that side of the room with a spindly framework of two-by-fours, but there was still a gaping hole—and since we were on the fifth floor of the Nathan Hale Administration Building, this meant that a misstep could result in a quick plummet down to the campus quadrangle. The furniture hadn't been replaced and was all slightly charred, while what remained of the carpet smelled like a doused campfire. The principal's beloved desk, which had been incinerated in the blast, had been replaced by a wobbly piece of plywood laid across two sawhorses—although the principal had managed to procure a new rolling chair.

"I recognize that it's still a work in progress," the principal said weakly. "They won't be able to start the repairs until December. But I just couldn't take working in that broom closet anymore. And now that it's spring, it's not so bad. I kind of like the open design. All the fresh air is invigorating."

"I can see that," I said as supportively as I could. The hole in the wall certainly let in plenty of fresh air. And pigeons. A dozen of them were roosting in what remained of the ceiling, which meant that a good amount of the floor was speckled with pigeon droppings.

The principal ignored them and made a show of taking a deep breath. "Ah. It's far better than all the stale, recirculated air you'd get in a normal office. I suppose, in a way, I ought to thank you for destroying this place." He attempted another smile for me, although I had the sense that he didn't feel like smiling at all, and that he was only playing at being nice to mask his natural enraged state.

I wondered what was going on.

There was a knock at the door. The principal started back for it, intending to open it, but this proved unnecessary when the hinges simply tore free from the damaged frame, and the door toppled into the office.

This revealed four more people standing in the doorway, all of whom had apparently also been summoned to the meeting.

Two were fellow students from spy school: Mike Brezinski and Erica Hale. Mike had been my best friend in my normal life, back before I had been recruited to the academy. I was supposed to keep the academy's existence a secret from Mike (as well as everyone else on earth), but he had eventually figured out where I was really going and been rewarded for his cleverness by getting recruited.

Meanwhile, Erica had known about the academy for her entire life, as she was a legacy. She came from a long line of spies and had been training since a very young age to follow in her family's footsteps. Thus, she was significantly more talented than any of her fellow trainees at school—and most actual spies as well.

The other two invitees were Erica's parents. Catherine Hale was an exceptionally talented agent for Britain's MI6—and a doting mother. Somehow she found a way to balance both lives and was as adept at thwarting criminals as she was at baking cookies.

Meanwhile, Alexander Hale was a fraud. Until very recently, his greatest skill as a spy had been convincing people that he was skilled as a spy. This had worked for him for quite a long time, and he had been respected and admired by his peers, until he was finally found out and disgraced. Since then, he had managed to redeem himself slightly, after ending up on a few missions with me—along with Catherine, Erica, and Mike.

"Greetings!" the principal exclaimed as pleasantly as he could. "Welcome, everyone! I'm glad you could make it!"

The other four responded to this in varying ways. Catherine and Erica both regarded the principal suspiciously, probably wondering what could explain his friendliness, while Mike was more cautious, as though he suspected that perhaps the real principal had been kidnapped and replaced with an impostor. Alexander didn't appear to notice any difference at all.

"It's good to see you, too," he said, shaking the principal's hand. "I like the new layout of the office. Very spacious. So, what's the reason for this get-together?"

"I'd be happy to explain that." A woman I had never met brusquely swept into the room. She appeared to be in her forties, wore a tailored business suit, and had a briefcase handcuffed to her right wrist. She didn't seem at all surprised by the state of the principal's office, which indicated to me that she had been there before. "I'm Indira Kapoor, deputy director of operations at the CIA. I've been paying close attention to your careers, and I must say, most of you have done some very impressive work." She turned slightly away from Alexander as she said this, as if to make it clear that the phrase "most of you" didn't apply to him.

Alexander appeared not to notice this, either. "Why, thank you," he said, flashing Indira a suave smile.

Alexander was a very handsome man, and I had seen his smile make other women go weak in the knees, but Indira was impervious to it. Instead, she kept her gaze locked on Erica, Mike, and me. "I recognize that, due to many mistakes on the part of the Agency, the three of you have ended up on missions far earlier than would normally be recommended for young agents. But you have all handled yourselves capably and acted with ingenuity and skill, which is obviously a testament to the education you have received at this institution." She shifted her attention to the principal. "So I suppose I owe you congratulations as well."

The principal now flashed what appeared to be an actual smile. "Thank you, Deputy Kapoor. I've done my best to whip these junior agents into shape." He plopped down into his desk chair and waved the rest of us to a charbroiled sofa.

I suddenly understood the reason for the principal's shift in personality. *We were making him look good.*

To my side, Erica bristled with anger. There were plenty of good things about the Academy of Espionage, but the principal wasn't one of them. If anything, he'd been a deterrent to our education. The idea that he was getting credit for anything we had accomplished was upsetting enough to me; for Erica, who had achieved her excellence in espionage with zero help from the principal, it was infuriating.

Her mother was aware of this as well. I saw her catch Erica's eye and mouth, *Let it go.*

Erica petulantly sat on the blackened sofa, sending a small puff of soot into the air. Mike and I took spots beside her. The sofa still reeked of burnt leather from the mortar blast.

Catherine sat primly in a gently seared armchair close by.

Alexander stayed by the makeshift desk, reaching into a bowl of jelly beans that the principal kept there. Then he made a face of disgust. "Er . . . do you have any other snacks? A pigeon appears to have pooped in these."

Deputy Kapoor ignored this, setting her briefcase on the desk and unlocking it from her wrist. "The reason I'm here with all of you now is directly related to the lead you discovered on your most recent mission, indicating the latest whereabouts of Murray Hill."

I sat up at the mention of the name. Murray had been a fellow student at spy school when I had arrived, but I had discovered he was working as a mole for a covert organization known as SPYDER. Over the next sixteen months, Murray had double-crossed both the CIA and SPYDER multiple times, doing everything he could to stay alive and get rich. I had last encountered him making a shady deal for an organization known as the Croatoan, which we had subsequently defeated, although Murray had escaped. However, I had recovered a piece of evidence that indicated where he might have been spending his time. . . .

"Is he in Nicaragua?" Erica asked, intrigued.

"We believe so." Deputy Kapoor entered a combination to unlock her briefcase, then lifted out five dossiers. "We've had a team working down there, following up on your lead, and while they haven't seen Hill, they *have* heard rumors about his whereabouts." She began to hand out the dossiers, first to Catherine, then to Mike, then me.

My dossier was a thickly stuffed manila envelope stamped with TOP SECRET. HIGHLY CLASSIFIED INFORMATION.

HAND-DELIVER ONLY TO BENJAMIN RIPLEY. OPERATION DEADLY MANATEE.

"Deadly Manatee?" Mike asked, sounding disappointed. "Manatees aren't even remotely deadly."

"Of course they are," Deputy Kapoor replied. "They have razor-sharp teeth, and schools of them have been known to skeletonize a human being within a minute. You don't get much deadlier than that."

"I'm afraid you're thinking of piranhas," Catherine said diplomatically. "Manatees are rotund, herbivorous mammals also known as sea cows. They're quite docile."

"Oh," Deputy Kapoor said, looking slightly embarrassed. "Really?"

"The only way one of them could ever kill a human is if you dropped it off a tall building onto someone's head," Mike informed her. "Don't you have any biologists at the CIA?"

"We're not a zoo," Deputy Kapoor said testily. "We're an espionage organization. And besides, I'm not in charge of naming operations. That's the Department of Mission Nomenclature. If you have a problem, you can take it up with them." She quickly handed off the remaining dossiers to Erica and Alexander.

"Um . . . ," the principal said meekly. "I think you forgot me. I didn't get a dossier."

"Why would you get a dossier?" Deputy Kapoor asked. "You're not going on assignment. *They* are."

"I just figured, since they're my students, and I'm responsible for their education—"

"That's not the way it's done," Deputy Kapoor interrupted. "The nature of this mission is highly classified. In fact, I'll need you to leave this office while we discuss it."

"What?" The principal snapped to his feet so quickly that his brand-new desk chair rolled across the room behind him and tumbled through the gap in his wall. The principal was so upset, he didn't even notice. "But this is *my* office!"

From outside, there was a distant yelp of surprise, followed by the distinct sound of an office chair thudding into the quadrangle lawn.

Deputy Kapoor said, "We need a secure place to discuss this mission. When you volunteered your office, I thought you understood how these things worked."

The principal was definitely upset to be cut out of the meeting; I could see the rage in his eyes. He simmered for a moment, then managed to tamp down his emotions in front of Deputy Kapoor and forced a smile. "I *do* understand," he said through gritted teeth. "I just thought that I might be included this time, seeing as I have molded these students into the fine agents that they are today."

"No," Deputy Kapoor said firmly. "Now, if you'll please leave us, I'd like to proceed with this debriefing."

"Fine," the principal said peevishly. He stormed out of the room, shooting me an angry glare on the way. If his office door had still been attached to the doorframe, he probably would have slammed it.

While all this had been going on, everyone else had opened their dossiers and begun examining the contents. Even though we were all going on the exact same mission, Erica and Catherine were pointedly holding their official orders so that no one else could see them, indicating that we might not all be getting the same information. I noticed Erica look up from hers and give me a glance of concern.

"Oh," Catherine said suddenly. "This is intriguing."

She was holding a big, glossy brochure. I found one in my dossier as well and pulled it out.

It was for a cruise ship. The *Emperor of the Seas*. There was a photograph of it on the front cover, docked at a tropical island. The ship was absolutely enormous, eighteen stories tall and nearly a quarter mile in length. It looked like a floating office building.

"I've heard about this ship!" Mike exclaimed. "It's the biggest cruise ship ever constructed!"

"That's correct," Deputy Kapoor agreed, looking pleased

by Mike's knowledge. "It's the first of a line of mega-cruisers being built by a Chinese conglomerate in Beijing. The *Emperor* launched last winter and has been cruising in the South Pacific, but it is currently en route to the Caribbean. Its last port of call, ten days ago, was in Hawaii, and it will be making some stops in Central America before passing through the Panama Canal."

"I assume one of those stops is Nicaragua," Erica deduced.

"Yes. Our agents on the ground have learned that Murray Hill plans to board that ship in the port of Corinto tomorrow morning."

"Why?" Alexander asked.

"We have no idea," Deputy Kapoor admitted. "Which is why we are sending all of you to Nicaragua. It's a joint operation between us and MI6. You'll be boarding that ship in Corinto tomorrow as well."

"We get to go on the *Emperor of the Seas*?" Mike exclaimed. "Awesome! It's supposed to be the most amazing ship ever built! There's a bunch of swimming pools and miniature golf and a ropes course and a rock wall and a water park!" He excitedly pointed to a photograph from the top deck of the ship: a spaghetti tangle of waterslides that dumped into a large pool.

It looked like a whole lot of fun.

Deputy Kapoor gave Mike a sharp look. "The purpose is

for you to be investigating Murray Hill, not going on water-slides."

"Do you want us to blend in and look like normal tourists?" Mike asked.

"Of course."

"Well, normal tourists go on waterslides."

Deputy Kapoor frowned. "I suppose you have a point."

"Are you sure this is prudent?" Catherine asked her, then looked to Mike, Erica, and me. "I know that you children have served your country well and faced considerable danger on several other missions. But you're still . . . well, *children*. Michael, you're only in your first year of training here. And Benjamin, your instructors still won't let you carry a firearm for fear that you'll accidentally shoot yourself with it."

I didn't take offense at this. I was in no hurry to carry a firearm for the exact same reason. And while I had been proud to serve my country on those missions, I hadn't been a big fan of the "considerable danger" portions of them.

It was only four weeks since I had thwarted the last enemy plot, in which I had nearly been blown to pieces— along with a significant chunk of Washington, DC. That had landed me in the hospital for a few days with some cracked ribs. They had healed, but I was still supposed to be taking it easy.

Deputy Kapoor said, "The Agency is not taking this

decision lightly. However, we have our reasons for activating the children. First, they have faced Murray Hill many times and are familiar with his behavior." She turned to me. "In fact, Agent Ripley, you probably understand Murray Hill better than anyone else at this agency."

"That's right," Mike said supportively. "You probably know what Murray's thinking before *he* knows what he's thinking."

I started to deny this, as Murray Hill had hoodwinked me plenty of times, but Deputy Kapoor continued talking before I could. "Secondly, this cruise ship has been designed for *families*. It turns out, there are many places on the ship where adults aren't even allowed to go, such as the teen clubs. And Murray is a teenager—albeit an extremely unscrupulous one. If he ventures into any of these adult-free areas, we need agents who can follow him without causing alarm."

"Good thinking," Alexander Hale said. "Only . . . don't you think it will look suspicious for the children to be traveling alone?"

Deputy Kapoor gave him a stern look, indicating she was disappointed that he hadn't grasped the nature of the mission yet. "They won't be alone. They'll be posing as part of a family. With *you*. You and Catherine will pose as the parents, while Erica, Mike, and Ben will pretend to be your children. Er, well, Erica won't be pretending, as she actually *is* your child. But the boys will be posing as your sons."

"We get to be brothers?" Mike asked, thrilled. "Best mission ever!"

"But we don't look alike," I pointed out. "And we don't look like the Hales, either."

"You're adopted," Deputy Kapoor replied. "Which also explains how you can be so close in age."

"This is so cool!" Mike exclaimed. "I always wanted a brother!"

"You *have* a brother," I reminded him.

"A *good* brother," he corrected. "One who doesn't pin me down and fart on my head."

Inside all of our dossiers were elaborately detailed biographies of the characters we would be portraying. I quickly perused them. We would all be posing as the Rotko family, since the Hales already had aliases under that name. Erica would resume being Sasha Rotko, who she had impersonated on previous missions, while her parents would be Bill and Carol. Mike's alias was Jack Rotko, a gifted middle-school athlete, while mine was Quincy Rotko. I was thirteen—which made sense, as it was my own age—and I was captain of the math team at St. Smithen's Science Academy for Boys and Girls—which also made sense, as St. Smithen's was the cover for spy school, and I was quite gifted in mathematics. (Among other things, my math skills gave me an unusually accurate sense of time, and so I knew that we had been in our meeting for thirteen minutes and twenty-seven seconds without even looking at my watch.)

"I'm an accountant?" Alexander said disappointedly, perusing his own file. "That doesn't sound very exciting."

"It's not supposed to be exciting," Catherine told him. "You're supposed to blend in and not draw attention to yourself."

"So what are you?" Alexander asked.

"An ophthalmologist."

"You're a doctor?" Alexander cried jealously. "Awww. Can't I be an ophthalmologist too?"

"Do you know what part of the body an ophthalmologist studies?" Deputy Kapoor asked.

"The spleen?" Alexander guessed.

"Not even close," Deputy Kapoor said. "Which is why we made you an accountant."

"This is going to be great!" Mike was so thrilled, he was practically vibrating. "We get to go on another mission—on the coolest cruise ship in the world. And I get a fake brother." He turned to Erica exuberantly. "And a fake sister, too!"

Erica gave us a faint smile in return, as though she wasn't nearly as enthusiastic about this as Mike.

Which was understandable. Erica and I had an unusual relationship. I'd had a crush on her since the very first moment

I saw her at the academy. Meanwhile, she had thought I was a pathetic loser who'd wash out within a week—if I didn't get killed first. Over the ensuing months we had ended up on several missions together, during which she had slowly come to respect me—and even consider me a friend. However, this made her extremely uncomfortable, as she believed relationships were a liability in the spy business. (Her parents were a prime example of this; being spies had been hard on their relationship, leading to a divorce, although they had recently been trying to work things out.) So Erica often dealt with her feelings by pretending they didn't exist. On our last mission, she had actually hugged me, but since then, she had been avoiding me completely.

So, in theory, going on a cruise with her should have been a good thing. As my fake sister, she would be forced to spend plenty of time with me—and I had heard that cruises could be very romantic. The glossy brochure for the *Emperor* was filled with photos of loving couples walking hand in hand on tropical beaches and standing at the railing of the ship, staring out at the sunset.

But going on a cruise with Erica *wasn't* a good thing. Not at this point. In fact, it promised to be a disaster.

Because, for the first time since I had met her, I wanted to avoid Erica Hale.

PREPARATION

Armistead Dormitory

Academy of Espionage

May 15

1600 hours

"I can't go on this mission," I told Mike.

"Come on," he insisted. "It's going to be great. Look! The ship has a roller rink!" He held up the brochure to show me.

He was seated on my bed in my dorm room, eagerly leafing through the brochure, having spent an entire ninety seconds packing for the mission. (He had simply crammed all his bathing suits, shorts, and T-shirts in a duffel bag.) I was taking a bit longer to get packed, as I was busy panicking.

"You and I screwed up big-time," I reminded him. "And when Erica finds out, she's gonna kill us."

A few weeks earlier, we had accidentally let Erica's younger sister, Trixie, know that everyone else in her immediate family was a secret agent. And her grandfather, too. Up until then, the family had kept Trixie in the dark about this, believing that it was safer for her not to know their secrets. Trixie had been shocked and dismayed. (A connoisseur of spy movies, she had always imagined that she had great potential to become a secret agent, so it was upsetting to discover that her skills were massively inferior to her sister's.) Still, she had handled it well, promising not to tell her family that we had spilled the beans—and insisting that Mike owed her dinner. This last part wasn't really a punishment; she and Mike were obviously attracted to each other. The date had gone well; Trixie and Mike had been texting relentlessly ever since. Which was another thing I knew Erica would be upset to learn.

"Erica's not going to kill us," Mike said dismissively, then thought to add, "Although she might maim us a little bit."

"She's definitely going to be angry." I nervously paced across my room, which didn't take long, as my room was extremely small. "Really, really, *really* angry. I mean, I've made mistakes before, and she wasn't happy then. But this mistake involves her *sister*."

Erica was extremely protective of Trixie—so protective,

in fact, that she hadn't even let me know she *had* a sister until our last mission, and that was only because Trixie's life had been in jeopardy.

Now we had potentially put Trixie at risk again. And possibly Erica and her family as well. Because information was dangerous. If Trixie accidentally let the truth about her family slip and the wrong people got wind of it, that would cause serious trouble. Bad guys might try to harm Trixie to get more information—or use her as leverage to manipulate the Hales.

"There's an easy solution to this problem," Mike assured me. "*Lie.* All we have to do is be completely dishonest with Erica about what happened for the rest of our lives, and everything will work out just fine."

I stared at him in disbelief. "It's not that simple. Erica is like a human lie detector. She *always* finds out the truth. The only reason she hasn't learned about Trixie yet is because I've been avoiding her. But if we go on that ship, I won't be able to keep that up."

"I'm not so sure about that. This ship is freaking enormous." Mike unfolded a map of the *Emperor* that had been contained in the brochure. It was so long, he had to fully extend both his arms to hold it up. "There's over three thousand guest rooms, plus all the restaurants and pools and everything else. It'll be like vacationing in a floating city."

"I still won't be able to avoid Erica the entire time! We're supposed to be siblings!"

"A lot of siblings never talk to each other. Especially teenage ones. My brother barely said anything to me the whole year he was fourteen—and he spoke to my parents even less. We're supposed to be posing as a normal family, right? Well, nothing's more normal than acting like you don't want to be around your sister or your parents."

"We're going to be sharing a suite," I reminded Mike. "How can I avoid Erica in one of those?"

"Some of these suites are awfully big." Mike pointed to another page of the brochure. "Look at this one! It has six rooms, two balconies, four bathrooms, and a private hot tub."

I stopped pacing to look at the photo. The suite was bigger than my parents' house. It was spacious and beautifully furnished and had an incredible view of a tropical island.

Despite my concerns about the mission, I had to admit that the ship *did* look amazing.

"Still . . . ," I began.

Mike cut me off before I could say another word. "I know you won't be able to avoid Erica the whole time. But you'd have the same problem here, right? You're at the same school as her. Your plan isn't to avoid her for the next five years, is it?"

"Of course not," I said, although it wasn't that convincing. Because I had actually considered that plan. "I know

Erica will find out sooner or later. I was just hoping it would be later. *Much* later."

"It's possible that her finding out what we've done won't be nearly as bad as you think. Maybe she won't be mad at all."

"I highly doubt that. . . ."

"Or maybe she *won't* find out what we've done. Not right away, at least. I mean, we're going on a mission. Which means Erica and her family will be laser focused on that." Mike paused to consider his own words. "Well, Erica and her mother will be laser focused. Her father will probably fall overboard within the first hour."

He tossed me the brochure. I leafed through the pages. The *Emperor of the Seas* was so opulent, it almost didn't seem possible. It had an aquarium, a laser tag arena, a Broadway-size theater, and even a park with actual trees growing in it. Everyone in the photos looked like they were having a wonderful time. Of course, I was well aware that everyone in the photos was a model who was being *paid* to look like they were having a wonderful time, but still . . . it was all very convincing.

"It'll be fun," Mike said. "And you know it."

"Fun? We're supposed to be figuring out what Murray Hill is up to. . . ."

"On the world's coolest cruise ship! Most spies get sent

on missions to crummy places like Afghanistan and Siberia. We get to go on a tropical cruise!"

"Remember what happened the last time we went to the tropics on a mission? We ended up nearly dying in a plane crash. And then nearly dying in a lake filled with crocodiles—and in a cave—and some Mayan ruins—and . . ."

"This will be different. We're more experienced now. And we'll have Catherine there to protect us."

"Catherine was with us in Europe, and we almost died several times on that mission too!"

"But we didn't. Not only did we stay alive, but we also saved the day and thwarted the bad guys. Face it, Ben, we're pretty good at this spy thing. That's why they're sending *us*. . . ."

There was a knock at my door. "Ben?" Zoe Zibbell called from the hallway. "Are you in there?"

I was sure Zoe *knew* I was. She was a talented spy-in-training. So pretending like I *wasn't* there would make her suspicious.

"Hold on!" I quickly shoved my suitcase—which I had failed to pack anything in yet—back under my bed while Mike hid our classified dossiers beneath the pillows. Then I opened the door and welcomed Zoe in, doing my best to act like nothing unusual was going on.

"Hey, guys!" Zoe swept into the room, looking like her

typical nice-and-friendly self. She was in my year at spy school and had been my first friend there, although we had hit a slight rocky patch a few weeks before when Zoe had suspected Erica of being a double agent and teamed up with DADD—the Double Agent Detection Division—to try to capture her. In Zoe's defense, Erica did look guilty, having attacked CIA headquarters with a rocket-propelled grenade, but she had been forced into it by the Croatoan, which was threatening Trixie. (Which was why it was so important to Erica to keep Trixie's identity a secret.)

Zoe was only two steps into my room before she froze in her tracks. "Is the CIA sending you on a cruise ship to track down Murray Hill?"

"Who told you that?" Mike asked, surprised.

"*You* just did." Zoe gave him a proud smile. "I only suspected it up until now."

Mike immediately grew annoyed at himself. "How? We just found out about the mission ourselves."

"I heard that the school notified all professors that you would be missing class for a few days but that your absence has been sanctioned. The only school-sanctioned absences are for missions. There's a brochure for the *Emperor of the Seas* on Ben's desk, and since neither of you has the money to even *think* about that sort of vacation, that means you're being sent aboard. Given that Murray Hill is still at large and

Ben knows more about him than anyone else, it makes sense that's the reason they're sending you."

"You put all that together in two seconds?" Mike asked, startled.

"I'm a good spy," Zoe said proudly.

"Or, you were leaning against my door, eavesdropping on our conversation," I said accusingly. "You still have some flakes of paint from my door stuck to your ear."

Zoe reflexively lifted her hand to her ear to brush the paint away.

There wasn't any paint, though. I had just lied about it.

"Aha!" I exclaimed. "I knew it! You were spying on us!"

"It *is* a spy school," Zoe said, sounding disappointed in herself.

"We're your friends," Mike said disapprovingly. "It's not cool to spy on your friends."

"I know, but . . . I was worried you wouldn't tell me the truth." Zoe flopped on my bed beside Mike. "The part about your professors being notified is true. Everyone's talking about it. . . ."

I rolled my eyes at this. The communications with the professors were supposed to be top secret, but secrets never stayed secret for long at a spy school.

"And I wanted to know what was going on," Zoe continued. "This stinks. Why aren't they sending *me* on this mission too? I've been a student here way longer than Mike has. And I contributed just as much to our missions as Mike did in Mexico and London."

"You also agreed to be a junior agent at DADD," I reminded her. "Which means you're now supposed to be rooting out double agents instead of going after crooks like Murray."

Zoe frowned. "Double Agent Detection isn't as much fun as I thought it would be. We've only found two moles since I joined, and both of them gave up right away when we caught them. You'd think that at least one of them would have made a run for it. Or tried to fend us off with martial arts. But instead, they both just started crying. It was pathetic."

"Still, you busted two double agents," I said supportively. "And I know there's lots more to come. SPYDER corrupted a lot of spies. I'm sure some of them will try to escape. . . ."

"Or maybe even try to kill you in self-defense," Mike added.

"You're only saying that to make me feel better." Zoe sighed. "DADD is a dud. I spend all my time going through phone call transcripts in the basement of CIA headquarters. Meanwhile, you're going to face off against Murray Hill on a cruise ship. He'll probably have his henchmen try to kill you in some exotic location," she said jealously. "And then you'll get to have action sequences on speedboats or Jet Skis or something cool like that."

"Actually," I said, "I was kind of hoping that we'd just find Murray and arrest him and that would be it."

Zoe shook her head. "Nothing's ever that easy with Murray. There's definitely going to be a double cross and some attempts on your life. And then, knowing you, you'll end up defusing a bomb with only seconds to spare. You have all the luck."

"Most people probably wouldn't consider that lucky," I remarked.

"We're training to be spies here," Zoe said. "Most of our fellow students only *dream* about getting to do the kind of stuff you get to do. You're lucky, whether you realize it or not."

I understood her point, but it still didn't make me *feel* lucky. In fact, our conversation had given me a growing sense of dread about the mission. Zoe was right: Nothing was ever easy where Murray Hill was concerned. So I had that to worry about—along with whether or not Erica would find out about Trixie.

I desperately wanted to believe that everything would work out, that we'd catch Murray quickly and even score a few relaxing days of vacation aboard the cruise ship. But I had a nagging feeling that the mission wouldn't go the way I hoped.

As it turned out, things went worse than I could have ever imagined.

EMBARKATION

Corinto Cruise Port

Pacific coast of Nicaragua

May 16

1600 hours

I was actually looking forward to seeing Nicaragua, which I had heard was beautiful. Unfortunately, I spent most of my time there in the cruise ship terminal, which was quite likely the ugliest spot in the entire country, if not all of Central America. At one point, the island of Corinto had probably been very picturesque, but everything that had made it that way had been chopped down, steamrolled, and paved over. It was now basically a container port, full of rusty tankers, groaning cargo cranes, and semi trucks belching diesel fumes. The cruise ship terminal was a drab and charmless building designed simply to shunt tourists onto the ship, like cattle moving into a slaughterhouse.

In fact, the entire cruise ship experience so far seemed designed to let us have as little interaction with the country of Nicaragua as possible. After flying to Managua from Washington, DC, we had been greeted at the baggage claim by exceptionally cheerful cruise employees who immediately directed us onto tour buses, along with all our fellow cruise ship passengers—which was almost everyone else on our flight. The employees held little flags to let us know where they were and treated us all like kindergartners, right down to their insistence that we stay in line and have a buddy. Several other planeloads of cruise passengers had arrived from other cities, so more than fifty buses were needed to shuttle us all to Corinto. The entire caravan had driven straight from the airport to the cruise ship terminal, without even so much as a pit stop (there was a bathroom on the bus), so all I saw of Nicaragua was a blur of roadside businesses as we barreled past them.

Now, inside the terminal, we stood in a series of lines with all the other passengers, passing through an endless maze of sterile hallways. There was one line to have our passports examined, another to have our tickets verified, and yet others to check our luggage, pass through security, get our room keys, and so on. There was no chance to even get food, short of a few vending machines, and the air-conditioning was almost nonexistent. We were hot and sweaty—and so was everyone else—so the whole place smelled like body odor. It was like being in the world's largest department of motor vehicles.

The Hales, Mike, and I were doing our best to blend in, which was rather easy, as every single tourist was wearing almost the exact same outfit: T-shirts, shorts, sandals, sunglasses, and baseball caps (or floppy sun hats for the women). The hats and sunglasses helped to conceal our faces, not that anyone else was even looking our way; almost every one of them was riveted to their phones, taking advantage of the free Wi-Fi in the terminal. Thus, we didn't even have to be that cautious about what we were saying. Mike and I found the casual style extremely comfortable, since this was what we wore most of the time anyhow. It wasn't Erica's or Catherine's style at all, but both of them managed to blend in perfectly, as usual; Catherine didn't look one bit like her customary, fashionable self. However, Alexander, who was partial to tailored three-piece suits, looked as uncomfortable as a cat that had been dressed in a costume. He kept tugging at his T-shirt as though it were giving him hives.

The CIA had issued us all fake passports declaring us the Rotko family from Annapolis, Maryland. I had spent much of our travel time trying to memorize my character's backstory to the point where I could recite details like my fictitious birth-date and school name without hesitating (which was quite important when passing through customs and ship security).

Despite the fact that there were dozens of busloads of people in the terminal, waiting to board the *Emperor*, it still wasn't anywhere close to the number of people the ship could hold. "There are two types of cruises," Alexander explained as we were waiting in our ninth line of the day. "Round-trip cruises, where everyone boards and disembarks at the exact same location and stays aboard for the same number of days—as opposed to one-way cruises, where the ships continue going in the same direction and people can board and disembark anywhere along the line. We're on the one-way type. So there will be lots of people who've already been on board for a while, although they might be taking advantage of this stop to go ashore today."

He pointed through a grimy window. The *Emperor* was too big to dock directly at the terminal, so it was anchored out at sea. Dozens of small, festively painted shuttle boats were zipping back and forth between it and the terminal. Some were ferrying new passengers out to the ship, while others were bringing passengers who had gone ashore for the day back from excursions. There were also several larger, slower cargo boats piled high with crates marked with things like BEEF, CABBAGE, and PUDDING. Feeding the thousands of guests and crew required a staggering amount of food; each crate was so big, a forklift was needed to move it.

The passenger shuttles could only hold fifty people, and it took a few minutes to load each one, which explained why we were waiting so long to get aboard. Although, thankfully, we were finally getting close to the front of the line.

"Do you think there's an Internet café anywhere in this building?" Mike asked, glancing around the cavernous terminal. "I want to check my messages."

Erica, Mike, and I hadn't been allowed to bring our phones on the mission. There were two reasons for this: First, phones could be tracked, and on a mission, being tracked was a bad thing. The CIA could requisition special phones that didn't constantly pinpoint your location, but they weren't easy to get; Catherine and Alexander both had them, but Erica, Mike, and I didn't. Second, the coverage fees for cellular service at sea were exorbitant, and the CIA said they couldn't afford it.

"There are several computer centers on the ship," Catherine told Mike. "You'll be able to check your messages once we're settled."

"But that could be *hours* from now," Mike protested, sounding a little desperate.

I tensed beside him. I knew *why* Mike wanted to check his messages so badly; he wanted to get in touch with Trixie.

Of course, this was the last thing he should have been thinking about; we had a mission to focus on—and any contact with Trixie had the potential to get us in trouble. But Mike wasn't thinking clearly. I had never seen him like this where a girl was concerned. When he had dated Jemma Stern, the president's daughter, he had regularly gone whole days without bothering to text her (a behavior that hadn't gone over very well with Jemma). But now he looked like a child who had been denied candy on Halloween.

Catherine picked up on this as well. "What messages could you possibly have to check that are so important?" she asked suspiciously.

"Has anyone seen Murray?" I asked quickly, trying to change the subject. I made a show of scanning the crowd in the terminal. "I haven't noticed him anywhere yet."

"I wouldn't expect to," Erica told me, though not in her normal voice. She was in character for our mission, using her usual alter ego, Sasha Rotko. Sasha was the anti-Erica. Whereas normal Erica was cool, calculating, and emotionally detached, even when beating up bad guys, Sasha was bubbly, enthusiastic, and slightly vapid. It was always a bit unsettling to see how easily Erica could shift into being the kind of person who she probably would have detested in real life. "This area's only for the passengers in economy class, like us. The rich ones get waaaaaay better service. They have their own private terminal—and even private shuttles to the ship." She pointed out the window.

Beyond the portion of the dock where the economy-class passengers were climbing aboard the shuttle boats was a far less crowded area. This was cordoned off from the rest of the dock with a velvet rope and patrolled by burly guards, the same way that the entrance to an exclusive nightclub would be. There was a much smaller, sleeker private terminal, with tinted windows and a dozen air conditioners on the roof. A single black speedboat that looked like a maritime limousine was docked beside it. It was all quite obviously designed for wealthier passengers. I noticed a few of them boarding the speedboat; they looked relaxed and happy, and all the adults were drinking festive cocktails served in coconuts.

"Oh," I said. "Murray's definitely coming in that way. If there's a cushy route, he's taking it."

"Why aren't *we* taking the cushy route?" Mike asked, upset. "If Murray's going to be staying in first class, shouldn't we be there too? So we have a better chance of finding him?"

"I'm afraid neither of our agencies can afford to send us first class," Catherine said, keeping her voice low so that none of the other tourists would overhear her. "Espionage may be extremely important, but most operations still have shoestring budgets. We should consider ourselves lucky that we're even being given a suite. If it hadn't been necessary to bring you children along, the agencies would have probably sent Alexander and me in undercover as cleaning staff."

"And they wouldn't have even let us keep our tips," Alexander groused.

The fifty people ahead of us were led onto the loading dock by a cheerful crew member, and we moved up to the front of the line. Around us, our fellow passengers began to buzz with excitement, realizing we were almost ready to board the *Emperor of the Seas*.

I said, "If the wealthy patrons have different loading areas and shuttles, are they also separated from the regular tourists on the boat?"

"Oh yeah. There's a huge first class section." Mike unfolded his map of the ship, which was well creased, as he had been studying it a lot. "There are special dining rooms and clubs only for the rich people. There's even a whole floor of the ship that only they can access, with their own spa and pool deck." He pointed it out.

I took the map from him, realizing that I'd been so busy learning my fake identity that I hadn't taken much time to familiarize myself with the ship. Sure enough, there was an entire level marked *Exclusive First Class Area: Access Restricted*. It was one of the highest floors of the ship, and the private pool deck jutted out over the stern. "We need to figure out how to access this level," I said. "Because Murray's definitely going to be on it."

"But Murray's not much older than you," Alexander observed. "And those suites are thousands of dollars a night. How could he afford such a thing?"

"The Croatoan paid him a lot of money for helping with their evil scheme," I replied. "We saw it. And Murray likes to treat himself well. There's no way he'll be in economy class. In fact, knowing Murray, he's probably in the most expensive suite on the ship."

"Oh! I know where that is!" Mike pointed to a group of rooms at the bow end of the Exclusive level. "This is the Emperor Suite. It has like six bedrooms, so there's plenty of room for Murray and any henchmen he might have."

I examined the suite on the map. It was easily the biggest accommodation on the ship. In addition to the bedrooms, there was a gourmet kitchen, a dining room, a game room, and a private movie theater.

I said, "When Murray was working for Leo Shang, Shang rented out an entire hotel. And when SPYDER was operating out of the Atlantis resort in Mexico, they took the entire penthouse suite there."

"SPYDER doesn't exist anymore," Alexander reminded me. "Murray is working for someone else now."

"But he's learned from his previous employers," I said.

"These big suites give you plenty of privacy—and lots of luxury. I promise you, if Murray is anywhere on this ship, he's in this suite."

Catherine nodded thoughtfully. "You're on this mission because you know Murray. So if you say he's in that suite, then we'll need to infiltrate it as soon as possible."

"That will be quite a challenge," Alexander cautioned. "The Exclusive level alone will have its own security, and then that suite will certainly have even more. Its usual clientele is probably sheiks and oligarchs. Plus, any evil organization worth its salt will establish additional protection. . . ."

"I can get inside," Erica said confidently. "It's easy."

Alexander looked at her curiously. "Easy? How . . . ?"

"Hello, cruise ship travelers!" a young woman at the front of the line exclaimed. She was Aboriginal Australian, with a major Australian accent—and she was the perkiest person I had ever seen in my life, with a huge smile, big bright eyes, and dimples the size of golf divots. She wore a flamboyant pink uniform with a sailor's cap perched atop her head at the jauntiest angle possible. When she spoke, everything she said had an understood exclamation point after it. "My name is Kit Karoo, and I'm one of the many hospitality crew members on the *Emperor of the Seas*! Our job is to make sure you're having the best vacation of your life! It's your turn to board the shuttle to the ship! So who's ready to have some fun?!"

Her enthusiasm was infectious. Everyone around us cheered with excitement. Erica, still in character, gave a loud whoop of fake joy.

"That's what I like to hear!" Kit declared. "So let's stop lollygagging and get on that shuttle!"

There were more whoops of excitement from the nearby passengers.

Kit counted off the fifty people at the front of the line and then led us outside onto the loading dock, where a magenta-colored shuttle boat from the *Emperor* had just discharged a group of tourists who were ending their cruise. All of them looked quite depressed that their vacation was over.

After spending well over an hour in the stifling, overcrowded terminal, it was a joy to be out in the fresh air of the dock—even if it reeked of diesel fumes from the shuttle boats.

We all filed onto the shuttle. Kit stood by the door, handing out life jackets to each of us with staggering zeal. "Hey, kids!" she said when Mike, Erica, and I reached her. "Are you on spring break?"

"That's right!" Erica responded ebulliently, in full Sasha Rotko mode. "Our school's on a year-round schedule, so our break's super late."

"Well, you need to come by the teen club on board!" Kit exclaimed. "I'm one of the FunMasters there! It's called Koolnezz, and it's totally amazeballs!" She handed us each a large pin that said KOOLNEZZ KID on it, confirming that the name of the club was indeed spelled as badly as she had pronounced it.

Real Erica would have chucked the pin in the garbage at the first opportunity, but Sasha Rotko acted like it was the greatest gift she had ever received. "I love this! It's gorgeous! We will definitely be at the club first chance we get!"

"I love your spirit!" Kit cried. "I can tell you're gonna have a blast on this trip! There's so much fun stuff to do on the *Emperor*, it's incredible!"

"Like what?" I asked, trying to sound as eager as Erica.

"Ooh! Let me show you!" Kit hopped aboard the shuttle boat as the last of our group of travelers crammed on. A crew of sailors quickly untied the boat from the dock, and we set off across the bay toward the *Emperor of the Seas*.

The moment we were on open water, Alexander Hale turned a light shade of green. "Uh-oh," he said, and staggered toward the railing of the boat.

Meanwhile, Kit removed a tablet computer from a holster on her belt. Both the holster and the tablet had *Emperor of the Seas* logos embossed on them, indicating that they were official items for employees. Kit used her thumb to log in, then maneuvered through a few menus until she found the one she wanted. "Here we go! Teen-friendly activities! For starters, do you guys like to dance?"

"I *loooooooooove* dancing!" Erica proclaimed. Even though, in real life, Erica *hated* dancing. She had once declared that she would rather be tortured by enemy agents than go clubbing.

"Then you've come to the right ship!" Kit announced. "Because at Koolnezz, we have dance parties every night! Plus, there's arcade games, Ping-Pong, air hockey, pool, a half basketball court, trivia contests, karaoke . . ." She went on breathlessly for another good minute, although I didn't really pay attention to the rest of it, because I was staring at the cruise ship.

The *Emperor of the Seas* had looked big from the terminal, but as we got closer, the enormity of the vessel became more and more staggering. Our shuttle boat, which was a sizable craft, was dwarfed by the ship like a piece of plankton beside a whale. The *Emperor* had been designed for maximum occupancy, rather than an eye for beauty, so while there were some graceful lines at the bow, the center of it was really just an eighteen-story building. It was as though a colossal apartment complex had somehow broken off the mainland and floated out to sea.

High above, at the top of the ship, was the pool deck. I couldn't see it from my angle, as I was down at sea level, but I could glimpse the tops of the smokestacks and a few blue curls of plastic where some of the waterslides curved out over the edge of the boat, adding the thrill of potentially plummeting to one's death in the ocean to what would have been an otherwise normal water-park ride.

We were approaching the cruise ship from the bow, so I had a good look at the exterior of the Emperor Suite. It was located just below the top deck and spanned the entire ship from port to starboard, giving it sweeping views of the horizon. A balcony ran the entire length, backed by floor-to-ceiling windows that gleamed in the sun.

Directly beneath the Emperor Suite was the bridge, from which I knew the captain and crew manned the ship. This, too, had floor-to-ceiling windows and spanned from port to starboard—although it was actually slightly wider than the rest of the ship, with glassed-in wings protruding from the sides. I figured the protrusions probably served the same purpose as rearview mirrors on a car, allowing the crew to look backward along the length of the ship during maneuvers.

". . . baking competitions, pottery lessons, and bingo tournaments!" Kit finished, sounding slightly winded. She had rattled off all the Koolnezz amenities without taking a breath. "Does any of that sound fun to you?!"

"It *all* sounds fun to me!" Erica exclaimed. "When can we start?"

"Right after you get checked in!" Kit said. "And the club is open until two a.m. tonight! Although we do close for an hour at eight so that everyone can attend the pirate party!"

Every night the *Emperor of the Seas* hosted a themed party, and for our first night, the theme was pirates. It seemed odd to me that we would be celebrating the very people who would have pillaged a ship like the *Emperor* in real life, but I also had to admit the brochure made it sound like a good time.

"I'd love to keep telling you about all the fun!" Kit went on. "But we're almost at the ship, and I've got to help everyone get aboard safe and sound! I'll see you at Koolnezz, though!"

"You sure will!" Erica chirped.

Kit slipped her tablet back into her holster and stepped away to give all the passengers a cheerful round of safety tips for getting off the shuttle.

As Kit moved past us, Erica deftly swiped her tablet. She did it so quickly, Kit didn't notice a thing. The tablet hadn't even gone into sleep mode yet, so we still had access to all the screens.

Erica turned around so that Kit couldn't see what she was doing and began searching through the menus. All the other guests surged toward the exit, wanting to be the first to step foot aboard the *Emperor*. They were so focused on getting off the shuttle, no one noticed as Catherine, Mike, and I clustered around Erica.

Alexander didn't join us, as he was still leaning against

the railing. He had turned even greener, like an apple ripening in reverse, and was now a shade of emerald.

"Are you okay, Dad?" Mike asked, doing his best to stay in character.

"I'm fine," Alexander said reassuringly. "I just felt a twinge of motion sickness, but I've been out on the briny many times. I'm sure it will pass soon . . . oh dear." He bent over the railing and vomited into the ocean.

"I *warned* him," Catherine said under her breath. "He's always like this at sea. But every time, he thinks he can beat it. He booked us on a cruise for our honeymoon and spent the entire trip with his head in the toilet."

Our shuttle boat pulled up alongside the *Emperor of the Seas*. A few feet above the waterline, a portal was open in the hull of the ship, which would allow us to step inside. To our left, toward the stern, several much larger portals were open. Cargo was being loaded through these, with dozens of porters moving it from big, flat scows into the ship. The one closest to us was unloading the thousands of pieces of luggage the new passengers had brought, while the scows closer to the stern were delivering the huge pallets of food.

On the other side of us, toward the bow, the dark black speedboat bearing the exclusive guests pulled up in front of an open portal, where a tuxedoed waiter stood with a tray full of champagne glasses at the ready. The powerful engines cut out, and a gull-wing door in the side of the boat rose. A horde of cruise ship employees set a gangplank across the small gap between the speedboat and the portal, then helped the wealthy passengers across.

The elite didn't really look any different from the passengers on my shuttle. For the most part, they were dressed in T-shirts and shorts as well. They were simply being treated far better than we were. And, given the refreshed looks on their faces, it appeared that the indoor cabin of their speedboat must have been air-conditioned. I kept a close eye on them, hoping to spot Murray Hill.

Meanwhile, beside me, Erica was busily searching through Kit Karoo's tablet, completely ignoring her father's puking. "Here we go!" she announced. "Just as I figured, they have everything about the ship on this. Including current passenger lists." She brought up the manifest for the Premier level and found the Emperor Suite. "The guests listed on the manifest are . . . Harry and Ophelia Butz."

Mike giggled at the names.

"That definitely sounds like Murray's sense of humor," I said.

"Looks like we've found where he's staying," Catherine observed, then glanced over at Alexander. "Are you all right, darling? It's time to get on board the ship."

Alexander turned from the railing, his T-shirt bedecked

with a few flecks of vomit. A weary look in his eyes indicated he was questioning his decision to accept this assignment. "Coming, dearest," he gasped, then wobbled toward the exit.

We were the last passengers off the shuttle. As Kit helped us disembark, Erica deftly slipped the tablet back into her holster. Kit never noticed it was missing.

Unlike the wealthy passengers, we didn't get a nice gangplank between our shuttle and the *Emperor*. Instead, we had to step across the narrow gap over the water. The seas were calm, but the shuttle was still bobbing on the waves, making passing from one craft to the other slightly treacherous.

As I stepped over the gap, I glanced toward the first-class speedboat once again, still on the lookout for Murray Hill.

He wasn't among the crowd disembarking—but someone else I knew was. Someone whose presence startled me so much that I almost fell into the sea.

It wasn't hard to see him, as he was at least a foot taller than everyone else on the boat.

It was Dane Brammage, a hulking thug for SPYDER and other evil organizations who had tried to kill me on multiple occasions. I had thought he was dead.

Apparently, he was not. And now I was going to be stuck on a cruise ship with him.

ILLEGAL ENTRY

Great Hall

The *Emperor of the Seas*

Just off Corinto, Nicaragua

May 16

1700 hours

"Dane Brammage is on this ship," I informed my fellow spies. "I just saw him!"

"Really?" Alexander asked, concerned. "Are you sure it was him?"

"Of course I'm sure! He's the biggest human being I've ever seen—as well as the palest. He looks like an abominable snowman without hair."

I probably should have been doing a better job of keeping

my voice down, or at least pretending to be a normal teen-age tourist, so that none of our fellow passengers would notice—but all my fellow passengers were very distracted at the moment. Kit Karoo was giving everyone from our shuttle boat a welcome tour. She had led us up a few flights of stairs from the loading area into the great hall of the ship, which was enormous and magnificent, and everyone else was oohing and aahing in amazement. Several other groups of new passengers were scattered about, having followed their guides there, and they were all equally awed. The hall was the length of a city block and stretched five stories high. There were gilded rail-ings and luxurious carpeting and sparkly glass elevators and a sweeping grand staircase. On a mezzanine balcony, a quintet of musicians was playing Caribbean versions of pop music. I probably would have been oohing and aahing myself if I wasn't on the verge of freaking out.

"How can Dane Brammage possibly be alive?" Mike asked. "The last time you saw him, he was plummeting off the Eiffel Tower. That should have killed him."

"*Nothing* kills that guy," I replied. "He's also been buried in an avalanche and sunken in a frozen lake. He fell into a shark tank, and the *sharks* were the ones who ended up in danger. The man is indestructible."

In the center of the great hall, seven distinguished-looking people in crisp uniforms were greeting guests and taking pictures with young children. There were five men and two women of varying ethnicities, although the man in the center was the oldest and appeared to be the most senior, given the number of medals on his chest.

Kit pointed him out to the rest of the group. "That's our incredible captain, Dean Steinberg, along with several of the co-captains of this ship! The *Emperor of the Seas* has the finest crew on earth. As you can see, Captain Steinberg is a highly decorated officer!"

"Highly decorated for *what?*" Catherine asked suspiciously.

Kit's bubbly demeanor faded for a brief moment. Apparently, a guest had never questioned her about this before, and she had no idea what the answer was. "Er . . . important cruise-captain things!" she declared gamely, then quickly changed the subject. "Now, while there is obviously a tremendous amount to see on this ship, I know what all of you are *really* excited about right now: our all-you-can-eat welcome seafood buffet!"

Our fellow travelers cheered enthusiastically, although Alexander groaned at the thought of eating anything in his condition.

Catherine kept her eyes locked on Captain Steinberg the whole time. "I'll bet my granny's knickers those decorations are fake. Just to fool the masses into being impressed."

"The buffet is at the Hook, Line, and Sinker Café toward the stern on this deck!" Kit announced. "Grab all you want—and by the time you're done there, our bellhop service will have delivered your bags to your suites, so you can head to your room and relax—or explore the ship before our pirate party!" She turned to Mike, Erica, and me and said, "Come find me at Koolnezz! You'll have the best time ever!"

Our fellow guests stampeded toward the buffet. We stayed with them until they reached the restaurant, which allowed me a glimpse of all the food arrayed inside. So much seafood was laid out, it was hard to imagine anything was left in the ocean; there were separate stations for grilled fish, oysters, clams, mussels, calamari, lobster, and sushi. A device that dispensed cooked shrimp like a slot machine sat beside a three-foot-tall pyramid of king crab legs. Despite all this, the passengers were devouring food as though they feared they wouldn't get to eat again the entire vacation. I saw one glutton with two plates piled with shrimp and entire lobsters tucked under each arm.

Before we could enter the buffet, Erica and Catherine pulled Alexander, Mike, and me into one of the glass elevators. Erica jabbed the button for the pool deck, and we were quickly whisked upward.

Erica and Catherine seemed to have agreed on a plan without even discussing it, although the rest of us were in the dark. "Aren't we going to eat?" Mike asked. "We've barely had anything all day. I was really hoping to get some food. And maybe find a computer room to check my messages."

"What is it with you and your messages?" Erica asked suspiciously.

"He probably just wants to let his parents know he's okay," I said, then gave Mike a hard stare. "Isn't that right?"

"Yes, that's exactly it," Mike agreed, relatively convincingly. "And I really am hungry, too."

Through the walls of the glass elevator, we had a lovely view of the entire great hall. Then we rose through the ceiling and passed through several floors of other amusements. The upper levels of the *Emperor* were designed with guest rooms along the outer edges of the ship—so that they could have windows and balconies—while the interior space housed entertainment venues. Through the glass walls of the elevator, we saw the laser tag arena, a dance club (which wasn't being used, as it was the middle of the afternoon), a bingo hall (which was packed), and the roller rink.

"There will be plenty of time for eating later," Catherine told Mike. "The food service on a cruise ship never stops. But right now is the optimum time to infiltrate the Emperor Suite and confront Murray Hill. All the new passengers are busy gorging themselves, and most of the passengers who were already on board have gone ashore for the day."

I had spent enough time with the Hales to understand

their thought process. "Plus, if Murray *is* on board, the sooner we find him, the better."

"Exactly," Erica agreed.

Alexander Hale groaned again. The *Emperor of the Seas* was so big that it didn't even feel like we were on a boat, but that didn't seem to have made Alexander's seasickness any better. His skin was moving into the darker shades of green, and he was now the same color as an iguana.

The elevator arrived at the highest level of the ship. The doors slid open, revealing the activity deck.

It wasn't quite what I'd hoped.

Mike and I had spent a lot of time examining the photos of this deck in the brochure; now it was apparent that they had all been taken from angles that made everything look bigger and more spacious than it was in real life. Even though the top deck was quite large, the designers had still tried to cram too much into the space. The rock wall and the ropes course were smaller than we had expected, while waterslides coursed everywhere overhead, blocking out the sun and dripping cold water. It felt as though we were in a pump room at a hydroelectric plant. In the center sat the swimming pool, which turned out to be the most disappointing element of all, a shallow pond smack-dab in the middle of all the chaos, packed so full of small children they could barely move.

"That's the *pool*?" Mike cried with disgust. "I've seen bathtubs that are bigger!"

"We're not here to swim," Erica reminded him, leading all of us toward the rock wall. "We're here to find Murray."

"Even so," Mike muttered, disappointed. "That's false advertising."

Alexander belched ominously. Given how much he had puked on the shuttle, I'd assumed he had nothing left to vomit up, but now he looked like a volcano ready to blow.

"Your husband looks terrible," I whispered to Catherine. "Why did you let him come on this trip if you knew how seasick he gets?"

"In this line of business, it's always important to have someone who can create a good diversion," Catherine replied. Then she turned to Alexander and said, "No point fighting to keep it in, darling. Let it go."

Alexander clutched his stomach, folded over, and upchucked all over the tanning deck.

The tourists gathered there immediately sprang from their lounge chairs and evacuated the area before the smell hit them.

We were directly beside the rock wall, so the closest ship employees were the ones manning the ropes. The wall was designed mostly for children and people who had never tried rock climbing before, so it wasn't much more challenging than climbing a ladder. It was wide enough for ten people to climb at once, but since this was the least-crowded time of day, only two young children were using it, and both had only made it two feet above the deck. The rock-climbing guides belaying them were obviously bored—or they had been up until Alexander barfed. Now both guides were desperately looking around for someone to handle the puke instead of them.

Erica ran over and gave them her most imploring damsel-in-distress look, which was extremely effective. "My father's sick!" she cried. "Can you please help him?"

The guides couldn't resist her; plus, it was probably their job to help anyhow. They quickly belayed their young climbers to the deck, which took all of two seconds, unclipped them from their climbing harnesses, and ran to Alexander's side.

While they were distracted, Erica deftly swiped a coil of climbing rope, and Catherine nicked four harnesses. The other guests were all too busy evacuating the area to notice. The Hale women quickly headed in the direction of the ship's bow, so Mike and I hurried after them, leaving Alexander behind.

One thing I had learned from the Hales was that you could get away with almost anything if you behaved confidently enough. Even though Erica was only a teenager, she strode along so purposefully with the climbing rope that no one gave her a second glance. We swiftly made our way to the foremost section of the activity deck; this area was reserved for adults, as it was as far from the waterslides and other activities as possible and, thus, much quieter. There was another pool here; it was also disappointingly small, although since there were no young children using it, far fewer people had probably urinated in it.

Even though teenagers weren't allowed on the adult deck, we all looked as resolute as possible, so no one seemed to mind our presence. There weren't many adults there anyhow, and the few that were all appeared to be drunk. They were clustered around the bar, busily consuming tropical drinks served in hollowed-out coconuts and pineapples; it was possible that, in their inebriated states, they didn't even realize we were teenagers.

This section of the deck had a commanding view of the harbor. Since we were eighteen stories up, we could see long stretches of beach and green mountains in the distance, indicating that there was plenty of Nicaragua that was far more beautiful than Corinto.

I now realized what Erica's plan was; the Emperor Suite was directly below us. "We're rappelling onto the balcony?" I asked.

"Don't panic," Erica told me. "This is far less dangerous than a lot of other things I've made you do."

That was true. For example, the last thing Erica had made me do was parachute out of a helicopter while two F-16s were pursuing us. This was considerably safer—although, so was poking a grizzly bear in the eye with a stick. Still, I was pleased to realize that I wasn't panicked about rappelling down to the suite at all.

Instead, I was panicked about running into Dane Brammage again.

"What if Dane's there?" I asked, concerned. "Or any other henchmen?"

"We'll go down first and take care of any trouble," Catherine assured me. "You concentrate on finding Murray." She tossed climbing harnesses to Mike and me while Erica expertly knotted the rope around a flagpole.

If anyone could take out a horde of enemy thugs, it was Catherine and Erica Hale. Catherine had even bested Dane the last time we had encountered him. So I simply nodded agreement and slipped into my harness.

"Attention, all passengers!" a sunny voice announced over the loudspeakers. "All guests are now aboard, and we are about to get underway. Next stop, Costa Rica!"

The drunks at the bar gave a hearty cheer and toasted with their coconuts so violently that one man was knocked off his barstool.

A distant clanking arose as the anchors began winching

up. Far below us, I could see the chains slowly retracting at the bow of the ship. I calculated that, to hold a ship the size of the *Emperor*, each anchor must weigh multiple tons, and that each link of the chain was certainly several hundred pounds, but from our distance, they looked as small as the links on a bracelet.

Erica had knotted the climbing rope in the center, leaving both ends loose so that two of us could rappel down at the same time. She and her mother fed the ropes through their belay devices, casually hopped over the guardrail, then slid out of view.

The ropes pulled taut for a few seconds while they dropped down onto the balcony of the Emperor Suite, then went slack as they unclipped.

Mike and I prepared to follow. I looked to him, wondering if he was thinking the same thing that I was, how our lives were so bizarre that within minutes of boarding the biggest cruise ship in the world, instead of pigging out at the buffet or racing down waterslides like normal people, we were rappelling off the top deck to infiltrate an enemy hideout.

"I'm really bummed about the size of that swimming pool," Mike grumbled.

Apparently, we weren't thinking the same thing at all.

"All clear!" Erica shouted from below.

Mike and I hopped over the railing and slid down to the

balcony. It was only fifteen feet below us, and thus the trip took a mere three seconds.

Erica and Catherine had already jimmied the locks on the sliding doors. The doors weren't alarmed, as it didn't appear to have occurred to the designers that anyone would be entering the suite from the balcony, rather than the front door. Mike and I unclipped from the ropes and followed the others inside.

As opposed to the activity deck, the Emperor Suite looked even better than the brochure. We had entered the main living room, which was lavish and spacious with expensive furnishings and chandeliers and fine art on the walls and a grand piano. A gourmet kitchen was directly ahead of us, while several doors led off to bedrooms, bathrooms, and the private movie theater.

We heard the sounds of someone approaching from behind one of the doors.

Erica and Catherine flanked both sides, ready to incapacitate whatever evildoer came through it.

The door swung open.

I gaped in surprise when I saw who it was.

And she gaped right back at me.

"Ben Ripley?" asked Jessica Shang. "What on earth are *you* doing here?"

REUNION

Emperor Suite
The *Emperor of the Seas*
May 16
1800 hours

"I want to thank you for arresting my father,"
Jessica told me.

It was a few minutes after we had barged into her suite. Jessica had graciously invited the four of us to have something to eat, then rung for a chef and a butler who were apparently on call solely for her. We were all now seated on the balcony, sipping freshly squeezed lemonade along with Jessica's mother, the only other resident of the entire suite.

I hadn't met Shayla Shang before. She was petite, but

with an enormous, boisterous personality; she and her daughter both loved to talk. From the way she was dressed, it was obvious that she enjoyed being exceptionally wealthy; each finger and several of her toes sported rings with diamonds the size of garbanzo beans; more jewels dangled from silver necklaces draped around her neck; and she wore a garish, sequin-studded designer dress that cost fifteen thousand dollars. (I could tell because she had neglected to remove the price tag from it.) In the direct sunlight, with all the sequins and diamonds, she sparkled like a disco ball.

There had been no need to explain that we were secret agents. Jessica knew this because the last time she had seen Erica, Mike, and me, we had been in the process of apprehending her father.

I was still recovering from the dual shocks of discovering that I had been completely wrong about Murray hiding out in the Emperor Suite—and that it turned out I knew the people staying there anyhow.

Meanwhile, Jessica didn't appear remotely fazed by this. Instead, she was obviously pleased by our sudden appearance and excited to catch up. "I mean, it was definitely a shock to find out that you'd been lying to me about who you were," she went on. "But the fact is, Daddy getting busted was the best thing that ever happened to me and Mom."

"Really?" I asked.

"Absolutely," Shayla Shang chimed in. "Leo Shang was a world-class jerk."

Jessica said, "That ski vacation was the only time he ever acted like he really cared about *me* and not making money. Then it turned out that he had only brought me along as cover to commit a crime. Plus he hid a stolen nuclear bomb in our room. Ooh! Crab puffs!" She looked eagerly to the butler as he emerged onto the balcony with a platter of appetizers the chef had whipped up. "You all *have* to try these."

The scenery was shifting around us, indicating that we had gotten underway. We were so high above the engine room and the ocean was so calm that I didn't have any sense we were moving, save for the fact that the green mountains of Nicaragua were gliding past.

We each took a crab puff—except Mike, who helped himself to a half dozen. "Sorry," he explained. "We haven't eaten all day."

"Take as many as you want," Shayla said graciously. "There's plenty more where that came from."

I took a bite of mine. It was delicious. So I quickly grabbed a few more off the plate.

So did Catherine and Erica; all of us were starving.

"Leo treated me the same way he treated Jessica," Shayla said. "He only cared about making money. I was only an accessory to him, like a fancy watch or a piece of jewelry."

She looked wistfully at her own jewelry as she said this; all her diamonds glistening at once were almost blinding. "Mind you, he'd earned most of his money legitimately. He only got *really* greedy right at the end, when you caught him. . . ."

"So Mom and I got to keep all the money," Jessica concluded. "And the legal businesses he owned. Like this cruise line."

Catherine, Erica, and I paused in the midst of devouring our crab puffs at once, stunned by this last bit of information. If Mike was surprised, he didn't let showing it get in the way of his eating.

"This is *your* ship?" I asked.

"More or less," Shayla replied. "We're the majority shareholders in the company, although Leo set up a dozen shell companies to conceal that. He always thought it was better if people didn't know exactly what he owned."

"Daddy liked keeping secrets," Jessica added. "He owned all sorts of things that we didn't know about until he went to jail. Like a soccer team. And a few skyscrapers. And Fiji."

This even got Mike's attention. He stopped chewing for a moment and spoke with his mouth full of crab puffs. "You own *Fiji?*"

"Well, not all of it," Shayla corrected. "A lot of it, though. The good parts, really. If any of you ever want to go on vacation there, let us know."

"No way!" Mike exclaimed. "I've always wanted to go to Fiji! Could you hook us up on a trip this summer?"

"Of course," Shayla said. "You can stay at one of our homes there. It's the least we can do to pay you back for arresting my husband."

Mike pumped a fist enthusiastically. "Score!"

"Actually, I don't think we can accept that offer," Catherine said, giving Mike a sharp look. "We can't have it look like our agencies are taking gifts in return for doing things that have benefitted you. It shows a lack of decency."

"To heck with decency!" Mike cried. "We're talking about Fiji here! One of the most beautiful places on the planet!"

"I'm sorry," Catherine said. "It's wrong."

Mike sulked in his deck chair. "This is so unfair."

Shayla asked, "Then how about an upgrade to a first-class suite? I assume your current rooms aren't on this level, seeing as you came in by rappelling off the upper deck instead of knocking on the door."

Mike snapped upright in his chair. "A first-class suite?! That'd be incredible!"

"But an even worse breach of ethics," Catherine chided, which sent Mike right back into a sulk. "We're on a mission right now, so it's even less appropriate to accept gifts." She looked to Shayla apologetically. "It's not that we don't appreciate the offer . . ."

"I understand," Shayla said diplomatically.

"Speaking of our mission," Erica said, "we have reason to believe that Murray Hill might be on this ship."

"Murray?" Jessica asked, seeming genuinely surprised. "What's he doing here?"

"That's what we're trying to find out," I said. "In fact, the whole reason we thought he might be in this suite was due to the name you're registered under."

"Harry and Ophelia Butz?" Jessica asked, and then giggled. "We're trying to keep a low profile on this ship— although, come to think of it, Murray *did* teach me those names, back when he was working for Dad in Colorado. I didn't realize he was helping plot an evil plan at the time. I thought he was just an intern. And a goofy one at that."

There was a sudden, frantic knocking at the front door of the suite. "Mrs. Shang?" a voice called from the other side. "This is security. Are you all right in there?"

I froze at the voice, not because it was that of a security guard, but because I recognized the unusual singsong accent and knew exactly who it belonged to: Dane Brammage. I glanced at Erica, who had also gone on alert; she was scanning the balcony for anything she could use as a weapon.

Before I could warn him not to, the butler opened the front door . . .

And a man who was not quite Dane Brammage stormed through.

He *looked* like Dane Brammage, though. So much so that for a few terrifying moments, I thought it was actually him. Both men were hulking Scandinavians, so muscular that they had to rip the arms off their uniforms in order to accommodate their enormous biceps. But upon reflection, there were some subtle differences. This man's jaw was even squarer, and his skin was even paler—which I hadn't thought was possible. He was so fair-skinned, he was practically translucent.

The man who wasn't quite Dane cased the suite, then stared suspiciously at Catherine, Erica, Mike, and me. "I received a report that four people had rappelled off the adult deck down to your suite, perhaps with malicious intent."

"They did rappel down here," Shayla said calmly, "but not maliciously. I'm auditioning some new acrobats for our theatrical productions on board." She pointed to us with a lacquered fingernail. "Bjorn, these are the Flying Mazurkas. Mazurka family, this is Bjorn Turok, my head of security."

Catherine, Erica, Mike, and I all said hello at once—in four completely different accents, as none of us were quite sure where the Mazurka family might be from. Catherine's was Italian, Erica's was Russian, Mike's was Irish, and mine was just my own, because I'm not that good at accents.

"Hello," Bjorn replied in his real Scandinavian accent. He continued to regard us warily, as though he didn't quite believe Shayla's story—which made sense, as it was ridiculous. "Acrobats? Really?"

"Yes," Shayla answered, in a sharp tone that said she was the boss and didn't care to be questioned.

Bjorn got the message. "I'm sorry to bother you, Mrs. Shang," he said, although in a tone that made it clear he knew something strange was going on. "I was merely concerned for your safety. In the future, if you're going to have any more acrobatic auditions, I'd appreciate it if you would let me know."

"Of course," Shayla agreed. "I apologize for any concern I might have caused you. Thanks for dropping by."

Bjorn bowed slightly and let himself out, locking the door behind him.

Catherine, Erica, Mike, and I all looked to one another at once, thinking the exact same thing.

Mike was the first to put the thoughts into words. "That was *really* freaky."

"What do you mean?" Shayla asked.

Catherine said, "Your head of security bears an uncanny resemblance to someone else we know. . . ."

"Dane Brammage!" Jessica exclaimed, putting it all together. "I forgot you'd all met Dane before!" She turned to her mother to explain. "Dane was working with Daddy in Vail. So he had some run-ins with these guys. . . ."

"He tried to kill us," I clarified, then thought to add, "more than once."

"Oh goodness." Shayla seemed genuinely upset that she'd caused us any stress. "How many times?"

"I think we're up to seven," I said.

"No, it's eight," Erica corrected.

"It depends how you count," I told Shayla. "Sometimes, it's hard to say whether an attack was one prolonged attempt to kill us or two shorter attempts to kill us that were really close together."

"The point being, he hasn't exactly been convivial where we're concerned," Catherine concluded. "I can't believe how much your man Bjorn looks like him. . . ."

"They're first cousins," Jessica said. "Dad hired both of them at once. Dane was the more dangerous one by far. You don't have to worry about Bjorn. He wouldn't hurt a fly." She paused, then thought to add, "Unless he thought the fly was going to harm us in some way. Then he'd hurt it bad. Because that's his job."

Erica looked to me thoughtfully. "So maybe it *wasn't* Dane that you saw boarding the ship earlier. Maybe it was Bjorn."

I had been wondering this myself. "It sure looked like

Dane. Although it was only a glimpse. Is there any way to find out if Bjorn went ashore today?"

"I'll have Yi go ask him." Shayla looked to her butler, who had just returned to the balcony with a tray full of pigs in a blanket, and spoke to him in Chinese.

"Oh!" Mike said, struck by an idea. "And maybe Bjorn could get us a list of all the guests on the ship, so we can go through it and see if we can figure out which one is Murray's real alias."

"Capital idea," Catherine told him, then looked to Shayla. "I'd be particularly interested to see the names of the other guests registered on this level. Could Bjorn take care of that?"

"Certainly." Shayla continued instructing Yi, who listened carefully, then nodded agreement, set the tray of pigs in a blanket down, and hurried out the door.

Mike and I quickly grabbed several pigs in a blanket apiece.

Jessica's brow was furrowed with concern. "So you really think that both Murray Hill *and* Dane Brammage might be on this ship?"

"Yes," I answered.

"That sounds like a whole dress of trouble," Jessica said.

"A whole *mess*," I corrected. Jessica's English was very good, but sometimes she got her idioms wrong.

"Right," she said. "A whole mess of trouble. I don't want those guys using our ship as some sort of evil lair."

"Neither do I," Shayla agreed. "I have enough legal headaches as it is after being married to a lawbreaker like Leo Shang. If the government thinks I'm harboring criminals as well, I'll never hear the end of it."

"Then we could really use your help," Catherine told them. It was hard to eat a pig in a blanket and still look refined, but somehow, she was managing to do it. "We'd like to keep our identities as covert operatives a secret from all of your employees, for fear that Murray and Dane might be in cahoots with them. But it would also be nice to be able to search this ship for any hint of what their evil plot might be. Is there any way you could arrange a special tour of the bridge or the engine room for us, as though we were all regular passengers with an interest in the operations of this ship?"

Shayla frowned. "I'm afraid not. Due to security issues, those areas are restricted with no guest access. *I* can't even visit them—and I own this ship. I suppose, I could try to pull some strings, but not without attracting a lot of attention. Bjorn would certainly get even more suspicious of you than he is now."

"Why is visiting all those places considered a security risk?" I asked.

Shayla shrugged. "Concerns about terrorism, I suppose.

We don't want any bad eggs taking control of the ship . . ."

". . . or trying to blow up the engine room," Jessica added. "Seeing as this ship is nuclear."

Mike gagged on a pig in a blanket in shock, sending it flying out of his mouth and over the railing. It dropped past all the suites below us and splatted onto the bow, where it was immediately set upon by a horde of seagulls. "This ship has a nuclear reactor on it?!"

Although Erica and Catherine had done a better job of hiding it, I could tell that they were equally as surprised. I felt the same way.

Shayla shot Jessica a disapproving look, obviously upset at her for sharing this, but then pasted a smile on her face for us. "Yes, it does. Just like every aircraft carrier in the US Navy. It's very safe—and far better for the environment than running a ship this big on diesel fuel. Unfortunately, most people have a flawed view of nuclear power." She gave Mike a sharp look, which made him shrink in his seat. "Everyone *says* they want us to care more about the environment, but then they go bananas when you so much as mention the solution. So we've kept the fact that this ship is nuclear powered as quiet as possible."

"Is there *any* chance the reactor could blow up?" I asked, trying my best to sound like I wasn't completely terrified by the possibility.

"Of course not," Shayla replied curtly, as though she was offended by the thought. "There are a dozen fail-safes built into the system to prevent that from happening. This technology has been used by navies all over the world for decades without incident. It's much safer than traditional diesel-powered systems. Plus, our engineering team is extremely competent and well trained. Which is exactly why they don't want random passengers taking tours of the engine room."

Catherine nodded. "That makes sense. I suppose we don't have to go down there—as long as you can guarantee that Murray and Dane don't have access to that area somehow."

"They couldn't," Shayla said. "Since the engine room is so important, the doors require entry codes that change every four hours. That also goes for the bridge. No one gets into either one of those places unless they have authorization—and I can promise you Murray and Dane do not."

"How about the crew areas, then?" Erica pressed. "Could we at least get into those?"

"What would you even want to do that for?" Shayla asked. She wasn't antagonistic so much as slightly repulsed by the idea.

Erica explained, "Given your maps, it appears that about a third of this ship is reserved for the crew. That's an awfully large portion. It might be helpful if there was a way we could move through those areas freely."

Shayla nodded understanding. "I suppose it wouldn't be hard to get you some employee passes—or even some spare uniforms. There are thousands aboard."

"And you guys could even walk around there without it being suspicious," Jessica said to Erica, Mike, and me. "A lot of the highest-ranking employees have their families live with them on this ship. They don't want to leave them behind, since they're at sea all year. There's even a school for their kids."

"Do you go there too?" I asked. As far as I knew, May was part of the school year in China.

Jessica made a face as though I had asked if she regularly ate her boogers. "Ugh. No. I have private tutors aboard. And I'm even taking lessons from some of the other staff. Like, Bjorn's teaching me Norwegian."

"Those passes would be great," Catherine told Shayla. "Thank you."

The last traces of land slipped out of sight behind the ship; we were now out in the open ocean. A pod of dolphins was frolicking in the wave made by the ship's bow, although we were so high above them that they looked like a school of hyperactive anchovies.

Yi returned to the suite with a sheaf of papers in his hand. He came out to the balcony, handed them to Shayla, and spoke to her in Chinese.

She thanked him, then translated for us. "It seems that Bjorn did go ashore for a bit this afternoon, returning only a short while ago."

Catherine and Erica both gave me a look. I immediately understood what they were thinking, because I was thinking it too: There was a good chance that I had seen Bjorn, rather than Dane Brammage. I wasn't sure what to think, although in truth, I *hoped* it was Bjorn I had seen. Because Dane Brammage was extremely dangerous, and he didn't like me very much.

Shayla continued. "Yi has also procured the manifest you asked for. And he reports that there is a man vomiting profusely in the infirmary who is asking if anyone could track down his wife, Carol Rotko."

"That'd be my husband," Catherine said with a sigh. "He's *still* vomiting? My goodness, I thought he'd have run dry by now." She accepted the manifest from Shayla and stood from her deck chair. "I suppose I should go check on him. And I think we've taken advantage of your hospitality long enough." She looked to Erica, Mike, and me expectantly.

We promptly stood as well. Catherine was generally very even-keeled, but you didn't want to cross her where good manners were concerned.

"Thanks for the food," Mike said.

"And for not having us arrested for breaking and entering," I added.

"It was the least we could do for the people who put my husband in jail," Shayla said graciously.

"It was nice to see all of you again," Jessica said. "I'd love to hang out some more while you're on board."

"That'd be great," Erica said. "We'll be in touch."

Yi opened the door for us, and we exited into the main hallway of the Premier level. Since we had arrived by rappelling off the top deck, this was our first time in the hall. It was quite luxurious, paneled in dark wood with plush carpeting. Every few feet there was a cut-glass vase filled with fresh flowers.

However, I was less interested in the hall's decor than I was in Erica's behavior. "What was that all about?" I asked her once Yi had shut the door behind us.

"What was what all about?"

"You were being *friendly*. Jessica asked to get together, and you said, 'That'd be great.' Are you really planning to hang out with her?"

"No," Erica replied. "I'm planning for *you* to hang out with her. I think the Shangs might still be up to something."

"Me too," Catherine agreed.

"Really?" I asked. "They seemed perfectly innocent to me."

Erica and Catherine exchanged a brief glance, like they

were amused by my amateurism. Although before I could ask why, Catherine stopped in her tracks, staring at the manifest Yi had procured for us. "Oh my."

"What is it?" Mike asked. "Did you find where Murray is staying?"

"No. But here's something else." Catherine pointed to the very first page of the manifest.

This page didn't list the individuals who were staying in each room. Instead, it listed the facilities that had been reserved on board by various groups. For example, the Enriquez family was celebrating a wedding that night in the Lotus Ballroom.

But of far more interest was what Catherine was pointing to: That evening, the Chrysanthemum Ballroom had been reserved by the International Tulip Growers Association.

Back in London, two months earlier, Murray Hill had told us that the ITGA was a front for a consortium of evildoers.

"You think Murray's working with them?" I asked. "Because he didn't sound like he was a big fan of theirs when he told us about them."

"What did you expect him to say?" Erica asked me. *"By the way, there's yet another group of bad guys, and I'm secretly working for them while pretending to work for you?"*

"I suppose not," I admitted, feeling kind of foolish.

"We ought to infiltrate that banquet hall and see what we can find out," declared Catherine.

"When?" Mike asked.

"When else?" Catherine replied. "Tonight. During the pirate party."

COUNTERFEIT PIRACY

Suite 1722

The *Emperor of the Seas*

Somewhere off the coast of southwestern Nicaragua

May 16

2030 hours

According to the brochure, the nightly themed parties aboard the *Emperor of the Seas* were thrown to create a sense of camaraderie and merriment amongst the passengers. They were also a good way to sucker all of us into forking over extra money for costumes.

Before attending, we had to visit one of the many shops on board the ship and procure pirate outfits, which I suspected weren't remotely close to what real pirates had worn.

Instead, they seemed to have been inspired by the Pirates of the Caribbean ride at Disney World, featuring things like loose-fitting white shirts, red-and-white-striped bandannas, and eye patches. There was an entire aisle of plastic hooks, as though it was a rarity for any pirate to have more than one hand. If any *real* pirates had seen us, they probably would have taken offense at our stereotyping—but it appeared that, in our increasingly compassionate times, pirates were one of the few remaining groups of people whose culture we were allowed to insensitively appropriate.

The costumes were cheaply made, but not cheaply priced. However, Catherine felt that we needed them. "We'll be much less conspicuous when dressed the same way as everyone else," she had explained, and then reluctantly charged all the outfits to our room.

Acquiring them turned out to be significantly easier than putting them on. Partly because they were so shoddy that half the buttons and snaps didn't work. And partly because our suite was so small, there wasn't enough room for all of us to change at the same time.

It was a far cry from the spacious opulence of the Emperor Suite. We technically had two adjoining rooms, but even combined, the suite was slightly smaller than our dorm rooms at school—and those were notoriously cramped. Catherine and Alexander had the master bedroom, while

Erica, Mike, and I had the kids' room. We all had to share a bathroom the size of a Porta-Potty. The suite was designed with what the brochure referred to as "cruise ship efficiency," but that turned out to be a euphemism for cramming way too much into one space. Between our small beds and our luggage (which had been delivered by the staff while we were with the Shangs) there was barely even room to turn around. It didn't help that Alexander had practically taken up residence in the tiny bathroom, his head poised over the toilet.

To make things worse, we didn't even have a balcony. Those were luxuries for people with more money. We merely had a small porthole in each room.

"Are you *sure* this is a suite?" Mike asked, skeptically surveying the tiny space. "Maybe they made a mistake and put us in a storage closet."

"We're in the right room," Catherine replied grumpily. "The cruise ship company appears to have a very flexible definition of what 'suite' means." She and Erica were getting dressed in the master bedroom, but the wall between us was so thin, we could talk right through it.

"Maybe we ought to take the Shangs up on their offer of a bigger room," Erica suggested.

"Erica!" Catherine gasped. "You know that would be unethical."

"You know what else is unethical?" Mike replied. "Saying

this suite sleeps five people comfortably. I believe the official term for this space used to be 'steerage.' If this was the *Titanic*, we'd be the people who didn't get life rafts."

"At least we don't have to worry about hitting an iceberg," Catherine replied, trying to sound positive. "Not down here in the tropics."

"That's the *only* good thing about this ship," Mike muttered under his breath. Since leaving the Shangs, he had been growing increasingly sullen as we discovered more and more ways in which the *Emperor of the Seas* didn't live up to its own hype. He and I had taken some time to explore the ship and found that the laser tag arena and the escape room were disappointingly small. The waterslides were too short, while the lines for them were too long. Koolnezz, the teen club, had been a decent size, although it was filled with out-of-date arcade games, many of which were broken. Kit Karoo had greeted us enthusiastically and tried to get us excited about the imminent karaoke tournament, but we had bailed instead. I wasn't a fan of butchering pop songs in public, and Mike desperately wanted to check his messages.

However, when we finally tracked down the computer center, we discovered that the Wi-Fi access wasn't free. In fact, it was exorbitant. Mike could only afford to log in for five minutes, which was barely enough time to skim through the dozens of messages Trixie had sent him. He then dashed off a quick message in return, claiming that all was okay and that he missed her a lot but that, sadly, it might be a while until he could write again. (He'd asked me to stand guard in the computer lab in case Erica or Catherine came in, and I had read his messages over his shoulder. I learned, among other things, that he and Trixie *really* liked each other, and that his pet name for her was Pookums.)

In addition to all that, we had been forced to attend a mandatory safety training for all new guests, which involved standing on a deck in the blazing sun for a half hour while a crew member explained how to work a life jacket.

Therefore, Mike was in a surly mood. "Nothing about this ship is anything like they advertised," he grumbled while adjusting his pirate shirt. "Unless you're rich. The Shangs have a giant suite, while we're staying in a bread box. I'd write a nasty review about this boat if I could afford the Wi-Fi."

"Oh, it's not so bad," Erica said.

Mike and I reacted to this, stunned.

"You *like* this ship?" I asked. "You don't like *anything*."

"That's not true," Erica replied.

"You don't like ice cream," I reminded her.

"What's to like about ice cream? It's full of empty calories, and it gives you brain freeze. All I'm saying is, there are some positive things about this ship. Like the safety training."

Mike goggled in astonishment. "You enjoyed that? All

they did was tell us how to operate the lifeboats in case of an emergency!"

"Emergency training is always fascinating," Erica said. "And important. In addition, a cruise is an extremely convenient environment to conduct an operation. If Murray was running his scheme in some random city in Nicaragua, he could go anywhere in the country he pleased. But now, he's limited to the confines of this ship, which should make tracking him down much easier. And when we *do* find him, he won't be able to escape."

Mike said, "So then, the reason you like this ship is because there's a focus on safety, and it's a good place to catch bad guys."

"Yes," Erica agreed. "Oh, and the food is good."

"It *is*," I had to admit. "And there's a *lot* of it." Even though I was disappointed by many of the same things on the *Emperor* as Mike, I had also been pleased to discover that there was a ridiculous amount of food available for free, including a well-stocked make-your-own ice cream sundae bar that actually opened at eight a.m. every day, just in case you wanted a fully loaded banana split for breakfast.

A disturbing gagging noise suddenly arose from the bathroom, reminding me that, even though the *Emperor of the Seas* hadn't fully lived up to our expectations, we were all still having a much better trip than Alexander. He was no longer green, but instead a ghostly white, as though he had vomited all the color out of his body. The doctors in the ship's infirmary had given him plenty of anti-motion-sickness remedies, and none of them were working. He was wearing so many therapeutic wristbands and adhesive skin patches, he looked like a bear that had been tagged by park rangers, but despite them all, he remained nauseous, clutching the toilet bowl and moaning despondently.

I finally managed to get all my pirate gear on. My outfit was the same as Mike's—we each had a puffy shirt, a bandanna, an eye patch, and a fake sword in a plastic scabbard— but I felt he looked significantly more roguish than I did. Somehow, I looked more like a hobo than a buccaneer. I finished it off by cinching my utility belt around my waist. Catherine had given it to me as a present: She and Erica both wore them all the time and made them look quite fashionable. Mine wasn't as well stocked with espionage supplies as theirs, but I still had a few useful items, like my junior CIA agent badge, a small flashlight, a canister of mace, and breath mints. (One of the few things Alexander Hale had taught me was that it was always a good idea to have fresh, minty breath; it made people like you.) I hid the utility belt beneath the waist sash that had come with my costume, yet another item of clothing no real pirate had ever used. Then, while Catherine and Erica finished dressing in the other room, I sat on my bed and perused the manifest again, trying to deduce where Murray might be.

There was no one else registered in the Premier level of the ship with a name that jumped out at me, the way Harry and Ophelia Butz had. I did find a Seymour Heinie and a Weldon Rumproast listed in the cheapest section, but I assumed those were real people with horribly unfortunate names. I was sure that Murray would never stay in quarters like ours—and he was probably now wise enough to use a false name that didn't draw attention to itself.

Many of the guests registered to the Premier level had last names that indicated they were from China, Japan, Korea, Indonesia, and the Philippines, which made sense, seeing as the *Emperor* had begun its journey in the western Pacific. But I had no way of knowing if any of those might be a fake to hide Murray, Dane Brammage, and whatever other henchmen Murray might have aboard.

Assuming Dane was even on board. It was entirely conceivable that I had seen Bjorn, rather than Dane. In fact, it was conceivable that neither Murray nor any of his cohorts were even on the ship at all and that this mission was merely a wild-goose chase.

Although the International Tulip Growers Association did bear investigating.

"Any luck?" Catherine asked.

I looked up from the manifest to find her and Erica standing in the narrow doorway between our rooms, dressed in full pirate gear.

They were easily the two most beautiful pirates there had ever been.

With her costume bandanna around her hair, Erica's resemblance to Trixie was even more pronounced. Mike noticed it too and was stunned. "Whoa, Erica," he said. "For a moment there, I thought you were . . ."

I swallowed hard, fearing he was going to say Trixie and inadvertently reveal that we'd met her, but he caught himself at the last second and trailed off.

"Thought I was who?" Erica asked.

"Anne Bonny?" I suggested. "The famous female pirate?"

"Yes!" Mike agreed quickly. "That's exactly who I was thinking of. Let's go see what the ITGA is up to!" He immediately left the room.

I leapt to my feet and followed him, with Erica close behind me.

Catherine paused before leaving to call to Alexander. "We're heading out," she said through the bathroom door. "Will you be all right without us?"

There was a pained but affirmative wail in response.

"Good," Catherine said, and then joined the rest of us in the hallway.

The halls on our floor were far less opulent than those on the Premier level. They were so narrow that you couldn't even walk two abreast and decorated with cheap fake wood paneling and floored with linoleum. We hustled through ours quickly.

"You never answered my question, Quincy," Catherine said.

It took me a half second too long to recall that was my alias. "Oh, right! The manifest. I couldn't find a name that tipped me off on the Premier level, but if Murray is holed up anywhere on this ship, I'm sure he'd be there."

"Then we'll have to get access to that level," Catherine said.

"You know what would give us access to that level?" Mike asked. "Taking the Shangs up on their room upgrade offer."

"For the last time, we are not accepting bribes," Catherine said sternly. "Plus, you boys need to lose the eye patches. I admit, they give both of you a knavish charm, but they completely bollix up your depth perception."

"I can handle an eye patch just fine," Mike told her peevishly, then promptly misjudged the width of a doorway due to his lack of depth perception and walked straight into the wall.

"Very smooth," I teased, removing my own eye patch as I passed him.

We entered one of the several "vertical integration passages" on the ship. There was a bank of four elevators and a wide staircase. We opted for the staircase, as we had already learned that the elevators were in high demand and thus the slowest way to get from floor to floor.

Our room was on the lowest guest level, so the stairs only went up. Although there were two levels of crew quarters, engine rooms, and other facilities below us, the stairs to them were concealed behind locked doors marked CREW ACCESS ONLY.

We were still waiting for the Shangs to obtain our passes to those areas.

The stairs were much wider than the hallway, so I was able to ascend them beside Catherine. "Why don't you trust the Shangs?" I asked her. "Jessica isn't a bad person. We never would have caught her father without her help."

"Even so, her mother's reticence to allow us to visit the bridge or the engine room is suspicious."

"She had a good argument as to why. . . ."

"To heck with her arguments. She's the owner of this ship. If she wanted to bring an elephant into the engine room, they'd let her do it. And yet, we made it very clear that there are criminals operating on board here, and she still refused. Ergo, I suspect she's hiding something. Which is why we'll need you to spend more time with Jessica. If she *is* honest, then maybe you can talk her into getting us a tour somehow."

"I'll do my best," I agreed. I was wary of taking advantage of Jessica Shang's friendship once again, but the idea of spending time on the Premier level of the ship was far more appealing than hanging out at Koolnezz or waiting hours in line for the waterslides.

Mike seemed to be thinking the same thing, because he immediately piped up, "I'll help too!" Then he walked straight into a railing, because he still hadn't removed his eye patch.

We emerged from the stairs into the great hall to find the pirate party in full swing. It appeared that whatever money the cruise company had saved on building larger guest rooms had all been blown on decorations. The hall was now bedecked with streamers and bunting, and fake cannons on the higher levels were blasting confetti bombs into the air. Even though the party had just begun, the room was jampacked with passengers, all of whom were wearing almost the exact same pirate costumes we were. (And since many of them were as insistent upon wearing the eye patches as Mike was, they were all bumping into one another or the furnishings.) Along the walls, banquet tables were piled high with food that could be eaten with your hands, the idea apparently being that pirates hadn't mastered utensils; there were mounds of spare ribs, corn on the cob, and giant turkey legs. Bartenders were handing out goblets of pirate grog (which was really just apple juice). On the mezzanine level, a pirate band—which was made up of the same five musicians as the Caribbean band from earlier in the day—was playing a lively reel while fake buccaneers danced around them. High above us, actual acrobats and aerialists swung from trapezes and dangled from long silks.

I had to admit, it looked like a great party.

Unfortunately, we weren't planning to attend it.

It was the perfect time to do some snooping. It appeared that virtually every guest and staff member on the ship was distracted by the festivities, and since everyone was dressed nearly identically, we could easily move about without anyone realizing who we were. We had learned the layout of much of the ship by now and knew that the Chrysanthemum Ballroom was on this level, so we worked our way through the crowd, with a brief stop at the banquet tables to grab turkey legs and grog. (Since almost everyone else was eating and drinking, this helped us blend in even more, and besides, we were hungry—and the turkey legs were delicious.) As we went along, I caught a glimpse of Shayla and Jessica Shang on the mezzanine. Shayla was holding court with several guests, wearing a sequined couture costume that looked like the sort of thing a pirate would wear to the

Oscars. Meanwhile, Jessica looked bored. If I hadn't been on a mission, I would have gone to talk to her.

We were almost out of the hall when Kit Karoo leapt into our path. "Tell me you're not leaving the party!" she exclaimed.

"We're not leaving the party," Mike said, even though we were quite obviously doing exactly that.

"You can't go!" Kit pronounced. "There's so much fun ahead! We're about to have a dance competition! And then there's going to be a reenactment of a real-live pirate attack! And then we're making s'mores!"

"S'mores?!" Erica asked exuberantly, back in full Sasha Rotko mode. She sounded as though Kit Karoo had promised her a million dollars. "I love s'mores! We are definitely in for s'mores! We're just running out to get some more bandannas at the store, and then we'll be right back!"

"You promise?!" Kit asked.

"Cross my heart and hope to die!" Erica replied.

Mike and I echoed this sentiment as enthusiastically as we could.

"All right!" Kit whooped. "That's the spirit! See you at the s'more pit!" She let us pass and went off to badger some other teens into having fun.

The party had spilled out beyond the great hall into the shopping mall, where plenty of guests who hadn't planned ahead were still grabbing costumes at the last minute, but the crowd thinned out as we got to the onboard theater, where the night's pirate-themed juggling performance wasn't scheduled to begin until after the celebration had died down. The ballrooms were just beyond the theater, at the stern of the ship.

There were four of them, arranged around a large foyer. A placard on the wall indicated that over the course of the next few days, there would be three weddings, six corporate retreats, and one bar mitzvah. However, none of them were scheduled at night, probably to avoid conflicting with the shipboard parties—except for the meeting of the International Tulip Growers Association, which was supposed to be taking place right then.

The door to the Chrysanthemum Ballroom was locked, and when we pressed our ears to it, we couldn't hear a thing inside.

"Sounds like no one's there," I observed.

"Which means it's the perfect time to break in," Erica concluded. She considered the lock and coded keypad entry for the door. "There's some decent security on this. It'll take a while to crack it." She removed her favorite set of lockpicks from her utility belt and went to work.

Catherine handed Mike and me some radio earpieces so that we'd all be able to stay in touch. "Benjamin and Michael, why don't you be our lookouts while we handle this?"

"Sure thing," Mike agreed. We both inserted our radios in our ears and returned to the main entrance for the ballroom area, leaving the Hale women to jimmy the lock.

We ended up in a long hall that stretched from port to starboard across the ship. There was another vertical integration bank in the center, with elevators and a staircase, while at each end was a door that led outside to the Promenade Deck.

This was the same deck that we had visited for our mandatory safety training. Besides the Activity Deck on the top level, it was the only other public outdoor space on the *Emperor of the Seas*. It was five stories above the water and was a sort of indentation in the bulk of the ship, like the beginning of a paragraph, so that it ran on top of the suites below it and was roofed by the suites above it, with one side open to the air. The deck circled the entire ship like a belt and was a half mile around. It had a walking track and a few shuffleboard courts, but the real reason for it was to store the emergency life rafts, which had to be deployed relatively close to the water.

"There's probably a window from the Chrysanthemum Ballroom out onto the Promenade Deck," I suggested. "I'm gonna go check it out. You stay here and keep watch."

"Good plan." Mike remained where he was and dug hungrily into the turkey leg he was lugging around.

I still had a turkey leg myself. It was so large, I had barely made a dent in it.

I headed out onto the deck. Even though it was night, it was sultry and humid, but the ship's movement created a slight breeze, and we were so far from shore that there was no light pollution. A million stars were visible in the ink-dark sky. It was so beautiful, I had to stop at the railing for a moment to take it in.

The deck was actually two stories tall, with the life rafts stored overhead so as to not block anyone's view of the sea. They were all wadded up inside white metal canisters the size of oil drums, which the crew would drop overboard in case of emergency. Ideally, upon striking the surface of the ocean, the canisters would burst open and the rafts would automatically inflate. There were hundreds of them, lined up in ceiling-mounted racks like bullets in an ammunition belt. In addition, the sleek-looking speedboats used to ferry the wealthy passengers were suspended on davits that jutted from the edge of the ship above. I realized that the gaily colored shuttles we had used to access the ship before must have belonged to the port of Corinto, but for the exclusive guests, the *Emperor of the Seas* had its own craft. The speedboats were so dark, they were hard to see against the night sky.

The shuffleboard courts and the walking track were all

currently unused, as everyone appeared to be at the party. The deck was eerily empty.

The *Emperor*'s running lights illuminated the surf below, which churned and foamed as the ship plowed through it. Even though there were another thirteen stories of ship above my head, I still felt like I was surprisingly high up.

It occurred to me that this was the farthest I had ever been from land while still on the surface of the earth and not in an airplane thirty-five thousand feet up. The sea looked massive and endless from where I was, even though I was only seeing the tiniest fraction of it. I was on the starboard side of the ship and since we were heading south, I was facing west, which meant there wasn't another speck of land until the Philippines, almost ten thousand miles away. Even a ship as colossal as the *Emperor of the Seas* was really just a flyspeck in the great expanse. I had always known that the ocean was enormous, but I had never really felt *how* enormous until then.

I turned my attention away from the water to the ship itself.

The windows of the Chrysanthemum Ballroom were dark, indicating that no one was inside. Still, in the interest of being thorough, I went to the closest window and attempted to peer through it.

I couldn't see a thing.

The planks of the deck creaked behind me. For reasons I couldn't explain, a chill went down my spine. Since my turkey leg was as big as a medieval mace, I figured it might make a decent weapon. So I tightened my grip on it and whirled around, ready for action.

Dane Brammage was standing there. And this time, I was sure it was him and not Bjorn Turok for three reasons:

1) I was close enough to see the slight differences in their faces that set them apart.

2) Murray Hill was right next to him.

3) He immediately tried to kill me.

CONFRONTATION

Promenade Deck

The *Emperor of the Seas*

May 16

2115 hours

Dane and Murray were both dressed like pirates as well. They had the same style of costume that I did, with the puffy shirt and the bandanna and the eye patch, although it appeared that instead of fake swords and scabbards, they had real ones.

Still, Dane didn't need a sword to harm me. Instead, he simply clamped a massive hand around my neck and squeezed. He didn't appear to be working that hard, exerting no more energy than a normal person would to crumple a piece of paper.

But instead of paper, Dane was crumpling *me*. The flow of air to my brain instantly stopped, and it felt like my head was about to pop off like a bottle cap. I did my best to fight back, clubbing him on the skull with my turkey leg, but it was like an ant kicking a rhinoceros. Dane casually wrested the turkey leg from my grasp and started to eat it himself.

Next, I tried yelling for help, hoping to alert Catherine, Erica, and Mike over my radio, but that failed too. I couldn't make a sound with Dane's hand around my larynx. Plus, Murray deftly plucked the radio from my ear and flicked it over the railing and into the sea.

"Don't kill him yet," he told Dane casually. "We're not quite done with him."

Dane relaxed his grip on me, allowing air to blessedly return to my brain. If he was pleased or disappointed to not finish me off, he didn't show it.

On the other hand, *I* was extremely pleased he hadn't finished me off. I sucked in great gulps of air, trying to make sure oxygen got to all the important parts of my body that needed it.

I considered making a run for it. Dane was powerful but not fast, and Murray had the athletic ability of an anemic koala, but both of them had swords, and I was reeling from my near strangulation. If I tried to escape, there was a decent chance that Dane would shishkebab me.

Murray smiled brightly, as if we were old friends, although there was also a self-satisfied cockiness to it. "It's good to see you again, Ben. I was wondering how long it'd take you to come snooping around here."

I winced, grasping what had happened. "There is no ITGA meeting here, is there? It was only bait to lure us."

Murray's smile jacked up a few notches. "Still as sharp as ever, Ben. But not quite sharp enough."

"The ITGA isn't even on this ship, is it?"

Murray broke into mocking laughter, the way you did when you had just played a great practical joke on someone. "The ITGA doesn't even exist! I made it up!" He paused a moment, then corrected himself. "Well, there is a *real* International Tulip Growers Association, but they're actually tulip growers, not evil conspirators. I was kind of hoping the CIA would do a big raid on them in Amsterdam and end up looking like idiots, but I suppose there's still time for that."

I was feeling dumber by the second as I put everything together. Murray had told us about the ITGA a few weeks before, back in London, when we had thought he was working with us. Which meant he was already plotting against us.

However, the real concern was his comment that the CIA might still raid ITGA. Because that implied I wouldn't be around to *tell* the CIA that ITGA wasn't evil.

"When did you figure out we were on the ship?" I asked.

"I spotted you the moment you stepped aboard," Murray said proudly. "I figured you might show up. Every time I plot something, there you are. So I reserved this ballroom with the ITGA, and sure enough, you walked right into my trap."

A set of doors farther down the deck burst open. We all looked that way, me hoping that it was Catherine, Erica, and Mike coming to my rescue—and Murray and Dane hoping that it wasn't. To my chagrin it turned out to be a group of inebriated pseudo-pirates. They quickly grabbed shuffleboard sticks and began sword fighting with them. They didn't even seem to notice us, but their presence was enough to concern Murray.

"Let's take a walk," he said, then started in the opposite direction of the drunks, toward the stern, although he promptly walked into a support post. "Dang it," he muttered, tearing off his eye patch. "I've got no depth perception with this thing." He tossed it overboard and continued toward the stern.

Dane roughly shoved me after him, then followed closely behind so I couldn't escape.

This was bad. The farther we got from the doors, the farther we were from my friends, who obviously had no idea that I was in trouble. Which meant I'd have to save myself.

In my utility belt there was a small aerosol container of mace, which I could spray into an assailant's eyes. However, deploying it would be tricky. I assumed it would take more than the normal dose to incapacitate Dane, as he had routinely proven to be impervious to things that would kill another person. And while Murray had virtually no tolerance for pain—I had once seem him reduced to tears by a hangnail—he *did* have a sword. So I would have to be cautious and time my attack perfectly.

As we approached the stern, I tried to reach into my utility belt and grab the canister of mace without it *looking* like I was reaching into my utility belt to grab a canister of mace. This involved subtly slipping my hand underneath the pirate sash cinched around my waist and fumbling around there while keeping my eyes forward so as to not appear suspicious. Thankfully, it was quite dark, which made it hard to see what any of us were doing—although that was also a concern for me. For all I knew, Murray was reaching into *his* costume for something to incapacitate *me*.

The stern of the ship was the least popular section of the Promenade Deck, probably because people liked to look where they were going, rather than where they'd been, even if all directions looked exactly the same at night in the middle of the ocean. Plus, little had been done to make the stern very inviting. The deck there had no shuffleboard or lounge chairs. The wall opposite the railing was simply a flat white expanse, punctuated every now and then by a restricted-access door marked with various warning symbols that indicated dangerous things like electrical grids, heavy machinery, or toxic chemicals were concealed behind them.

"So," I said to Murray, "what are you plotting here?"

Murray gave a sharp laugh in response. "Why on earth would you think I'd tell you that?"

"It looks like you're planning on killing me," I said. "So it couldn't hurt to let me know what brilliant plan you've cooked up this time."

"Nice try, but flattery isn't going to work," Murray replied, although I could see it was a struggle for him to say this. Murray loved to talk, especially about how smart he was, and it was killing him to keep his plans to himself.

"Come on," I pleaded. "I always love hearing about your plans. They're so devious."

Murray wavered, but didn't crack. "You're the one who's being devious here, Ben. Very cunning of you. With your mind and my schemes, we would have made a great team. But I'm not gonna do the James Bond villain thing and tell you my whole plan, *thinking* you're going to die, only to have you not die and then ruin it all."

"That's very unlikely," I said, hoping it wasn't true. "I'm in a tremendous amount of peril here. You've done an exceptional job of luring me into a trap. I'm completely outmanned, and I don't have any weapons. The chances are pretty high that I'm not going to survive. So why not tell me what you're up to? I'd really like to know."

"Oh, I'm sure you would. But the only reason you're even alive right now is that I need some information from *you*." Murray suddenly stopped in his tracks and spun around to face me.

Luckily, in the second before this, I had managed to locate the mace in my utility belt and palm it. So Murray didn't catch me looking like I had my hands in my pants. Unfortunately, I couldn't use the mace yet, because Dane was still directly behind me. I needed to maneuver things so that my back wasn't to at least one of my opponents.

"What kind of information?" I asked.

"How much do you know about what I'm plotting here?"

"Why would I ask you what you were plotting if I knew what you were plotting?"

"To make it *sound* like you didn't know anything about what I was plotting," Murray explained. "So that I wouldn't know that the other spies knew, and thus assume that everything was fine and dandy, only to have them thwart everything. But I'm not about to take that chance. And I know you must know *something* about my plans, because you figured out that I was on this ship. So . . . tell me what you know, or I'll kill you." He attempted to dramatically whip out his sword but lost his grip on it. It clattered noisily on the deck.

Behind me, I heard Dane giggle.

Murray quickly snatched the sword back up and pointed it at my chest. "Spill your guts," he said menacingly. "Or I'll spill them for you."

I could tell from the smirk on his face that he'd been practicing that line and thought he'd delivered it well.

"You already let me know you're planning to kill me," I said. "So why would I share any information with you at all?"

"There's two ways to die: quick and painless, or slow and really, really painful." He jabbed me in the sternum with the tip of his sword, which hurt. A lot.

"Good point," I conceded. "Okay. I'll tell you what we know. First of all, we used forensic geology on a rock from your shoe to figure out you were in Nicaragua."

"Clever," Murray noted. "What else?"

"And we think you're plotting to steal the nuclear reactor from this ship and use it as a bomb." This last part was obviously a lie. But I told him it for two reasons. First, I was stalling. The longer I talked, the longer I stayed alive, and the better chance I had of getting the jump on Murray and Dane. Or having Erica or Catherine come along and rescue me.

Second, I figured that maybe I'd guess right and catch Murray by surprise.

That didn't happen.

Instead, Murray burst into laugher. "Wrong!" he crowed.

"Incredibly wrong! You really thought we were going to steal the reactor off this ship? That thing's enormous! It's inside a locked room inside another locked room inside a restricted area. And it's welded into the keel! I might as well try to steal the Washington Monument!" Murray laughed so hard, he doubled over.

Behind me, Dane was laughing too.

I thought I saw an opportunity for escape. "Oh," I said, doing my best to sound truly upset. "We thought you were going to set it off on the San Andreas Fault to create a massive earthquake that would knock Los Angeles into the ocean." That was the plot of the original Superman movie, although I was hoping that Murray wouldn't know it.

He didn't. And he laughed even harder. "That scheme is ludicrous. Wow, Ben. I expected better from you. You're losing your edge, buddy."

Dane was laughing heartily as well. So much that it sounded as though he was having trouble catching his breath. And Murray was so racked with laughter that he'd lowered his sword from my chest.

I wasn't going to get a better opportunity than this.

Even though Murray had a sword, I figured it was more important to incapacitate Dane first. He was big and dangerous and trained to kill, while Murray was small and weak and extremely uncoordinated.

So I spun around, catching Dane off guard, held the canister of mace in front of his eyes, and depressed the plunger.

Only to discover I wasn't holding a canister of mace at all. I had accidentally grabbed my flashlight from my utility belt instead.

In retrospect, it was an easy mistake to make. Both were compact metal cylinders of the exact same size. The on/off switch for the flashlight was located in the same spot as the plunger for the mace, at the end of the cylinder, and felt exactly the same.

So, instead of disabling Dane Brammage with an incredibly painful spray of mace in his eyes, I merely illuminated the deck of the ship a tiny bit better.

Dane immediately stopped laughing and seized me around the neck once again.

Murray stopped laughing too. "You were just trying to get the jump on us?" he asked, sounding betrayed. "You can sure be a jerk sometimes."

"Me?" I squeaked, gasping for air. "You're trying to kill me!"

"Not *trying*," Murray said angrily. "We're doing it. I've had it with your shenanigans. You've thwarted me for the last time."

"You can't kill me!" I said desperately, already feeling myself start to grow weak. "Then you'll have a dead body on your hands and nowhere to run. It won't be long before someone catches you red-handed."

Murray laughed again, but this time, it was mocking. "Oh, Ben. You really are slipping. Maybe it's the lack of oxygen to your brain, but you've missed a key element here: We're on a ship. And on a ship, you can kill someone and get rid of the body at the exact same time. Show him how it's done, Dane."

Dane dragged me to the railing at the stern.

To my horror, I now realized what Murray's plan for me was.

"It was nice knowing you," Murray said.

And then Dane threw me off the ship.

SURVIVAL AT SEA

The Pacific Ocean

Somewhere off the coast of northwestern Costa Rica

May 16

2130 hours

The five-story drop into the water was terrifying, but it wasn't even close to the worst part of being thrown overboard.

I had fallen from great heights into water surprisingly often in my brief time as a spy, so I knew how to plummet in the safest way possible. I assumed the pencil position, keeping my arms to my sides and holding my legs together, and thus plunged straight into the water like a needle going through a piece of fabric, rather than painfully thwacking into the surface. Still, I got a great deal of seawater up my nose, and the ocean was shockingly cold.

And yet, this also wasn't the worst part.

Since I had been dropped off the stern, I landed dangerously close to the three enormous propellers that drove the *Emperor of the Seas*. Each was the size of a house and spun rapidly, churning the ocean and creating turbulent vortexes of water. My pencil position had prevented me from fracturing every bone in my body on the ocean's surface, but it also sent me slicing down deep into the sea, where I was immediately caught in the maelstrom behind the propellers. In the cold, dark water, I was spun wildly, tossed about, nearly torn apart by dozens of currents acting at once upon me—and then finally sucked right toward the blades of the propellers themselves. I was nearly diced like a carrot in a food processor, but at the last second, a gyre of water yanked me upward and spit me out on the surface, racked with pain and coughing up salt water.

This still wasn't the worst part.

When you are aboard a giant cruise ship, it's hard to get a good idea of how fast they move. But when you are in the water *behind* a giant cruise ship, you have more perspective. The ships travel surprisingly fast for objects with the mass of the Empire State Building. The *Emperor of the Seas* was quickly leaving me behind in the ocean. The enormous, dark, incredibly deep ocean. Now that I was bobbing on the surface, I discovered that the waves were far bigger than they had appeared from the Promenade Deck. Each was at least ten feet high. Meanwhile, the coast of Central America was many miles away. I was already exhausted and aching after nearly being julienned by the propellers. I would have been lucky to swim the length of a swimming pool, let alone dozens of miles through choppy, shark-infested waters. And that was assuming that I could keep my bearings straight and not get turned around or dragged farther out to sea by currents.

There was nothing in my utility belt that I could use as a flotation device.

So the chances of my survival were slim. It was extremely likely that I was going to drown out in the ocean, all alone, and no one would ever see me again.

Or I was going to get eaten by a shark.

This was the worst part. The realization that I was doomed, and that my end wasn't going to be sudden and merciful, but drawn out, dismal, and terrifying.

For a moment, I considered simply giving up. What was the point of struggling to go on? All I would succeed in doing was making the next few hours of my life miserable before I died. So why fight the inevitable? I could just stop trying, let the ocean suck me down into its depths, and have the whole horrible ordeal be over within only a few seconds.

But I didn't do that.

Erica Hale wouldn't have given up. And neither would Catherine. Or Mike. Alexander probably wouldn't have given up either (although there was a good chance he might not have grasped how dire his situation was). Because giving up would be letting Murray Hill win. It wasn't only my life at stake; when the forces of evil were at work, there were countless other lives at stake as well.

I had to at least try to survive.

The *Emperor of the Seas* was already disappearing from sight, getting smaller as it moved away and being blocked by the swells of the waves. I treaded water, fixing its location on the horizon and then looking up to the sky above. It was a crystal-clear night, allowing me to easily pick out the constellations. Since the ship was heading south, I could figure out which way east was. The constellation of Virgo hung in the sky in that direction.

So now I had my bearings. I started swimming toward Virgo, battling my way through the rolling waves.

It was only now that I realized I was still clutching my flashlight. Somehow, despite everything that had happened, I had kept a firm grip on it, as though some part of my subconscious felt I was going to need it. I was about to tuck it back into my utility belt when I heard someone calling my name.

I was quite sure this was a hallucination. Even though I had been lost at sea for only two minutes, my mind was obviously playing tricks on me. The ship was too far away for me to hear anyone yelling from the decks, and there was no way someone who knew me could be all the way out here in the middle of the ocean.

But then I heard it again. It was faint, almost swallowed up by the roar of the surf around me, but it was definitely my name. And this time, I recognized the voice.

Mike was yelling for me.

I treaded water once again, trying to keep my head as high above the surface as possible, desperately searching the dark expanse of the ocean for what was going on.

The beam of a searchlight swept over my head.

I looked toward the source and spotted a life raft bobbing on the waves.

My heart leapt, but I tried to restrain my emotions. There was still a great distance between myself and the small boat, and the night was pitch-black. Even though Mike was coming for me, the chances of him spotting me in the dark, churning expanse of ocean were minuscule. I couldn't assume I was rescued yet. I had to do everything in my power to get Mike's attention.

Which was where the flashlight would be useful.

I held it over my head, aimed it in the direction of the

life raft, turned it on and started screaming at the top of my lungs.

The beam of light was thin but strong, and it was the only light out there on the ocean.

I was already exhausted, and the cold water was sapping my energy. The waves kept sucking me under. Every time I yelled, I got a mouthful of seawater. But I fought as hard as I could to scream and keep the flashlight high above my head.

It worked.

I knew Mike heard me, because the tone of his voice changed. It went from despairing to hopeful. And then the searchlight stopped sweeping the ocean and focused in my direction. Several times, it lit me up, only to bounce away due to the motion of the water. But it was definitely coming closer.

I hoped Mike could get to me before I drowned.

I struggled to keep afloat, well aware of how annoyingly ironic it would be to die when rescue was so close. But I could feel my strength flagging quickly. Every time the ocean pulled me down, it was harder and harder to get back up again. Twice, I saw the life raft come close, only to have Mike lose sight of me and head off in the wrong direction.

It was a big inflatable raft, designed for twenty-four people (I had learned this during safety training), although it appeared that Mike was the only one in it. It was propelled by a small outboard motor attached to the stern, which Mike had to steer manually, making it difficult for him to also search for me at the same time. Luckily, Mike had some skill with small boats, having spent many a summer day water-skiing on Chesapeake Bay. If our roles had been reversed, I would have been hopeless, but Mike had a possibility of success.

Each time he lost me, I managed to get his attention again, although the process was agonizingly slow. Minutes crept by, and with each one, the chances of my survival grew worse and worse. Even as the life raft got tantalizingly closer, I was losing stamina. My hands trembled from the cold and the effort of holding the flashlight. It was an ordeal to keep my head above water. And then, when the life raft was only a few yards away, I lost the light. A wave knocked it right out of my hand.

I tried to grab it as it sank into the depths, taking my eye off the ocean, and another wave caught me by surprise. It came over me from behind, swamping me and forcing me downward. I fought back toward the surface, and even got the tips of my fingers through, but then another surge came and shoved me down again.

I could feel darkness closing in all around me.

And then something splashed into the water beside me. Someone grabbed hold of my arm and yanked me back to the surface.

"You picked a heck of a time to go swimming," Mike said.

While I was relieved to have been saved, I was also terrified that Mike had sacrificed his own life to save me. "Why aren't you in the raft?" I screamed.

"Relax. I'm tied to it." Mike pointed to the safety line he had wrapped around his torso.

Even so, I knew he had taken a big risk. Getting both of us back to the life raft on the bobbing seas wasn't going to be easy, and I wasn't going to be much help. But Mike did it. He hooked an arm around me and used the safety line to find his way back to the raft, which was idling in the waves. That took another five minutes, by which point I was completely spent. It was all I could do to cling to the gunwale while Mike clambered aboard and then hauled me in.

Then, while I lay there, sputtering and trembling like a landed fish, Mike wrapped me in emergency blankets and handed me a cup of fresh water, which I gulped down quickly, and some emergency rations, which turned out to be a chocolate bar. "You probably ought to get out of your wet clothes," he advised.

He was right. So I shrugged them off and then clutched the blankets around me while Mike wrung several gallons of seawater out of my pirate clothes. My teeth were chattering so badly, I couldn't even ask a question. All I could manage was, "H-h-h-how . . . ?"

"Did I get here?" Mike finished. "I got worried when your radio went dead, so I came looking for you. Unfortunately, I went the wrong way, up toward the bow, so I lost valuable time. I got to the stern just in time to see Dane toss you overboard. If I'd gone that way first, I could have rescued you."

"Or gotten yourself tossed over as well," I tried to say, although it only came out as "Or-or-or-or-or . . ." through my chattering teeth.

"Anyhow, I called to Erica and Catherine, but I knew I couldn't sit around waiting for them to come to the rescue. You didn't have that kind of time. So I launched the life raft and jumped down into it."

"By-by-by-by . . ."

"Myself? Yeah. I guess Erica was right: That safety presentation *was* important. It actually wasn't too hard to launch this thing. The instructions were right on the side and easy to follow. They said the rafts were only supposed to be used in case of emergencies, but I figured this qualified." Mike grinned at me in the night.

It was so dark, I could barely see him, even though he was only a few feet away from me. The *Emperor of the Seas* was now long gone, only a distant blip of light on the horizon. There was no way we could catch back up to it. The life raft's motor wasn't nearly big enough to race after a cruise ship.

The raft was built for a lot more people than us, so we

had plenty of room. It was mostly made of a foul-smelling rubber—a rubber floor with inflatable rubber pontoons around the edges—but there was also a large box in the stern that held the emergency blankets, food rations, and drinking water.

I had warmed up to the point that I could now control my voice a bit better. "Is there an emergency beacon on this?"

"Kind of."

"Kind of?"

"There *is* one. But it might have been damaged when I jumped into the raft. I think I landed on it. And then the global positioning system sort of fell into the ocean."

"Ah." I scanned the night sky for Virgo. While Mike had been tending to me, we had been bobbing randomly around the waves. Eventually, I spotted it and pointed. "That way is east. Land's in that direction."

"How far away, do you think?"

"It might be up to thirty or forty miles."

"Then I guess we'd better get moving." Mike fired up the motor, pointed us east, and we set off across the ocean, hoping like heck that we'd find land before our fuel ran out.

9

HALLUCINATION

Near Ostional, Costa Rica
May 17
0700 hours

"Does that beach look weird to you?" Mike asked.

I focused on the horizon, squinting into the rising sun.

Mike and I had been trading shifts steering the life raft east all night, although Mike had taken the bigger share, as I was wiped out from nearly dying. I had caught sight of land on my shift, and when I had roused Mike to inform him, he had leapt to his feet and danced with elation. It was a gorgeous stretch of coastline, rolling hills covered with green jungle, but it was only now, as we got closer, that we realized something was wrong with the beach.

"It looks like it's moving," I said.

"Oh good." Mike heaved a sigh of relief. "I thought I might have been hallucinating. Like from scurvy or one of those other pirate diseases."

"Maybe we're *both* hallucinating." I kept my eyes fixed on the beach, worried about my own mental health. The entire stretch of land seemed to be alive. It was shifting slowly, a thousand different pieces moving in different directions at once, like a jigsaw puzzle that was assembling itself.

I was pretty sure you couldn't get scurvy after only a few hours at sea, but I was wondering if some other trauma from the night had fried my brain somehow. Or maybe it was my eyes that weren't working properly. They were definitely stinging from all the exposure to salt water. I had hesitated to use any of our drinking water to rinse them, fearing that my calculations might be off and that we'd be drifting at sea for weeks. But now that we were in sight of land, I felt we could spare some fresh water, so I poured it into my cupped palm and flushed my eyes with it. Then I looked back at the beach.

It was still moving.

By now, however, we were closer, and I could see it a little better. Enough to realize that it wasn't the sand moving around on the beach at all. Instead, it looked like individual rocks were moving around by themselves. Rocks the size of Thanksgiving turkeys.

This didn't make me feel any better about my mental state.

Mike seemed equally concerned. "Where do you think we are, exactly?" he asked.

"I'm guessing northern Costa Rica."

"I don't know too much about Costa Rica. Is it usual for the rocks to wander around here?"

"I don't think so."

"Rats. I think we've gone loopy."

I nodded agreement—but then realized what we were looking at.

"They're turtles!" I exclaimed. "Sea turtles! They must be coming ashore to lay their eggs!"

"Whoa," Mike said, realizing I was right. "There must be thousands of them!"

That was my estimate as well. Part of the reason I'd had so much trouble grasping what was happening on the beach was that I had no idea that so many sea turtles could be in one place at one time. But there they were. The beach was literally crawling with turtles.

The closer we came, the better we could see them. Their shells were smooth and brownish green, while the beach was an unusually dark brown. Since the turtles were built for swimming, they only had stubby little fins instead of legs, which made it extremely difficult for them to move on land.

And yet, they needed to come ashore to lay their eggs, so they were slowly dragging themselves out of the water, fighting their way up the beach, digging holes, filling them with eggs, covering them up, and flopping back down into the water again. The whole process looked like an ordeal, every inch of ground a struggle. The turtles were as slow and awkward on land as I had been when floundering in the water.

Now I noticed that the ocean around us was also full of turtles, some making their way to land, others heading back to sea. It was like sea turtle rush hour. So many shells were poking through the surface, it seemed as though we could walk to land atop them.

In the water, the turtles were far more graceful and considerably faster—although just about *anything* was more graceful and faster than a sea turtle on land.

However, as amazing as the spectacle was, what we really needed in that moment was civilization. We had to find a phone, get some help, and figure out how to return to our ship. But as luck would have it, we had come upon the least-inhabited span of coastline I had ever seen. There was nothing but sand, jungle, and turtles.

"Maybe we should head south," I suggested. "There must be a town somewhere close by."

"I hope so." There was a touch of worry in Mike's voice. "We're running low on gas." He turned the boat down the coast, and we motored slowly along the shoreline, trying to conserve our fuel and avoid running over any turtles.

We had only gone a few minutes before the motor conked out. It gave a cough and a wheeze and then sputtered into silence.

"Aw, come on!" Mike pounded the motor angrily. "Don't leave us stranded here in Turtle Town!"

"Look!" I exclaimed, pointing ahead of us.

We had just rounded a bend in the shoreline, revealing a whole new stretch of beach. About a half mile away was one of the most beautiful things I had ever seen: a seaplane. It was docked in the ocean beside a speedboat at the end of a long, lonely pier that extended across the beach. At the opposite end of the pier, perched atop a thickly jungled cliff, was a large, modern house. There were no other homes, or any sign of civilization at all, in sight. The house was as secluded as houses could be.

Between us and the pier were a few thousand more sea turtles.

The walls of the house facing the ocean were mostly glass, allowing us to see that the lights were on inside.

"Someone's home!" I exclaimed. "We can get help!"

"You might want to put your clothes on first," Mike advised me.

I was still wrapped in the emergency blanket, as my clothes

were wet and briny. But Mike had a point; when seeking the help of strangers, it was always a good idea to not be naked. So I pulled my wet and tattered pirate outfit back on. I had no way to see my reflection but suspected that I looked like someone who had recently been keelhauled. But that was still slightly more presentable than I had been when naked.

The water was shallow below us, so we hopped out of the life raft, dragged it ashore, and dropped its anchor on the sand to keep it from floating out to sea. Then we started across the beach, wending our way through the swarm of sea turtles.

This took some time, as I was battered and tired, and it was really hard to avoid stepping on turtles, because they were everywhere. Furthermore, the turtles weren't trying to avoid us at all. I had expected that our presence would make them skittish, but they didn't seem to care about Mike and me in the slightest. They kept flopping right into our path, forcing us to take a serpentine route. It was like walking across a minefield where the mines were actively trying to get in our way. Plus, we couldn't walk over any of the newly laid eggs for fear of crushing them. Fortunately, it wasn't hard to see where the nests were, as they were covered with little mounds of freshly turned sand. So we cautiously wove around them all.

The turtles themselves weren't showing each other nearly

as much respect. They clambered right over the sand mounds and one another, even if the others happened to be in the process of laying eggs, with no respect for anyone's privacy at all.

"What do you think our plan should be?" I asked, zigzagging through a phalanx of sea turtles.

"Let's just be honest," Mike suggested. "We knock on the door, tell them we're CIA, and say that we have an emergency and need a ride on their plane to get back to the ship."

"They'll never believe that. We're only teenagers."

"We have official badges." Mike fished his out of the folds of his costume. "I'm sure this will work. Costa Rica is a peaceful country. They *like* Americans here. In fact, tons of Americans retire in Costa Rica. For all we know, the owner of this house is one of them."

I realized Mike had a point. Some of my parents' friends from our old neighborhood had recently retired somewhere in Costa Rica, claiming that the land was cheap and the country was wonderful.

As we neared the house, it became evident that whoever lived there had a lot of money. The house was bigger than I had realized and looked as though it must have been quite expensive to build. It was all windows and balconies and was cantilevered over the edge of the cliff. There was even a swimming pool built directly into the cliff face, so that one side was a wall of glass, apparently so that they could even have a view of the ocean while swimming. A long, switchbacking staircase descended to the beach from the house, although there also turned out to be an elevator built into the cliff.

Three men emerged from said elevator at the far end of the pier. They were all big men, wearing suits, which seemed wrong for the weather and the location. They looked like locals, rather than expatriates, and they made a beeline toward us. Or as much of a beeline as one could make across a beach filled with turtles.

"They don't look happy to see us," I observed.

"We're on their property," Mike reassured me confidently. "They're probably wondering what's going on. Relax. We've got nothing to worry about."

The men had either overheard us speaking English, or they simply assumed that we weren't locals, because the biggest of them spoke to us in English as well. He was almost as brawny and imposing as Bjorn Turok. "Hey!" he barked as they approached. "Be careful around all those turtles! They're endangered!"

"We *are* being careful!" Mike responded pleasantly. Although in that moment, he was so busy watching the men that he stumbled over a turtle that had blundered into his path.

"Doesn't *look* like you're being careful," the big man said.

"What are you even doing on this beach? This is private property!"

"We didn't mean to trespass. This was an emergency." Mike held out his CIA badge for the men to see. "We're CIA, and—"

That was as far as he got. Because the moment the men heard "CIA" they snapped guns out of their belts and aimed them at us.

"Oops," Mike said quietly, his confidence draining. "I guess we might have something to worry about after all."

CONFRONTATION

La Casa del Diablo
Near Ostional, Costa Rica
May 17
0730 hours

Before I had enrolled at spy school, my response to this crisis would have been very different. I would have either tried to explain, in Spanish, why these men were making a mistake. Or I would have passed out in fear.

But by now, I had learned many tricks of the spy game. I had been in so many dangerous situations that I didn't pass out or panic. Instead, I managed to stay relatively calm and tried to focus on how to survive.

Which was why I didn't reveal that I could speak Spanish

yet. Erica had taught me that it often made sense to keep such things a secret at first. If people didn't realize that you spoke their language, they often said things in front of you that they never would have otherwise.

This was exactly what happened. The three henchmen directed Mike and me at gunpoint across the beach and into the elevator in the cliff, chatting amongst themselves in Spanish, assuming that they wouldn't be understood. Thus, I was able to quickly learn many things:

1) Mike and I had been trespassing on the private property of a drug trafficker known as El Diablo, which meant "the Devil."

2) The henchmen weren't quite sure what to make of our presence there but were concerned that the CIA was planning to infiltrate the compound.

3) They were taking us to El Diablo himself to have him decide what to do with us.

4) One of the henchmen had eaten something that was making him very gassy. The other two henchmen were teasing him mercilessly about this. They also didn't want to be in the elevator with him for fear that he would release a toxic fart in that small, enclosed space, so they made him walk up the stairs instead.

5) The big henchman, who was the leader, was unsure what to get his young daughter for her upcoming birthday.

The second henchman suggested that coloring books were always nice. (Henchmen could be surprisingly chatty when they didn't know you could understand them.)

The elevator brought us directly into the house, and we emerged into a great, glassed-in room with spectacular views of the beach. The furnishings were spare and modern. The gassy henchman entered through the porch doors, panting heavily after running up the stairs. The other two henchmen now forced us through the house at gunpoint.

While they were busy discussing the merits of coloring books versus something more splashy, like a video game system, I let Mike in on some of what I had learned, keeping my voice as quiet as possible so as to not let the henchmen know that I had understood them. "We're on a drug dealer's property. They're taking us to see him right now."

Mike's eyes went wide in fear. *What do we do?* he mouthed.

I could only shrug in response. We were outnumbered, unarmed, and on unfamiliar ground. I was trying to work out a plan but had come up with nothing so far.

The henchmen led us into a large, modern kitchen that also had an exceptional view. El Diablo was sitting in the breakfast nook.

On first impression, he didn't look that scary.

He appeared to be the same age as my grandfather, and he dressed the same way as well. He wore a green terry cloth bathrobe over his pajamas and slippers that matched the robe. A pair of unfashionable glasses was perched on his nose, and he was fiddling with his cell phone while eating a bowl of granola.

Despite his unimposing looks, he wasn't in a good mood. Just like my grandfather, he seemed completely stymied by his cell phone. "These ridiculous things," he said in Spanish as we entered. "I can never get them to work. I thought I downloaded a song, but now I can't find it. . . ." He finally looked up from his phone and reacted with surprise upon seeing all of us. "What's going on here?"

The lead henchman announced, "We caught these two kids on the beach. They're with the CIA."

El Diablo frowned. He looked from the henchmen to Mike and me. Then back to the henchmen. Then back to Mike and me again.

And then he burst into laughter.

"CIA?" he asked incredulously. "They're kids!"

"They have badges," the lead henchman explained.

"They're also dressed like pirates," El Diablo said. "Do you think that they're real pirates, too?" He made a face of mock terror. "Oh no! Maybe they're going to make us walk the plank!"

The henchmen all looked at their shoes sheepishly. "They *said* they were CIA," the leader said weakly.

"Look at them!" El Diablo exclaimed. "They're half-dead! They're probably delirious!" He suddenly shifted his attention to Mike and me and asked in perfect English, "Who are you?"

I figured the best way to stay out of trouble was to behave in exactly the way El Diablo had just suggested. So I answered him in my most delirious pirate voice. "Captain Long John Silver of the *Black Pearl*. Avast me hearties, thar be treasure buried on ye beach!"

Mike quickly realized what I was up to and joined in. "And I be his second mate, Jack Hawkins. Yarrrr."

El Diablo gave his henchmen a withering look. Then he asked us, "Are you with the CIA?"

"Yarrr," I said. "We be in the CIA pirate division."

"Yarrr," Mike agreed.

El Diablo looked back to his men, who all appeared to now be wishing they were somewhere else far away. "Where did you find these boys?"

"On the beach. They came ashore in a life raft."

"A life raft? So they're survivors of an accident at sea? And you held them at gunpoint?"

"We thought they might have been trying to steal turtle eggs," the leader explained. "And we know how much you care about the turtles. And then they said they were CIA, and we . . . well, we . . ."

"Made a bad decision based on faulty evidence?" El Diablo asked.

"Er . . . yes."

I was getting the impression that El Diablo wasn't very devilish at all. Although I had encountered far more evildoers than most people my age, the only drug kingpins I had ever seen had been in the movies or on TV. I had been expecting someone ruthless and terrifying, who would have immediately ordered his men to chop Mike and me up into tiny pieces and feed them to his pet alligators. Or something fiendish like that. But El Diablo actually seemed quite nice. Even though he believed his henchmen had messed up, he wasn't really angry at them. Instead, he made it a teaching moment.

"Jorge," he said to the leader, "you're a good man. And I appreciate your concern for the turtles. But if you want to move up in this organization, I need you to think carefully before you act."

Jorge nodded obsequiously. "I understand, El Diablo."

"These boys obviously mean us no harm. In fact, I think they could use our help. It looks to me like they need rest, food, and new clothes." El Diablo sniffed the air and wrinkled his nose. "They definitely need showers, too."

The gassy henchman farted loudly. El Diablo shifted his attention that way. "And you're working outdoors today, Enrique. At least until your stomach settles."

Enrique nodded and headed for the door.

El Diablo looked to Mike and me and spoke in English again. "Are you hungry?"

"Yarrr," I said. "Me mate and I have had nothing but hardtack and grog for days."

"Then let's get you some food," El Diablo said pleasantly. "And if you'd like warm showers and clean clothes, I can arrange that, too. Would you like that?"

"Yarrr," I said.

"Yarrr," Mike agreed, then thought to add, "And do ye have Wi-Fi? I'd love to check me messages."

REHABILITATION

La Casa del Diablo

Near Ostional, Costa Rica

May 17

0800 hours

Catherine Hale probably would have felt it was ethically wrong to accept any gifts from a criminal like El Diablo. But then, if Catherine Hale had been half-starved, filthy, and clad in only a sodden, tattered pirate outfit, she might have had second thoughts herself.

Mike and I couldn't even decide what gifts to accept first. We were ravenous but also desperate for showers. Thankfully, El Diablo suggested we could do both at once and let us carry enormous cinnamon buns off to the guest wing, where there were three separate bathrooms, each with its own shower. We devoured the buns along the way, while hatching a plan for how to deal with El Diablo: Once we had finished cleaning up, we would pretend to be refreshed and sane again, then use our official aliases as the Rotko boys, claim to have fallen overboard from the *Emperor of the Seas*, and ask if he could help us get back to the ship.

The guest bathrooms were as posh as the rest of the house; the showers were large and stocked with fresh soap, shampoo, towels, and loofahs. I took the longest, most luxurious shower of my life, scrubbing myself until I was finally warm again and every last vestige of salt was gone from my skin.

When I finally emerged, feeling fresh and clean, clothes were waiting for me. They appeared to belong to one of El Diablo's grandchildren, or perhaps a very small henchman. The T-shirt was a tacky souvenir from an American roadside attraction called Snakes Alive, the shorts were neon yellow, and the socks didn't match. However, I was in no position to complain. Plus, it was nice to be dressed as a normal tourist again, rather than a pirate.

I found El Diablo back in his breakfast nook, deep in conversation with Mike, who had apparently finished showering well before me. Mike was following our plan, no longer speaking in pirate dialect. He was teaching El Diablo how to work his cell phone, while El Diablo was talking to him about sea turtles.

"That species you see out there is the olive ridley sea turtle," El Diablo explained, pointing out the window. The beach was still thronged with them. "Like all sea turtles, they are endangered. This is one of the only places in the world where they lay their eggs in such numbers. However, the eggs are worth money, and people steal them. So I bought this whole beach and have my men patrol it to protect them."

"You must really like turtles," Mike observed.

"They are wonderful creatures," El Diablo said. "Originally, when I had to pick a nickname for myself, I wanted to be called 'El Tortuga.' But my wife said that wouldn't inspire fear."

"'The Devil' does sound a lot scarier than 'the Turtle,'" Mike agreed. Then he held up the phone. "If you want to see the songs you've downloaded, you just tap your music app."

"You mean this one?" El Diablo asked, tapping his phone.

"Uh, no," Mike said. "That app controls your thermostat."

El Diablo sighed heavily. "All these apps look the same to me."

Mike was about to show him the correct one when he noticed me. "Look who's finally out of the shower," he teased. "I'm surprised there's any water left in Costa Rica."

"Oh, you don't have to worry about hot water here," El Diablo said proudly. "All my water is heated by thermal power from volcanic activity. And all my electricity is solar. This house creates more energy than it uses!"

"Wow," I said. "You're really eco-conscious."

"Just because I'm a criminal doesn't mean I can't care about the environment," El Diablo said.

Since I only knew about this via eavesdropping, I pretended to be surprised. "You're a criminal?"

"A *minor* criminal," El Diablo clarified. "I have never hurt anyone—and I give back to the community. I also farm sustainably; I don't use any pesticides on my crops, and I water with drip irrigation. You know who the *real* criminals are? The gas and coal companies. They're destroying this planet. And yet, they get government subsidies for their businesses, while I'm branded a villain. Would you like some fresh papaya? I grew it myself."

"Sure," I said, taking a seat at the table. A papaya the size of a dachshund had been split open and drizzled with fresh lime. I used a spoon to scoop some into a bowl. "Thanks very much for your hospitality."

"Of course," El Diablo said. "What was I supposed to do, toss both of you back into the sea?"

"El Diablo also says he can get us back to our ship," Mike

said brightly. "As a thanks to me for teaching him how to use his phone."

"Really?" I asked, thrilled. "That's amazing!"

"We're still working on how to play the music," Mike said. "But we've mastered how to download it."

"I already bought three songs!" El Diablo said proudly.

I was starting to think that I had met kindergarten teachers who were more imposing than El Diablo. Still, I wasn't going to complain. I was clean, I had a way back to our ship, and the papaya was incredibly delicious. "How are we getting back?" I asked. "The seaplane?"

"Yes," El Diablo said. "Mike explained how you got separated from your family when you fell overboard last night. . . ."

"I told him about the drunk passengers who didn't know there was a pirate party," Mike said for my benefit. "And how, when they saw you, they thought you were a *real* pirate and tossed you overboard. So I had to deploy the life raft to save you."

"Right," I said, doing my best to play along. "Thank goodness you did that."

"Your brother is quite a hero," El Diablo said. "Much better than my lousy brother. Anyhow, we know your ship is scheduled to dock near Manuel Antonio National Park today. That's not too far. I can easily fly you down there."

"How soon can we leave?" I asked.

"Whenever you're ready," El Diablo said. "We were waiting for *you*."

"There's just one thing we have to do before we go," Mike said, then looked to El Diablo. "Do you mind if Ben and I talk in private?"

"Of course not," El Diablo said graciously.

Mike and I thanked him and stepped out onto the patio. This put us right by the pool that was built into the edge of the cliff. A railing led along the edge of the patio. Below us, turtles were spread out across the beach as far as the eye could see, in both directions. From our bird's-eye view, the sand looked like a piece of brown fabric that had been studded with very dull rhinestones. The three henchmen were posted at different points along the sand. Now that I realized they were there to protect the turtles, rather than kill any enemies, they seemed considerably less imposing.

Although it was possible that the men were there to protect the turtles *and* kill enemies.

"I checked my messages before showering," Mike said.

"You did that, showered, *and* showed El Diablo how to download music?" I asked.

"I didn't shower nearly as long as you did," Mike pointed out. "Anyhow, there were a couple messages from Trixie. The last one was from this morning. She said she'd been in touch with Erica—and Erica was really upset."

"About what?"

"About *you*, dummy. I mean, it's not like Erica told Trixie that, but what else could it be? Trixie just assumed that something had gone wrong with our mission—"

"How does Trixie know we're on a mission?" I interrupted, concerned.

Mike frowned. "Er . . . I might have mentioned it."

"Mike! This mission is supposed to be top secret! You're not supposed to tell Trixie about any of it! It's already bad enough that we let her know that everyone in her family is a spy!"

"Well, I couldn't just disappear for a few days without explaining *why* I was disappearing. . . ."

"Actually, that's *exactly* what we're supposed to do as spies!"

"You're missing the point here. Erica is upset about you. *Extremely* upset. Trixie talked to her last night . . . and she said Erica was *crying*."

"Crying?" I repeated. I couldn't have been more surprised if I'd heard that Erica had grown a third arm. Erica was not a person given to emotions.

"Crying," Mike confirmed. "She's obviously worried about you."

"And *you*," I said.

"I'm just a guy who's gone on a few missions with Erica. You're her friend—and as far as she knows, you've mysteriously vanished in the middle of an operation, which is never a good thing. You have to let her know you're okay."

I instantly felt like a jerk. In my rush to safety, and then my desire for food and a hot shower, it had never occurred to me that Erica might be worried about my absence. Or that Catherine and Alexander might be worried as well. Certainly, they would have noticed we were missing. But they always said emotions shouldn't interfere with a mission. I had just assumed that they would soldier on without us.

"You're right." I turned around and walked right back inside, not wanting to keep the Hales waiting another minute to hear from us.

El Diablo looked up from his phone as I entered. "Listen! I figured out how to work my music!" He cranked up the volume and played a Korean pop song he'd downloaded at full blast.

"That's great," I said supportively. "Is there any chance you have a phone I can borrow? I have to call our parents on the ship."

"Of course you do! There's a landline down the hall by the sauna."

I headed that way while Mike sat down to show El Diablo how to make a playlist.

I don't forget phone numbers. It's one of the benefits of my math skills. So I knew the number for the ship's operator by heart. I dialed it, then asked to be connected to our room.

Erica answered before the first ring was even done. "Hello?" she asked. I could hear the sadness in her voice. In that single word, I could tell that she was hoping for good news but was concerned it would be bad.

"It's me," I said. "Mike and I are safe."

"Ben!" she exclaimed, and now the sadness was entirely gone, replaced by a level of happiness that took me by surprise.

Behind her, I heard Catherine scream with joy and ask, "They're alive?"

"Yes," Erica confirmed.

There was another scream of joy from Catherine, and what sounded like Alexander vomiting, although vomiting as happily as one could.

Erica got back on the phone with me. The level of emotion in her voice had changed again, as though she was trying to control it because she didn't want me to know how worried she had been. "What happened to you?"

"I ran into Murray and Dane last night while you were breaking into the Chrysanthemum Ballroom. They threw me overboard."

"Murray and Dane?! I'll kill them. . . ."

"Erica," Catherine said sternly in the background, "you know I don't want you killing anyone. . . ."

"But they killed Ben first! Or they tried to, at least. He's lucky to be alive." Erica paused, then asked me, "*How* are you alive?"

I explained how Mike had seen me dumped overboard, found a life raft, and rescued me and how we had then made it to land and found a helpful local businessman who was willing to fly us to Manuel Antonio to meet them. I left out the part about what business El Diablo was actually in and made up a name for him—Mr. Gomez—instead of calling him El Diablo so that Catherine wouldn't chastise me for taking gifts from a criminal.

By the time I finished my story, Erica had returned to full spy mode. Any hint that she had been upset about my disappearance—or thrilled by my return—was absent from her voice. She sounded as businesslike as an accountant discussing tax returns. "Here's what you need to do," she said. "The ship just anchored offshore from Manuel Antonio. We'll go ashore with one of the excursions and meet up with you at the dock. Then we'll sneak you back aboard in the crowd. . . ."

"Why do we need to sneak back aboard?" I asked.

"Isn't it obvious?" Erica asked. "We don't want Murray and Dane to know you're still alive."

12

REUNION

Manuel Antonio National Park, Costa Rica
May 17
1500 hours

Erica's plan was simple: If Murray and Dane thought that Mike and I were dead, then they wouldn't be on the lookout for us, which would allow us more freedom to investigate them. Only, this required that we not return to the ship as ourselves. We would have to pose as other passengers.

El Diablo was eager to take us down to meet up with the Hales—who Mike had led him to believe were our *real* family, and not a group of CIA agents. Still, it took a while for us to get down there. First, El Diablo was insistent that we eat a full breakfast, seeing as we had been close to death and had to regain our strength. Then he kept getting distracted by the sea turtles, even on the short walk down the pier to his seaplane. ("This is an incredible event that few people ever have the good fortune to see," he explained to us, pointing to all the turtles laying eggs. "Never take an incredible event for granted.") Then, his plane wasn't particularly fast. It was old and outdated, because everyone would expect a drug dealer to travel in a sleek new jet, rather than a banged-up bucket of bolts. And finally, El Diablo didn't fly us to Manuel Antonio in a straight line, because there were dozens of places he wanted us to see along the way.

He flew us over his geothermal energy plant, his solar array, and the fields where he grew various illegal crops with sustainable methods. He veered over a coral reef that he'd had declared a national park and pointed out the Monteverde Cloud Forest and Arenal Volcano. He flew low enough over his brother's house to rattle the roof tiles because he thought it was funny. He even landed us in a river full of crocodiles because he thought crocodiles were amazing. (Mike and I were not eager to do this, as we had nearly been devoured by crocodiles on a previous mission, but we decided it wasn't prudent to share this information and feigned enthusiasm instead.)

Eventually, we made it to Manuel Antonio. This was a

relatively small national park bordered by a long public beach and a street lined with restaurants and souvenir stands. It was a far more beautiful spot than where we had boarded in Nicaragua. The *Emperor of the Seas* was anchored offshore while shuttle boats ferried passengers and crew back and forth to a pier, from which they dispersed for various activities. Even from the air, I could see that the surge of tourists had swamped the town. The beach was thronged, the cafés were packed, and the water was choked with so many speedboats, Jet Skis, and parasails that it looked like rush hour on the Beltway back home.

El Diablo came in smoothly and skimmed across the waves to a different pier that was reserved solely for seaplanes. I had expected that we would just say a quick thank-you, hop out of the plane, and let El Diablo head on home, figuring that drug dealers probably liked to lay low. But El Diablo wouldn't hear of it. "I'm not leaving until you are safely reunited with your family," he told us. "There are some nasty criminals in this area."

"Look who's talking," Mike whispered to me.

There was no way to refuse El Diablo's help without seeming suspicious—and he wouldn't have listened to us anyhow. He was already out of the cockpit, ready to escort us.

As we came down the pier to the beach, I spotted a group of uniformed police and grew concerned that El Diablo might end up in trouble, but El Diablo wasn't worried about being spotted at all. In fact, he was perfectly happy to be seen— which was a good thing, as all the locals seemed to know who he was: the fishermen, the souvenir sellers, the tour guides. It was as though Mike and I had shown up at a rock concert in the lead singer's limo. No one appeared frightened of him; instead, they smiled pleasantly or even called out to him. El Diablo responded kindly to everyone, waving and shaking hands. I heard one woman thank him for building a new wing onto her daughter's school, while a fishmonger told us El Diablo had funded a medical clinic in her town and tried to give him a freshly caught snapper as thanks.

Even the police seemed happy to see him. None of them shook his hand, but they nodded respectfully as we passed.

"Everyone here really seems to like you," I noted.

"I've done well, so I make a lot of donations to local causes," El Diablo explained. "I find, it's better to make friends in this life than enemies."

Beyond the crowded beach rose the forested hills of Manuel Antonio. At the front gates, tourists were lined up for guided nature walks, which promised them the chance of seeing wild sloths and monkeys. I would have loved to go on one of those, but sadly, I wasn't on vacation. I needed to reunite with the Hales and get back to work figuring out what Murray Hill was up to. So I consoled myself with the knowledge that I had already witnessed some incredible nature that morning and searched for Erica and Catherine.

Unsurprisingly, they spotted me first. They were waiting next to the shuttle boat pier, where they could keep a close eye on everyone coming and going from the *Emperor of the Seas*, and were dressed in full tourist regalia: T-shirts, sun hats, cargo shorts, and flip-flops. "My boys!" Catherine shrieked, then embraced Mike and me in a bear hug, the same way that my real mother would have. None of it seemed to be an act. She was obviously thrilled and relieved to find us alive and well again.

The real surprise came when Erica hugged me too. "I'm so glad you're alive," she said. I knew that it made sense for her, as my fake sister, to make a show of being happy that I was safe, but she still held on to me for far longer than I expected she would.

"It's nice to see you, too," I said.

"It looks like you're in good hands now," El Diablo told Mike and me. "So I'll leave you with your family."

Catherine turned to him, prepared to thank him profusely—but then I saw a flicker of recognition on her face. Her smile faltered for a fraction of a second, then returned in full force. "Thank you so much for rescuing my boys!" she exclaimed.

"Oh, I didn't rescue them," El Diablo said graciously. "They survived on their own. I only helped them get back to you."

"Even so," Catherine said pleasantly, "we owe you a huge debt, Mr. . . . What was your name again?"

"I'm just a concerned citizen." El Diablo turned to Mike and me. "Safe travels, boys. It was a pleasure to meet you." He flashed us a smile and headed back for his plane.

Catherine wheeled on us, her happiness slightly dimmed. "Did you two accept a ride here from a drug dealer?"

"Yes," I admitted, "but he was a *nice* drug dealer."

"It was either accept his help or starve to death in the wilderness," Mike added. "So we went with the option where we survived."

Catherine was about to say something in response, but Erica put a hand on her arm and said, "Mom, we can't always be saints. Sometimes, we have to make hard choices to get the job done."

Catherine pursed her lips, then gave in. "Speaking of which, as pleased as I am to see you boys, we have work to do. Let's get back to the ship. Erica has some items to prevent Murray and Dane from recognizing you."

Erica opened a shopping bag and handed us baseball caps and sunglasses from the local souvenir stores. These, combined with the tacky T-shirts El Diablo had given us, allowed us to easily blend in with the crowd of passengers lined up for the shuttles back to the ship.

I glanced down the beach. El Diablo was now accepting a sack of ripe mangoes from an adoring fruit seller.

"We've been keeping tabs on the shuttles all day," Erica said. "We haven't seen hide nor hair of Murray or Dane, so theoretically, they're still on the ship."

"But of course, we can't guarantee that," Catherine said with a sigh. "And short of your encounter with them last night, we haven't found a trace of them on board."

Mike asked, "So there was nothing in the ballroom?"

"Right. It was only a ruse to lure us into trouble." Erica sounded disgusted with herself for being tricked.

Catherine said, "While the two of you were gone, Shayla Shang got us access to the Premier level so that we could inspect each of the suites up there, which we did last night by posing as cleaning staff. Murray isn't staying in any of them. All the guests are legitimate tourists."

"Hold on," I said, feeling hurt. "You kept on with the investigation even though Mike and I were lost at sea?"

"We didn't know *where* you were," Catherine explained. "We thought that, perhaps, you'd been captured by those scoundrels. In which case, finding them made sense. . . ."

"But even if we *had* known what had happened to you," Erica added, "it's not like we would have stopped investigating. Then your deaths would have been in vain."

"Oh," I said. "I guess that makes sense."

"Of course it does." Erica sounded slightly annoyed at me for even questioning this. "If *I* had been the one tossed overboard, I wouldn't want *you* to stop investigating. I'd want you to find Murray and punch his teeth down his throat."

"Anyhow, it appears you were wrong about them staying in Premier class," Catherine told me with a hint of disappointment. "They must be in one of the regular rooms—or perhaps even crew quarters. But there are thousands of those, and we couldn't even begin to search them, seeing as our team was down to only two people."

"How's Alexander doing?" Mike asked. "He didn't want to come ashore and be on dry land for a bit?"

"He went to the ship's doctor this morning," Catherine reported. "And he got some new medicine that finally did away with his nausea. However, it's quite potent and has knocked him for a loop."

"That's putting it mildly," Erica whispered to me. "Dad's blathering like a lunatic."

We reached the end of the pier. Shuttles were pulling up and loading passengers one after the other, like cars on a roller coaster, so there was no wait to get on. We piled onto one with a large group of fellow tourists. In our cramped conditions, it reeked of sunscreen and body odor—and a few people who had gone deep-sea fishing had the additional funk of raw seafood.

"Why don't you tell us everything you can remember

about your encounter with Murray and Dane last night?" Catherine asked me. "Maybe they said something important that will help us decipher what they're plotting."

"Murray wouldn't say *anything* about that," I told her. "I tried to get him to talk, but he refused. And Dane didn't say anything at all."

"Think," Erica pressed. "Murray loves to talk. He must have said *something* of importance."

I did my best to recall my conversation with Murray, but to my frustration, it was eclipsed by the much more vivid memories I had of being tossed overboard. I could remember every terrifying second of that ordeal—even though I would have preferred to forget it—while the part of the evening that I *wanted* to remember was a hazy blur. "Murray has wised up," I reported sadly. "I know he wanted to tell me what he was up to—but he didn't."

The shuttle pulled away from the pier and headed across the bay toward the *Emperor*, dodging through a gauntlet of morons on Jet Skis, most of whom seemed to have no idea what they were doing. Two blindly cut right in front of the shuttle and barely missed getting plowed into, while one wiped out in our wake so violently that he was catapulted ten yards through the air.

"Uh-oh," Mike said, sounding concerned. "Look west."

The rest of us did. Although the sky above the bay we

were in was gorgeous and sunny as a postcard picture, storm clouds were gathering on the horizon, so dark that it looked like the dead of night.

"That's not promising," Erica observed.

"Just like this mission," Catherine groused. The joy she had felt at seeing Mike and me alive again had passed, and now her mood seemed as dark as those clouds. Which was a surprise to me, as I was used to her being incredibly upbeat no matter what the circumstances. "We've made no headway at all and nearly lost two of our team. And we're running out of time to get results. We need to either find Murray Hill or figure out what he's cooking up."

"There's four of us now," Mike said helpfully. "Maybe we can all search the other rooms and crew quarters."

I shook my head. "It'd be a waste of time. I *know* Murray. There's no way he'd stay in a room like ours if he could avoid it. And he's certainly not staying with the crew."

"Well, he has to be staying *somewhere*," Catherine said with surprising bitterness. "And he's not in the luxury suites. Face it, Benjamin, you were wrong about that." She gave a sigh. "However, I agree that searching every room on this ship one by one wouldn't be the best use of our time. It'd be like looking for a needle in a haystack."

"Then maybe we should go back to our original plan," Erica said. "And let Murray come to us."

"Erica!" Catherine snapped, then gave her a glare, warning her not to go on.

Erica glared right back. "Ben deserves to know."

She didn't have to tell me, though, because in that moment, I realized what had been going on. "Oh no," I said.

"What is it?" Mike asked blankly. "What's wrong?"

"I just realized why I was *really* brought on this mission," I replied sourly. "It wasn't because I understand how Murray Hill thinks. I'm the bait to lure him out of hiding."

DISILLUSIONMENT

Level Three

The *Emperor of the Seas*

Just off Manuel Antonio National Park, Costa Rica

May 17

1600 hours

"I can't believe you used me like this!" I yelled, storming through the narrow corridors of the ship toward our room. "I nearly got killed!"

"Obviously, that wasn't how the plan was intended to work," Catherine said, hurrying after me with Mike and Erica in tow. "We intended to catch Murray in the act of accosting you. It didn't occur to us that you'd abandon your post. I told you to act as a lookout while we broke into the

Chrysanthemum Ballroom, but you left the area and went onto the Promenade Deck without telling us."

"I was trying to help with the investigation! Because I *thought* that was what I was supposed to be doing! I didn't realize that my job here was simply to draw Murray out!"

"Benjamin, please keep your voice down," Catherine said nervously. "Or the whole ship will know that you're a secret agent."

"Isn't that the plan? To let Murray know I'm here so that he can come kill me?" I called out at the top of my lungs, "Murray! It's Ben! Your attempt to kill me failed! So come polish me off for good!"

A few passengers poked their heads out of the room ahead of me, wondering what the commotion was about.

"We're actors," Catherine told them. "Rehearsing for tonight's theatrical performance. It's a rousing spy thriller set on the high seas! You should come see it."

The other passengers now seemed excited to catch the show. I stormed past them all and barged into our room. Catherine, Mike, and Erica entered right on my heels.

Alexander was sitting on the bed in the adjoining room, looking surprisingly healthy, given that the night before, he'd been the same color as a watermelon rind. He was dressed, groomed, and back to his normal complexion. "Hello, everyone!" he said cheerfully.

Even though I was livid, I still paused to look at him, struck by his transformation. So did everyone else.

Mike told Erica, "I thought you said he was delirious."

"I'd like all of you to meet the Tralfamadorians," Alexander told all of us, pointing to some nonexistent beings. "They're from the Bingpot Galaxy."

"Oh," Mike said. "There's the crazy."

"Alexander," Catherine said with concern, "I don't see any aliens in that room."

"Well, of course you don't!" Alexander replied. "They're invisible to us. They exist in sixteen different dimensions, so we *can't* see them." Then he whispered to us in confidence, "That's probably a good thing, though, because I've heard they look like giant earwigs. But they have very lovely dispositions."

Catherine turned to Erica. "Why don't you and Michael deal with your father while I talk to Benjamin?"

Although she phrased this as a question, it wasn't really a request. It was an order. Erica didn't look pleased to be saddled with talking to her father about invisible aliens, but she nodded agreement and went into the next room with Mike.

"Do either of you have any cheese on you?" Alexander asked them. "The Tralfamadorians are absolute fiends for dairy products."

Catherine closed the door on them and then turned

her attention to me. "I know you're upset," she said. "And I understand why. But I can't have you jeopardizing this mission with emotional outbursts."

"And yet, jeopardizing my life is totally okay?"

"This is a dangerous business, Benjamin. You knew that when you signed up. I've been used as bait many times myself. . . ."

"But your partners *told* you that was happening, right?" I asked pointedly. "They didn't lie to you about it."

Catherine shifted from one foot to the other uneasily, then admitted, "That's true. I had my issues with lying to you, but the higher-ups felt it was better if you didn't know. They don't know you the way I do. They still see you as a child."

"A child whose life they're putting at risk."

"Yes." Catherine now looked far less upset with me and significantly more apologetic. "Just out of interest, if we *had* been honest with you, would you have agreed to this mission?"

"I don't know," I said truthfully, then slumped onto one of the beds. "What's most upsetting about all of this is that I was used as bait when I first came to spy school. I thought that maybe I'd proved myself since then. But apparently, bait is the only thing I'm qualified to be. . . ."

"That's not true." Catherine sat beside me and put

her arm around my shoulders. "You were brought on this mission for many reasons. You *do* know Murray Hill better than anyone. . . ."

"Maybe not. I was wrong about where he was staying on the ship. And you were obviously upset about that."

"I was upset at *myself*, not you. I agreed to this mission, thinking I could protect you—and I failed. The plan wasn't for you to confront Murray and Dane on your own. If they approached you, Erica and I were supposed to get the jump on them. But they caught us off guard. You almost died because of my mistake. If it hadn't been for Michael, you *would* have died. . . ." Catherine trailed off. There were tears in her eyes. "Oh, Benjamin, I'm so sorry."

"It's okay," I said, and was surprised to realize that I meant it. It seemed that I should have been angry at Catherine at that moment. *Really* angry. And yet, now that she seemed so upset with herself, I actually felt bad for her.

"No. It's *not* okay." Catherine pulled me even tighter against her and held me there for a bit, the same way my mother would have done if *she* had allowed a nefarious villain to throw me off a cruise ship. (Although, in my mother's defense, she had never put me in a situation nearly this dangerous; the worst she had ever done was to forget to pick me up after school one day when I was seven.) It was very comforting. Eventually, Catherine released her grip on me and said, "You're right, you deserve honesty. So here we go: I don't intend to drop my guard and let anything bad happen to you again—but of course, there's no way I can guarantee that. So if you want out of this mission, I'll understand."

"How would that even work?" I asked. "I mean, it's not like I can just leave the ship."

"True," Catherine agreed. "But we could have you lay low in here until the mission is over. Since Murray and Dane believe you're dead, there's little chance they'll come looking for you."

I considered what laying low might be like: sitting in our tiny room, watching TV and listening to Alexander rave like a lunatic. While that might have been safer, I certainly didn't feel like doing it. I realized I was far angrier about having been lied to than I was about being used as bait. "I want to stay on," I said honestly. "I want to find Murray and thwart his plans and make sure he and Dane are locked up for good so that they can't try to kill me anymore." Then I thought to add, "And so they can't kill anyone else, either."

Catherine smiled, blinking away her tears. "Sounds good to me," she said, then called out to the others. "We're good in here if you'd like to join us."

The door between the adjoining rooms opened immediately, as if Erica had been waiting desperately for the all clear. She and Mike came right in.

Behind them, Alexander was still in rapt discussion with his imaginary aliens. "My favorite cheese? Definitely Cambozola. You must try it some time."

Erica closed the door on him. "I liked it better when he was puking his guts up," she said.

"Benjamin and I have worked things out," Catherine reported. "But I'm against the idea of using him as bait once more. I'd rather keep his survival a secret and let Murray and Dane continue to believe that they've successfully gotten rid of him."

"Then we're right back at square one again," Erica said. "How are we supposed to find Murray and Dane on this ship? It's like searching an entire city. It's much easier to let them come to us." She looked to me. "No offense. I'm not trying to get you killed again. But the fact is, using you as bait *worked*."

"Except for the whole part where you dropped your guard and Dane threw me overboard," I reminded her.

"Er . . . yes," Erica agreed. "But we won't let that happen again."

Catherine said, "I propose that, rather than hunting down Murray and Dane, we search for what they've been plotting instead. Perhaps we'll catch them red-handed. Shayla Shang doesn't want us getting into the engine room. So let's get into the engine room."

"How?" Erica asked. "The Shangs got us the passes to access the crew areas, but not the engine room. And the restricted areas of this ship have tougher security than Fort Knox." This would have been an exaggeration for most people, but it wasn't for Erica; not only was she familiar with the security system at Fort Knox, but she also knew how to get past it.

The moment she said this, Mike's eyes lit up with excitement. "The Shangs got us the crew passes?"

"They had them delivered to us last night," Catherine answered. "One for each of us, as promised."

"Then I think I know how to get us into the engine room," Mike said.

MUSICAL THEATER

Restricted Crew Area

The *Emperor of the Seas*

Somewhere off southwestern Costa Rica

May 17

1800 hours

Mike had researched the map of our ship with the obsessiveness of a Talmudic scholar, which had led to his inspiration.

"Even though this ship is enormous, there's still limited space inside to contain everything the builders wanted to put in it, " he explained. "I mean, not only are there thousands of rooms, but there's also twelve restaurants and a disco and that ridiculously small swimming pool. And those things all fit together as tightly as possible, like the whole ship was crafted as a giant jigsaw puzzle. Well, after the great hall, the single biggest piece of the ship is the theater. Not only do you have a stage and three tiers of seats, but it also includes all the backstage stuff, like the dressing rooms and the space for them to store the sets when they're not being used. And there's even a whole big area *under* the stage, because sometimes they're raising and lowering the sets up and down through it, just like they would in a theater on Broadway. Actually, according to the brochure, it's even *bigger* than a lot of Broadway theaters, but then, some of those are really small and cramped. . . ."

"How many Broadway theaters have you been to?" Catherine asked, pleasantly surprised by Mike's knowledge.

"Plenty," Mike replied. "I *love* the theater."

I had known this about Mike, because he was my best friend, but I could understand how the others found it shocking. Mike often came across as the type of kid who'd rather put his hand in a toaster than sit through a musical, but he, like just about everyone else, had more layers than most people realized.

"Anyhow," he went on, "the only real place to fit a theater that big is at the rear of the ship, where it's the widest, and that also happens to be where the engine room is, as the propellers need to be at the stern. . . ."

"So the theater is sitting right on top of the engine room," Catherine concluded, growing excited.

"Exactly," Mike said. "And because it's a theater, there's all these hidden spots and crawl spaces underneath the stage. So I'm betting that if we can get in there, maybe there's some way to access the engine room without going through the main door."

"It's worth a try," Catherine agreed, sounding pleased.

Which is how, a few hours later, our team found ourselves infiltrating the theater—minus Alexander, whom Catherine had taken back to the ship's doctor to see if he could prescribe an anti-nausea medication that wouldn't cause cheese-loving-alien hallucinations.

We couldn't simply walk into the theater, as the public doors were locked until half an hour before that night's performance, so we had to enter through the crew area. This wasn't an issue, thanks to the passes Shayla Shang had procured for us, especially since the passes stated we were performers. The Flying Mazurkas. Although, due to the intricate way all of the parts of the ship fit together, we had to pass through quite a lot of the crew area to get to the theater.

The closest crew access point to the theater was in the grand entrance for the casino. Passing from the glitzy foyer into the crew area was a startling transition. The two zones were so different, it was almost as though we had stepped into a different universe. A significantly crummier one.

The casino entrance was glamorous and opulent, designed to evoke wealth and prestige, with inlaid marble floors, gilded columns, and crystal chandeliers. On the flip side, no attempt had been made to beautify the crew area at all; it was blatantly industrial, with unpainted metal walls, cheap linoleum floors, and naked lightbulbs. Pipes and wires were simply bolted to the walls. The rooms for the crew were claustrophobically small; we could tell because most of the crew who were inside had left their doors wide open, which cut down on privacy but gave them slightly more space. The rooms weren't much bigger than good-size closets—and each housed three people, with a tier of narrow bunks bolted to the walls. The only windows were small portholes an inch above the water, which didn't let much light in and were often blocked by large clumps of kelp. The bathrooms were communal, just like the ones in our dormitory at school, as evidenced by the great number of crew wandering back and forth in bathrobes, clutching shower caddies. And, though I hadn't thought it physically possible, their bathrooms actually smelled *worse* than ours at school.

"Wow," Mike said, sounding genuinely amazed. "These rooms make the ones in our dorm look big. Housing people like this can't possibly be legal."

"On land it might not be," Catherine said, "but the laws are significantly less stringent in international waters."

To make matters worse, the *Emperor of the Seas* had run into the storm that had been looming on the horizon earlier. And the storm was a big one. The upper decks were being pelted with torrential rain while gusting winds churned the ocean. Despite the ship's great size, it was still being pummeled by the waves. It was slowly rocking from side to side, which made walking through the tight hallways treacherous.

The crew members were from all over the world. I overheard at least a dozen different languages being spoken in only a short section of hallway. Although I couldn't comprehend all of them, I got the sense that most of the speakers were in bad moods, which was understandable. I had seen prisons that were more luxurious than the crew quarters. And then I picked up one voice I recognized. At least, I recognized the accent; the tone was radically different from what I'd heard so far.

"I'm so sick of these awful teenagers," Kit Karoo was grousing. "They're the worst. If I have to listen to one more pimple-faced wannabe pop star massacre a song at karaoke, I'm gonna kill someone."

We rounded a corner to find ourselves in an employee mess hall. It wasn't even a separate room; it was simply a widening of the hallway where a few tables had been crammed. Kit sat with several other crew members, all of whom were sullenly poking at what was theoretically food, although it looked like something you wouldn't even let your dog eat. Evidently, the attention to culinary detail on board only applied to the guests, not the staff.

Each crew member had a beer, which they kept their hands clamped around firmly to prevent them from sliding off the tables, given the rocking of the ship.

"If you'd like to change jobs, let me know," said a skinny man with an Eastern European accent seated next to Kit. "I'd be happy to spend my days getting kids to play games instead of cleaning toilets. You don't want to know the horrors I've seen. I think I might have post-traumatic stress disorder."

"Nothing is more horrible than an entitled teenager," Kit told him. "They're all snarky little jerks who you want to smack upside the head. . . ." She trailed off in surprise as she spotted us and then made a desperate attempt to cover. "But not you three!" she exclaimed gamely. "You guys are the best! Why didn't you come for s'mores last night?"

"We fully intended to," Mike said honestly. "But then Ben got thrown overboard."

Kit faked a laugh, assuming he was joking. "Aw, you're a pistol, kiddo! You know this is a restricted area, right? So, if you were to complain to management about something you *think* you overheard, I'd have to point out that you had been trespassing when you heard it—which you could be prosecuted for?"

"We're not trespassing." Erica displayed her official crew pass, which made Kit's eyes go wide with concern. "But don't worry. We won't tell anyone what you said."

Kit gave her a weak smile. "I don't *really* hate all teenagers. Just some of them. And the shifts on this job are torturously long. Try being chipper and perky while running dance-offs and air-hockey tournaments for sixteen hours straight and see if it doesn't give you a migraine the size of Tasmania."

"I get a headache after being chipper and perky for thirty seconds," Erica said truthfully.

"Still, I owe you one," Kit told us.

"We might take you up on that someday," Catherine said, and then led us onward through the maze of hallways until we came to the theater.

We had timed our visit in the hopes that it would be empty, assuming that the actors and crew might be grabbing dinner before performing two shows in a row that evening. However, the rough seas had forced some emergency rehearsals.

The theater presented a different show every night of the week, so that passengers who were on board for only a few days could see a variety of performances. Some nights, there were relatively simple acts, like magicians or jugglers or acrobats, but on others there were far more elaborate productions. This evening's entertainment was billed as a "Broadway-quality musical extravaganza" called *Symphony at Sea.* It was a love story between a sailor and a mermaid, and it seemed that several scenes were supposed to take place underwater, with the actors suspended by wires from the ceiling to give the impression that they were floating. This might have worked nicely in calm seas, but it was a serious problem on a stormy night. Now, during the rehearsals, the rocking of the ship was making the actors pendulum back and forth on their wires. Instead of appearing to be gently bobbling in a tropical lagoon, the unfortunate thespians dressed as tropical fish, turtles, and merfolk were being flung about wildly, occasionally clonking into one another like the bangles on an enormous bracelet.

This was causing a major crisis, seeing as the doors were supposed to open to the public for the early-bird performance in less than thirty minutes.

So instead of being empty, the areas behind and below the stage were packed with actors and crew desperately trying to figure out how the show would go on. And yet, this wasn't necessarily a problem for us. Once again, we simply pretended like we were supposed to be there, and no one questioned our presence. There were plenty of children in the cast, playing young crabs and squid and other marine life, and everyone was distracted by the crisis at hand, so we were able to blend into the chaos and wander about freely without drawing attention.

The area below the stage was in complete disarray. Props and pieces of scenery were scattered everywhere, the hydraulic lifts that raised everything up to the stage were constantly moving up and down, and actors scurried every which way. (Except for the ones playing merpeople; since their legs were bound together by their fish tails, they couldn't scurry so much as awkwardly hop from place to place.) It was also quite dark, requiring us to use flashlights to examine the floor.

I was the one who found the hatch. It wasn't hard to deduce that it led to the engine room, as it was clearly labeled ENGINE ROOM EMERGENCY HATCH: DO NOT BLOCK. The hatch was directly beneath center stage, next to a few bins holding swords and other weaponry for a climactic battle sequence. It was two feet square, with a handle built to lie flush with the floor so that no one would trip over it. I got the attention of the rest of my team, who hurried to my side.

By now, it was getting close to showtime. From somewhere off in the wings, a stage manager ordered everyone to get to their places, as the house was about to open. This provoked even more chaos, as everyone scrambled into position for the big opening number.

The hatch had even weaker security than the door to our room, which made some sense, as it was an emergency escape and its location was hidden. Catherine jimmied it within fifteen seconds, and then we all scrambled down through it and yanked it closed above us once again.

The engine room turned out to be extremely large, stretching from port to starboard and extending a hundred yards forward from the stern. Despite this, it wasn't hard to locate the nuclear reactor; it was directly beneath the emergency hatch, and thus, we found ourselves standing on top of it.

Or, more accurately, we were standing atop the housing unit for the reactor. Since the reactor used nuclear energy, it couldn't be left out in the open. Instead, just as Murray had said, it was inside a large metal housing, sort of a room within the engine room, a cube eight feet on each side. The reactor was producing so much energy that the housing was warm beneath our feet.

All around us, machinery that was powered by the reactor was hard at work. The reactor operated by turning water to steam, which then flowed out of the housing through a network of pipes into a turbine generator. The steam then moved to a condenser, where it turned back to water, which returned to the reactor, where it became steam once again. The gigantic shafts that rotated the ship propellers were encased in long metal tubes that extended across the floor from the engines to the stern, and all the electrical power for the ship was generated in this room as well. Everywhere around us were pipes for water and steam, many of them dripping with condensation. Despite the complexity of it all, the entire engineering staff was seated at a table a long distance away, playing cards. Either everything was operating so smoothly that they didn't need to keep a close eye on it, or they were incredibly negligent. There were four men, all only wearing shorts and tank tops, given the heat in the room.

The machinery was loud enough to easily cover the sound of our entrance, and there was a network of pipes obscuring us from the engineers' view—although the men were so riveted to their card game, they might not have even noticed us if we'd been in plain sight. A series of metal rungs was built into the side of the reactor housing to allow access to the emergency hatch. We quickly climbed down them to the floor.

The housing had two large windows built into it, allowing the engineers to monitor the reactor without having to go inside and be exposed to the radiation. As a further layer of protection, five separate radiation monitors were bolted to the housing; thankfully, all of them registered that it was safe. The windows were extremely thick and somewhat opaque, which gave them a yellowish tint. I figured they were probably lined with something to add even more protection from the radiation.

I peered through one window at the reactor. Given that it was capable of producing enough energy to level a small city, it looked surprisingly benign. The actual nuclear core was significantly smaller than the turbine generators and was housed in yet another metal case. This one was light gray and rounded, so that the core looked quite a bit like R2-D2 from *Star Wars*.

Just like Murray had told me, the housing for the reactor was welded to the metal floor of the ship. There was simply no way that anyone would be able to remove the core from both protective housings. . . .

"Oh," I said aloud, suddenly struck by a thought.

"What is it?" Erica asked.

"Murray *did* give something away when he was talking to me," I said.

However, before I got the chance to explain it, Catherine said, "Goodness me." There was a great deal of concern in her voice—and some anger as well—all of which made me forget about what I was about to say and try to figure out what had upset her so much.

Catherine was looking away from the reactor, across the engine room, toward some large objects that seemed very out of place.

There were twelve of them. Each was the size of a man, but then swaddled in so much protective plastic bubble wrap that it had grown considerably larger. Due to all the plastic, it was hard to tell exactly what was inside the wrapping, but I had the vague impression that I could make out human faces deep within them.

Catherine quickly made her way toward the objects,

weaving through all the hissing and clanking machinery. The rest of us hurried after her. Given the look on Catherine's face, I was concerned that, perhaps, real human beings were swaddled up in the plastic.

However, Erica appeared annoyed. "Mother," she said curtly. "You're getting distracted from the mission. We're supposed to be figuring out what Murray Hill is plotting. . . ."

"Our job is to thwart international crimes," Catherine said, then pointed toward the plastic-wrapped objects. "And *that* is a crime."

Erica said, "You always tell me not to lose focus of our objective. And these are not our objective."

"They are now." Catherine slipped beneath a dripping steam pipe and arrived at the plastic-wrapped items. She took a knife from her utility belt, slashed through some bubble wrap, and peeled it back.

To my relief, there was not a real human being inside. Instead, it was a statue of a human being: a soldier, dressed in a military uniform. He was sculpted from what looked like clay to me and had East Asian features.

Mike said, "I'm guessing that's not supposed to be down here."

"It's not supposed to be anywhere outside Xi'an, China," Catherine said angrily. "This is one of the terra-cotta warriors of Qin Shi Huang, first emperor of China. They're nearly two thousand years old, and they're national treasures."

I had heard of the terra-cotta warriors. The emperor had commissioned thousands of them, an entire army that was buried with him at his mausoleum. "So *that's* why Shayla Shang didn't want us in here?" I asked. "She's smuggling artifacts?"

"It appears so." Catherine's MI6 cover was as an art curator for the British Museum, but she had an actual art history degree and took crimes like this very seriously. "It makes sense. I'm sure that customs agents only inspect the cargo areas of a ship for contraband, not the engine rooms. But the conditions in here are awful for priceless artifacts such as these. The damp will destroy the clay they're made of. We have to get them out of here."

"Oh sure," Erica said sarcastically. "We've got plenty of room for them in our giant suite."

"Well, we can't just leave them here," Catherine replied, although even I could tell that her passion for cultural artifacts was clouding her judgment.

"We *can*," Erica told her. "And we will. We have to get out of here before the engineers notice us."

"Too late," Mike said.

I spun around. The engineers were no longer playing cards. They were coming toward us—and they were all holding weapons.

EVASIVE ACTION

Engine Room

The *Emperor of the Seas*

May 17

1900 hours

Three of the engineers were carrying crowbars, which they wielded like clubs. The fourth had a gun. He seemed to be in charge, although English was not his first language. "Put hands in air!" he demanded.

We ran instead. This was not my idea. Catherine bolted first, and the rest of us had no choice but to follow her.

The engineer with the gun promptly opened fire. There was plenty of machinery around to protect us, but since almost everything was made out of metal—including the walls—the bullets ricocheted about wildly.

"Careful!" Catherine screamed at them. "You'll damage the artifacts!"

"And *us*!" I added. "Don't damage *us*!"

The engineer kept firing as we ran. More bullets pinged off the metal surfaces. Pipes ruptured, venting steam, which created more cover for us, but also turned the engine room into a sauna—and made it hard for *us* to see. Suddenly, we found ourselves trying to run through a fog, surrounded by dangerous machinery and even more dangerous enemies. And if that wasn't bad enough, the floor was moving.

The storm outside appeared to have gotten worse just in time to complicate our escape. It would have been challenging enough to flee through an obstacle course of steam and gadgetry, but now we had to struggle to keep our balance as well.

Fortunately, the engineers were in the same situation we were. From somewhere in the fog, I heard the distinct sound of someone running headlong into a turbine, followed by cursing in a language I didn't know.

Catherine and Erica simultaneously recognized that the steam was an advantage and decided to make more of it. Each snatched up a wrench and deftly knocked the valves off other pipes, which resulted in more steam venting into the room, further concealing our escape.

"What was it you realized earlier?" Erica asked me casually, as though we were merely on an errand at the drugstore, rather than running for our lives. She had a habit of doing this. It was a little bit unnerving, as it always gave me the feeling that maybe Erica didn't think I was going to survive long enough to tell her the information later.

"Murray knew all about this reactor!" I explained, clambering over some pipes. "About the housing and how it was bolted down and everything!"

"So?" Mike vaulted over the same set of pipes with much more grace than I had.

"Why would Murray know about this unless it was important to him?" I asked. "Murray's not the kind of guy who just happens to read up on shipboard nuclear reactors. Or who reads up on *anything*, really. Plus, the fact that this ship even *has* a reactor is supposed to be a secret. His plot must have something to do with it."

"Nice thinking, Benjamin!" Catherine said, in a way that made me feel fantastic. "Oh, and duck."

I did, and she deftly lobbed her wrench over me. It whacked one of the angry engineers on the head as he emerged from the fog and promptly rendered him unconscious.

"Thanks," I said.

The other engineers all seemed to have lost their way in

the fog. We heard them shouting to each other—or possibly *at* us—as they bumbled around in it.

We arrived at the reactor, ascended the iron rungs on the housing, and scrambled back through the emergency hatch into the space under the stage.

While we had been down in the engine room, the evening's theatrical performance had begun. Now, instead of chaos under the stage, there was military precision. It was quiet, save for the overture music playing in the theater above us. Apparently, given the rocking seas, it had been decided that the actors would not be suspended from wires; instead, the entire cast was assembled beneath the stage, waiting silently to be lifted up on one of the many risers for the big opening number. There were dozens of people dressed as a menagerie of sea creatures: merfolk, tropical fish, sharks, octopuses, crustaceans, and what might have been either jellyfish or very large plankton (I wasn't quite sure). They all goggled silently as Catherine, Mike, Erica, and I suddenly emerged into this space.

Below us, the engineer with the gun emerged from the fog and took a shot at us. It sparked off the hatch, provoking startled gasps from the actors.

Mike and I slammed the hatch shut before another shot could be fired, but there was no way to lock it, given that it was an emergency escape.

We hurried for the wings of the stage but found them blocked by the ship's security guards. Hulking men bearing Tasers were waiting for us on both sides, boxing us in.

"Oh bother," Catherine said with a sigh. "The engineers must have called for backup." She plucked a knife from her utility belt to defend herself.

Erica did the same.

I reached for my mace, only to discover that I had lost it, probably after being thrown overboard. In fact, my entire utility belt was empty, save for a soggy packet of gum.

However, there was a bin full of weapons close by: the swords and broadaxes for the musical's many battle scenes. I quickly grabbed a broadax—which turned out to be made of Styrofoam. In retrospect, this made sense; the actors didn't want to fight with *real* weapons for fear that someone might accidentally have a body part lopped off. But at the moment, it was disappointing. The best I could do was wield it menacingly and hope that it fooled the guards.

By my side, Mike took a sword and did the same thing.

For a few seconds, it worked. The guards all hesitated in their approach, wary of the weaponry each of us held.

"Drop those," one of the guards demanded.

"Shhh!" a mermaid hissed. "There's a performance underway!"

Even though the woman was dressed as a half fish, she

was still quite imposing. "Sorry!" the guard said, and then dropped his voice to a whisper to threaten us. "There's no escape. You might as well surrender."

"Why don't *you* surrender?" Catherine suggested. "Put down your weapons, and we won't cause you grievous bodily harm." Despite the fact that Catherine looked as frightening as a rabbit, she *sounded* scary. The guards seemed to be seriously considering following her orders and might have even done it if one of the cast members hadn't decided to get involved.

A burly octopus-man grabbed Erica from behind, apparently under the impression that, as a teenage girl, she would be easiest to subdue. It took him exactly one second to discover that he had made a terrible error in judgment, as Erica promptly flipped him over her shoulder and dropped him to the floor like a sack of concrete.

But this distracted Catherine, Mike, and me, and the guards leapt at the chance to attack. The one facing me fired his Taser, but I had honed my reflexes at spy school—especially the ones that involved escaping harm—and sprang out of the way. The Taser prongs struck an unfortunate hammerhead shark behind me, who cried out in pain as electricity surged through him, and then collapsed.

"Shhhh!" warned the mermaid again.

The overture concluded dramatically, and one of the risers lifted the first group of actors up to the stage to begin the show. The octopus Erica had poleaxed happened to be one of them.

Their appearance above us was met with thunderous applause. If anyone was bothered by the prone octopus, I couldn't tell.

Around me, Catherine, Erica, and Mike were fending off their attackers. But I couldn't really focus on them as the guard who had fired the Taser now came at me bare-handed. I swung my Styrofoam broadax in a desperate attempt to scare him off, but he didn't falter, and my weapon broke harmlessly on his skull. I dodged him at the last second, and he barreled past, taking out three hapless lobsters.

Not far away from me, the engineers popped the hatch back open and started to climb out—although they paused in surprise upon seeing all the pandemonium around them. This gave me the opportunity to flip the hatch back closed. It clanged down on their heads, and they dropped back through the hatch into the engine room as though they had been bopped in a game of whack-a-mole.

While I was proud of this move, it left me open to an attack from another guard. I spun out of the way again and might have eluded him had the ship not lurched violently.

It had been rocking subtly all along, but this movement was something different altogether. We had most likely slammed into a very large wave; it felt as though we were all in a car that had just hit a speed bump at sixty miles an hour. I tumbled to the floor—as did half of the cast assembled under the stage.

And then the section of the floor I was lying on lifted into the air.

It was time for more actors to make an entrance. Only, most of the actors who were *supposed* to be on the riser had just tumbled off it—whereas I had fallen *onto* it. So I suddenly found myself at center stage before two thousand eager audience members, surrounded by toppled seahorses.

On the stage around me, things weren't going well. The big opening dance number had gotten off to an extremely rocky start—which might have been the case even if my friends and I hadn't barged into it. The actors who had originally planned to spend the scene suspended by wires didn't appear to know the choreography—and those that were merfolk couldn't really dance anyhow; since they had their legs bound together inside their fish tails, all they could really do was shimmy and take mincing steps. Their balance was precarious to begin with, and now the ship's most recent jolt had toppled most of them.

Plus, there was still a large octopus-man lying unconscious to stage right. No one had seemed to know what to do except dance around him.

Now I emerged into the midst of the chaos—at the exact

spot where, I later learned, the lead mermaid was supposed to arrive and belt out a power ballad about how she intended to rise above discrimination against her people. (It was titled "Something's Fishy—and It's Me.") But the mermaid was currently sprawled out somewhere below, while I was now blinded with a spotlight at center stage.

The audience applauded wildly, expecting something incredible. Thousands of eyes focused on me at once. The music swelled dramatically.

It was absolutely terrifying. My first thought was that I would rather be back beneath the stage, where people were trying to kill me, instead of in front of an audience.

The music for the power ballad kicked in.

I ran.

For a brief moment, I considered *dancing* offstage, so it would look like part of the show, but I quickly realized this probably wouldn't help—and I would only end up looking like an idiot. The audience gasped, apparently thinking I was an actor who had been struck by a massive attack of stage fright. Sadly, I didn't even get offstage as fast as I had hoped, because the ship was still heaving about in the rough seas. I stumbled over two different merfolk on the way.

Behind me, the mermaid's understudy tried to save the day, emerging from the chorus to sing, "In my life I have one wish: to no longer be half-fish." But before she could get any further, an enormous wave made the ship pitch dramatically. An extremely large cast member dressed as an orca fell on top of her, squashing her flat.

At this point, the stage crew seemed to realize that the show was an unmitigated disaster and dropped the curtain. It thumped down just as I reached the wings.

Bjorn Turok was waiting there for me.

He cuffed me on the side of the head. And everything went black.

RECOVERY

Emperor Suite

The *Emperor of the Seas*

Somewhere west of Panama

May 17

2230 hours

"Wake up, sleepyhead," a familiar voice said.

I returned to consciousness but didn't open my eyes right away. The world felt like it was pitching back and forth. It took me a few moments to realize that this wasn't because I'd been whacked in the head. It was because the world really was pitching back and forth. The ship was rocking wildly.

"Hello?" the voice asked again. "Earth to Ben. Come in, Ben."

I pried open my eyes. Jessica Shang was leaning over me, pressing a frozen steak against my forehead. I felt the area she was tending and found a lump the size of a walnut there.

"Are you all right?" she asked.

"My head hurts," I told her. "But I think I'm okay."

"Whew." Jessica heaved a sigh of relief. "I was worried that Bjorn might have hit you too hard and given you brain damage. That happened once before. Some guy tried to break into our house, and Bjorn punched him so bad that afterward, he couldn't use adverbs. Also, he thought he was a turnip. I asked Bjorn to just grab you, but he doesn't know his own strength."

I was lying on a couch in the main room of the Shangs' suite. It was dark outside, but every now and then, lightning flickered across the sky. We were in the midst of a serious storm. Rain was pounding against the windows so hard that it sounded like popcorn popping.

I sat up, just to see if I could do it. My head felt like it was full of rocks, but the rest of me seemed to be in good shape.

Something smelled delicious. My stomach growled.

"I thought you might be hungry," Jessica said. "Seeing as you were unconscious during dinnertime. So I had our chef whip up a little snack for you."

I noticed what Jessica considered a "little snack" on the

dining room table. There was steak with béarnaise sauce, lobster claws, green beans, mashed potatoes, freshly baked bread—and a chocolate soufflé.

I immediately forgot all about my headache and made a beeline for the table. Famished, I heaped food onto a plate, poured myself a glass of lemonade, and sat down to dig in. It was probably rude to not wait for Jessica—but then, Jessica had arranged for me to be knocked unconscious and hauled to her suite against my will, so I figured she had been rude first.

The food was amazing. "Where's everyone else?" I asked through a mouthful of steak.

"Your friends escaped from the theater. I'm not quite sure where they are now. But you were the only one I wanted to talk to."

"Why me?"

"Because you're the one I trust. Erica just sees the world in red and green. . . ."

"Black and white," I corrected.

"Right. To her, you're either good or bad. No nuance. I barely got to know her mother—and Mike wasn't a spy last time I met him, so I don't know how good he is at this yet. So I decided to talk to *you*." Jessica put a scoop of soufflé on a plate and drizzled molten chocolate on it. Either she'd had dinner already or she was skipping ahead to dessert.

"Okay. And where's Bjorn and your mother?"

"Bjorn's standing guard outside in the hall. And Mom had to go be the mistress of ceremonies at tonight's Fiesta of Fun."

I paused with a forkful of green beans halfway to my mouth. "There's a party *tonight*? With this storm going on?"

"It was already planned. And cruise people don't like it if you cancel events. If they paid for a fiesta, they want a fiesta."

"You can't move it to tomorrow night?"

"There's a whole different party scheduled for tomorrow. Plus, if we don't throw the fiesta, we have half a ton of guacamole that'll go bad."

"You could always give it to the staff. They're eating gruel down below. I'm sure they'd love some fresh guacamole."

"I think they get the leftovers," Jessica said, as though receiving the table scraps from a party you weren't invited to was a good deal.

It occurred to me that maybe I was in no position to judge. I was dining on lobster *and* steak while the crew subsisted on slop. "What did you want to talk about?"

"My mother's innocence. I know it looks bad to have those stolen statues in the engine room. But the engineers were smuggling them, not her. She didn't even know about them until *you* found them."

"How did she hear about that?"

"You broke into the engine room. Ship security noti-fied her immediately. They thought maybe it was a terrorist attack or something. We have a special link to the security system on our TV here. We can watch the footage from any camera on the ship—including those in the engine room. So we tuned in and saw it was you guys down there. And we also saw Erica's mother uncover the statue and realize what it was. Mom was shocked. She is very upset that her own ship was being used to smuggle away our country's heritage."

"So she asked you to have Bjorn bring me here so that you could explain all this?"

"Bongo."

"You mean bingo?"

"Yes, bingo. That's what I meant."

I rubbed my head. My mind was still fuzzy after being unconscious, but the timing of everything in Jessica's story seemed a little suspicious to me. However, I didn't want to upset her by questioning her mother's honesty outright. So instead, I asked, "If your mother didn't know about the stat-ues, then why didn't she want us to go into the engine room?"

"The engineers had told her it should be off-limits to everyone. Because there's a nuclear reactor down there. And all sorts of other dangerous machinery. So she believed them."

I cracked a lobster claw and dipped it in drawn butter. "How could the engineers get twelve huge stolen statues onto this ship without your mother knowing about it?"

"Mom doesn't run this ship. She *owns* it." Jessica was obviously annoyed at me for insinuating anything bad about her mother. "It's not her job to keep track of who brings what on board."

I raised my hands in mock surrender. "Then whose job is it?"

"I don't know. I have no idea if *anyone* keeps track of everything that's brought on and off. This ship is massive, and there's like three thousand employees."

"So any one of them can move whatever they want on and off whenever they want? That seems like a big security risk. Someone must be in charge of monitoring the cargo."

"I guess."

"Who's in charge of security on this ship?"

"Captain Steinberg, ultimately. He's in charge of *everything*. And then, there are all these other officers under him that run the other divisions, like security and safety training and all kinds of other stuff."

"Then we should talk to Captain Steinberg. Maybe he can direct us to the right person to help us. If I was the captain and there were crimes being committed on my ship, *I'd* want to know about them."

Jessica mulled that over while scraping the last morsels of soufflé off her plate. "I suppose that makes sense."

"Do you think you could arrange for us to talk to him? Right away?"

"I'm guessing he's awfully busy at the moment." Jessica pointed to the storm outside the window. "When it's a calm ocean, they can leave this ship on autopilot. But right now, it's all hands on duck."

"Deck," I corrected. "All hands on deck."

"Oh. Right. That makes more sense."

The storm was still raging. It didn't look like it was going to subside anytime soon.

"Maybe there's someone else we could talk to," I suggested. "One of the officers who reports to the captain. I mean, everyone can't be on the bridge at the same time. They must have shifts."

"Sure. But at times like this, they'd still be on call in their quarters."

"Where are those? Down in steerage with the rest of the crew?"

"No, silly. All the officers' quarters are behind the bridge."

I dropped a lobster claw that I'd picked clean, struck by this. "They're right below us?"

"Yes. So they're close to the bridge. It wouldn't make sense for the officers to sleep all the way down in steerage. This way, they're right by their posts in case of an emergency. Plus, the rest of the crew quarters are awful."

"The officers' quarters aren't marked on the map of this ship," I said. I hadn't spent nearly as much time perusing the map as Mike had, but I had devoted quite a bit of time to it.

"They're not?" Jessica asked, sounding surprised. "I guess the maps you've seen were designed for passengers. There's no real need to mark where the officers live on them."

That made sense. Our map hadn't shown other things, like the crew mess hall either. So I had simply assumed that the officers' rooms were all down with the rest of the crew.

"To get to the officers' quarters, you have to access the bridge?" I asked.

"Right. It's all in the same complex, but the access is restricted for security reasons."

"I need to get in there," I said. "Right away. I think that's where Murray Hill is hiding."

ORDERS

Emperor Suite

The *Emperor of the Seas*

May 17

2300 hours

Even without seeing the officers' quarters, I could imagine what would make them attractive to Murray Hill: They would be secure and cut off from the rest of the ship. On the Premier level, there were still other elite passengers, whereas the only people with access to the bridge were other officers. And the rooms would probably be quite nice: Any decent cruise line would probably make sure that its captain and officers were well taken care of. The lodgings might not be as luxurious as the Emperor Suite, of course; Buckingham

Palace wasn't as luxurious as the Emperor Suite. But Murray might have been willing to forgo a little luxury in favor of tighter security.

Still, I figured that I shouldn't go looking for Murray by myself. The last time I'd run into him, I'd nearly ended up dead. So I asked Jessica if there was a phone I could use in private. She pointed me to one of the several unused bedrooms, which turned out to be five times the size of our entire suite. I brought a serving of soufflé there, located the phone, and called my room. I was hoping to get Erica or Catherine. Mike answered instead.

"Where are you?" he asked me. "Are you okay?"

"I'm fine. I'm in Jessica's suite with her. . . ."

"Ooh!" Mike said. "Erica's gonna be jealous."

"I'm not here for anything romantic. . . ."

"You can tell me the truth. I won't rat on you to Erica. Jessica's cute. And nice. And *rich*. I mean, yes, her father did try to blow up Colorado, but I don't think she inherited the evil gene. . . ."

"Mike, I'm here for the mission. That's all. And I think I figured out where Murray and Dane are hiding." I quickly explained my reasoning for why they were staying in the officers' quarters.

"But how could they score those rooms?" Mike asked. "Aren't they reserved for officers only?"

"I assume some corruption is involved. Like, they bribed their way in—or offered Captain Steinberg a cut of whatever scheme they're plotting. Where are Catherine and Erica?"

"They're out tailing Dane Brammage, figuring he might lead them to Murray. Last I heard he was in the casino, playing roulette. I had to stay in the room to keep an eye on Alexander."

"Why? I thought they were getting him new medication that wouldn't make him hallucinate."

"They did. But it doesn't work. In fact, it's even worse. Now Alexander thinks he's Starbuck from *Moby-Dick*. He wants to mutiny and take over the ship. We had to duct-tape him to the bed, but we're still worried he'll escape. So I got stuck babysitting."

Sure enough, in the background, I could hear Alexander yelling deliriously, "I'm done with whaling! I hate it! I want to get to port, move to Seattle, and open a coffee shop!"

"Can you get in touch with Catherine and Erica?" I asked.

"Yes. We're using the radios. Let me try to reach them." Mike put me on hold for a few minutes. I ate my soufflé while waiting. It was fantastic.

Eventually, Mike got back on the line. "Catherine and Erica say you should investigate this by yourself."

I gagged on the last bit of my soufflé in surprise. "But what if I run into danger?"

"They say you won't have to worry about Dane, because they know he's in the casino."

"I still might run into Murray."

"You can handle Murray. You've dealt with him plenty of times. And you'll have the element of surprise, because he thinks you're dead."

"Still, wouldn't it be better if Erica or Catherine joined me?"

"Er . . . ," Mike stammered, obviously unsure of what to say. Which was an answer in itself.

"Oh," I said. "They don't think I'm right."

"Well, you *were* wrong about this once before—while they *know* Dane will eventually lead them back to Murray. And they've got eyes on him right now."

"I understand." I didn't try to hide the disappointment in my voice. It was upsetting to have my judgment questioned, no matter how valid Erica and Catherine's reasoning was.

Mike picked up on this. "I'm sure it's nothing personal. . . ."

"I know. But it still stinks."

"I'd come with you, but I can't leave Alexander alone. I left for three minutes to get some chips and guacamole from the fiesta, and by the time I got back, he'd torn himself free and was trying to recruit the eighty-year-old woman in the next cabin over to help him with the mutiny. It took me half an hour to duct-tape him back down again. I'm sure you'll be fine on your own, though. You're the best spy I know."

I knew that Mike was lying: Erica and Catherine were certainly the best spies he knew. But he *sounded* like he meant it, which bolstered my confidence a little. "Thanks. I better get going while Dane's still in the casino."

"Actually, before you go, there's one more thing," Mike said. "Since they have such good Wi-Fi in that suite, could you check my accounts to see if Trixie has written to me? And then maybe send her a quick message to say that I'm thinking of her?"

"No! It's bad enough that you're dating Erica's sister. Can you imagine how upset the Hales will be if they found out I delayed a mission to message her for you?"

"It won't take long! Just write 'I miss you' and sign it SnuggleBunny."

"SnuggleBunny?" I repeated with disgust. "I'm not doing that."

"Come on. . . ."

"I don't have the time. I don't know how long Dane's going to stay in the casino. If I want to get into the officers' quarters, I need to do it now."

"Okay," Mike said begrudgingly, like he realized I was right. "How are you going to get past all the security to access that area, anyhow?"

"Don't worry," I told him. "I have a plan."

18

INVESTIGATION

The Bridge

The *Emperor of the Seas*

May 17

2315 hours

Jessica Shang didn't have the access codes for the bridge. But she did have access to Bjorn Turok. And Bjorn, being part of the security team, had the access codes to every area of the ship. He also looked almost exactly like Dane Brammage—which meant he could pretend to be Dane if needed.

We met with Bjorn in the Emperor Suite. He was understandably skeptical when I told him that I was a CIA agent-in-training, although I managed to convince him of the truth when I showed him my badge and explained my uneasy relationship with his cousin. Bjorn was well aware of Dane's history of working for shady characters, and I still had the bruises on my neck from where Dane had throttled me the night before.

"That definitely looks like Dane's work," Bjorn said with resignation. "I'm sorry he tried to kill you. He has brought much shame upon our family. My aunt and uncle were devastated when he dropped out of medical school to become a hired killer."

I set down my second serving of soufflé in shock. (I knew I shouldn't be eating two desserts, but given that I was about to go on a potentially dangerous mission, I figured that I deserved a cheat day.) "Dane studied to be a doctor?"

"His parents really wanted him to be a pediatrician," Bjorn said. "But sadly, he seems to enjoy hurting people more than healing them."

Bjorn didn't much like the idea of posing as his sadistic cousin to give us access to a restricted area, but he recognized that it was necessary. So he led Jessica and me down to the level directly below the Emperor Suite, where the entry to the bridge was located.

The entrance was surprisingly pedestrian, perhaps to keep potential cruise ship hijackers from knowing where the bridge was. It was merely a door at the end of a hallway full of regular rooms. There was no indication that it led to the control center of the entire ship. The sign on it merely said RESTRICTED ACCESS—CREW ONLY, the same as a hundred other doors throughout the *Emperor of the Seas*. It had a coded-entry keypad and an ID card scanner.

Bjorn paused at the door. "I sure hope this works," he said. "You really think I look like my cousin?"

Jessica held up the tiny mirror from a makeup compact. "You look *exactly* the same."

"Really?" Bjorn scrutinized his reflection doubtfully. "I don't see it."

I had encountered something like this plenty of times before. People rarely ever seemed to have a good sense of what they looked like. Kids didn't think they looked like their parents. My mother, who was beautiful, thought she wasn't. While my father, who was out of shape and twenty pounds overweight, was under the delusion that he still looked like he had in college. (This seemed to be the case with most of my friends' fathers.) Bjorn didn't just look like Dane; they also had virtually the same accent.

"Trust me. This will work," I said, secretly hoping that was true.

Bjorn dutifully swiped his card through the reader and then entered the access code. The entry door clicked open.

We passed into what looked like an extension of the

hallway we were in, only the rooms lining the hall were now for officers rather than passengers. There were many rooms, as there were a lot of officers. The bridge was down at the far end of the hall. We could only see a small bit of it, but it was a hive of activity, everyone working to control the ship in the storm. Some officers were stationed at a bank of high-tech electrical equipment, while others scurried back and forth. A long row of windows stretched across the bridge, allowing for an unfettered view of what lay before the ship, which in this case was storm clouds, choppy seas, and rain.

This worked perfectly to our advantage. I had been concerned that we'd have to get past all the officers to find Murray's room. But since the rooms were *before* the bridge, that wouldn't be the case. There was only one problem. . . .

"Which room is Murray staying in?" Jessica asked me.

"I don't know," I admitted. I hadn't expected there to be so many options. I took them all in.

Most of the doors to the rooms were open. There was little point in locking your door in a restricted area that only the crew could access. We cased each of these rooms as we passed it. They were all built for two people, and while they were far less opulent than Jessica's suite, they were more spacious than my room—and cavernous compared to the crew quarters down in steerage. Each had two beds, a sitting area, and ample storage space, which was sensible, given that the officers would be living in these rooms for months at a time, if not years. The rooms were extremely tidy and well kept, as I would have expected from officers who had most likely had navy or coast guard training.

Not all of the doors were open, however. A few officers had still locked theirs. But seeing how shipshape the other rooms were gave me an idea for how to find Murray's.

Murray was the least shipshape person I had ever met.

Each locked room had its own coded keypad entry. I scrutinized them all as we passed but didn't see what I was looking for.

We were getting closer to the bridge. I had Bjorn walk in front of us, so that if anyone happened to glance down the hall, they'd think he was Dane. Plus, Bjorn was so big, he blocked us from view.

He also blocked our view of the bridge, but we could hear everything that was going on. Captain Steinberg was giving orders, while officers reported on visibility, weather patterns, engine performance, and how the crew and guests were handling the storm:

"Storm surge cresting at four meters with winds coming from the south-southwest."

"Starboard propeller experiencing some lag. We might have caught some kelp."

"Waitstaff at the fiesta claims the punch bowls are

sloshing around too much due to storm activity, resulting in punch spilling on the floor."

"Orient us to meet the waves head-on," the captain responded calmly. "Give the starboard prop a little more juice to clear it. And tell the waitstaff to not fill the punch bowls so darn high."

There were only two rooms left until we reached the bridge. Both were on the port side of the ship, as there was now an officers' mess hall on the starboard side. The mess hall had no doors on it, so as to allow constant flow from there to the bridge. It smelled strongly of coffee; the officers were probably drinking gallons of it to make it through the storm. I got a glimpse of the room. There was a lot of food laid out, and it was of far better quality than what the crew got. In keeping with that night's fiesta theme, it was tacos, tamales, chips, and guacamole. A few officers were gathered around a table, grabbing a quick bite. Luckily, they were focused on their food and not the hallway.

The doors to both of the remaining rooms were closed. The room closest to the bridge had a sign on it that said CAP-TAIN'S QUARTERS. The next room down had no sign at all. I looked at the coded-entry keypad.

The keys were smeared with a variety of foods. I noted traces of what appeared to be chocolate, salsa, and marshmallow fluff, along with streaks of what I was pretty sure was bacon grease.

"This is Murray's room," I said confidently. "If Murray's in there, we can catch him by surprise and subdue him."

"How?" asked Bjorn.

"The same way you subdued *me* tonight," I said. "Just bop him on the head. Although, knowing Murray, he might be asleep. So then you can just grab him."

"The door's locked," Jessica noted. "How are we supposed to get in?"

I looked to Bjorn. "A little help here?"

"You're *sure* this is the right room?" Bjorn asked warily. "If I break into an officer's quarters, I'll get fired."

"It's definitely Murray's room," I assured him, pointing to the soiled keypad. "Murray's the biggest slob I know. He was probably eating the chocolate and bacon at the same time."

Bjorn nodded agreement, although he didn't look happy about what I was asking him to do. He motioned for Jessica and me to stand back, away from the door. Then he waited a few seconds for the ship to pitch as it hit a wave and pretended to stumble. "Whoops!" he cried, slamming a shoulder into Murray's door.

There was a crack as the doorjamb splintered.

"You all right, Dane?" someone asked from the mess hall.

"I'm fine," Bjorn said quickly. "Just lost my balance." He beckoned Jessica and me forward.

The dead-bolt lock had ripped right through the jamb, allowing him to open the door. We all quickly slipped inside.

Murray wasn't there.

But my hunch had been correct: It was definitely his room. As opposed to all the neat and orderly rooms we had seen, this one was a disaster. It looked like a hurricane had hit it. Or, more specifically, *half* of it. Dane was apparently sharing the room. His side was clean and tidy, with clothes for an abnormally large person hanging in the closet—and the bed was sagging slightly, as Dane weighed significantly more than the average human being. Meanwhile, Murray's side was strewn with dirty clothes, crumpled papers, tangles of charging cables, and plates of rancid food scraps. Sure enough, there was one with traces of chocolate sauce and bacon.

At one point, it had been a rather nice room. It was spacious and well decorated, even compared to the other officers' quarters—although I presumed Captain Steinberg's room was about the same size. My original assumption about Murray had been right after all: He had secured some of the best lodging on board for himself—although he had sacrificed some luxury for security.

"We need to search all this stuff," I told Jessica and Bjorn, pointing to the garbage strewn about the room. "To see if there are any clues as to what Murray's plotting."

Bjorn cautiously poked at a balled-up pair of undies with his shoe, then wrinkled his nose in disgust. "*You* can search all this stuff. I'll guard the door."

I didn't bother arguing. Bjorn had already put his job on the line for me, and I didn't feel as though it would be smart to try bossing around a man who could crush me with his bare hands.

I reluctantly started picking through the detritus in Murray's room. I focused on the crumpled papers first, as they were far more promising to be evidence than the dirty clothes—and far less smelly as well.

Jessica gamely joined me, picking up papers and smoothing them out. "What are we looking for here?"

"I'm not sure. Anything that seems suspicious." I extracted a wadded hotel bill from a plate of congealed syrup. It was from the resort in Nicaragua where Murray had spent four nights before boarding the *Emperor of the Seas*. He had run up $750 in room service charges alone.

"Is *this* suspicious?" Jessica asked, holding up a piece of paper. It was a pencil sketch of a girl who looked very much like Zoe Zibbell dressed in a superhero unitard, holding hands with someone who looked a lot like Murray.

"No," I said. "It's *creepy*. But not suspicious."

"What's going on with you and Zoe and Erica?" Jessica asked me. "Are you dating either one of them?"

"It's complicated." I resumed rooting through the crumpled papers for clues.

"Why's it complicated? Because Mike's dating Erica's sister?"

I spun toward Jessica, startled. "How did you know that? Were you eavesdropping on my call?"

Jessica flushed. "Maybe a little. I couldn't help it. Your life is so exciting! And I'm just stuck on this cruise ship with nothing to do. I've been on here for four weeks already, and I'm bored out of my pelvis!"

"You mean your skull?"

"Yes. That's what I meant. This ship isn't anywhere as fun as our ski trip was. The waterslides are crummy, the laser tag area is small, the musical is terrible, and I've still seen it six times. So when you showed up in my room the other day, I was thrilled. Finally, something exciting was happening! I thought I'd see you last night, but you totally blew off the party. . . ."

"Actually, I was planning on going, but Bjorn's cousin threw me off the ship."

"I'm really sorry about that," Bjorn said. "I want you to know, most of my family isn't the slightest bit evil. Only Dane. We don't even invite him to the reunions anymore."

"He's really the black goat," Jessica observed.

"Black sheep," I corrected, then told her, "You can't tell

anyone about Mike and Trixie. Especially Erica and her family. It's a secret."

"All right," Jessica agreed. "I'll try not to. . . ."

"Trying isn't good enough. You need to promise."

"Fine. I . . . ," Jessica began—although she didn't finish. Because at that very moment, Murray Hill entered the room.

HOT PURSUIT

Officers' Quarters
The *Emperor of the Seas*
May 17
2330 hours

Murray was holding a churro in one hand and what appeared to be a blueprint in the other. He was humming happily and had a look on his face that indicated he was very pleased with himself. "Hey, Dane," he said to Bjorn cheerfully, mistaking him for his cousin. "Pack your bags. The deed is done. We've got just under thirteen hours to get really far away from here. . . ."

He froze in his tracks as he realized Bjorn wasn't Dane at

all—and that I was in the room as well. The happy look on his face turned to one of terror.

Then he threw his churro at me. And fled.

Murray wasn't very adept at throwing at the best of times. In his panic, he was even less coordinated. The churro missed me by six feet and landed in a pile of dirty laundry.

Bjorn made a grab for Murray as he scurried out the door but missed and then pursued him into the hall. Jessica and I weren't far behind.

But since Bjorn was in the lead, he was the one who Murray sedated.

Murray yanked a dart gun from his belt and started firing back over his shoulder as he ran. He was just as inaccurate with the gun as he was with the churro; the only reason he managed to hit his target was because Bjorn was so big. It would have been almost impossible to miss such a large target at such close range in such a confined space—and yet Murray still did. In fact, he missed Bjorn five times, striking both walls, the ceiling, a lighting fixture, and the leg of one unfortunate officer who had exited the mess hall at exactly the wrong time. Finally, on his sixth shot, Murray managed to hit Bjorn, who gave a cry of pain and then collapsed in a heap.

The officer Murray had hit also went down, though he did so a bit less dramatically. Jessica and I leapt over him easily, but Bjorn was a much bigger obstacle. The fallen Scandinavian filled up a considerable portion of the hallway. We had to clamber over his prone body, allowing Murray to get a decent head start on us. By the time we were past Bjorn, Murray was slipping through the exit from the bridge.

I raced that way with Jessica on my heels. "This is what I was hoping for!" she exclaimed. "Action! Adventure! Excitement! This is *way* better than laser tag!"

We burst into the hallway for regular passengers and spotted Murray ducking through yet another door in the distance. I heard a blast of 1970s disco music before it clicked shut.

Jessica and I followed, Jessica whooping enthusiastically the entire way. "We're chasing a real-live bad guy! I love it!"

We shoved through the door and found ourselves in the roller rink.

Throughout the trip, I had thought that a roller rink on a cruise ship was a questionable idea, but now it was evident that I had been wrong: A roller rink on a cruise ship was a *terrible* idea. Skating when the ship was gently rocking would have been difficult enough; during a storm, it was nearly impossible. And yet, the rink was surprisingly full, as an extremely ill-conceived skate party was underway.

Kit Karoo was DJing, blasting disco while glitter balls spun, strobe lights flashed, and fog machines spewed dry-ice clouds. Out on the rink, passengers were doing their best to skate, but since the boat was rocking, no one could really go forward. Instead, almost everyone was merely sliding back and forth across the rink from one railing to the other as the floor seesawed beneath them. And if that hadn't been bad enough, Murray Hill was now bulldozing his way through.

It was hard to see him directly, given the strobing lights, but I could see where he'd been. He had cut directly through the center of the rink, leaving a trail of toppled skaters in his path. So many people were sprawled out on the floor, it looked like a scene from a D-Day movie.

I went after Murray, Jessica on my heels. There was an intensely difficult obstacle course back at spy school, but crossing the rink was a close second. In addition to trying to stay upright on the pitching floor, I also had to avoid the fallen passengers and dodge the waves of wobbling skaters as they hurtled past, arms flailing. I didn't make it through unscathed. I stumbled over quite a few of the fallen and was clipped by several people, although since they were on wheels and I wasn't, I handled the collisions better than they did, sending them careening away or tumbling to the floor.

Jessica wasn't so lucky. A Bjorn-size passenger slammed into her like a freight train, lifting her off her feet and whisking her away. "Ben!!" she yelled as she disappeared into the dry-ice fog. "Help me!"

I didn't have time to go after her. I couldn't afford to lose Murray Hill.

Luckily, I was gaining ground on him. Murray had the athletic ability of a flounder; making it across the rink had been much harder for him than it had been for me. He reached the exit not far ahead of me, huffing and puffing, then spun around and opened fire on me with his dart gun. He missed by a mile, striking a disco ball, two speakers, and Kit Karoo, who yelped in surprise and then passed out on a heap of Donna Summer records. Murray's gun then clicked empty. "Stupid piece of junk," he cursed, tossing it aside, and then fled through the exit doors.

I came through them behind him and arrived at the central vertical access corridor for the ship. Here there was a bank of six elevators and a wide staircase. Rather than use the little energy he had left to run down the steps, Murray had opted to slide down the bannister. He was moving quite fast—much faster than he had intended, it seemed—and flew off the end at the next landing, taking out a group of festively clad revelers on their way home from the fiesta.

I leapt onto the bannister and slid down it myself, alighting at the landing with slightly more grace than Murray had. By this time, he had already hopped onto the next bannister, so I kept moving down with him.

We continued like that for the next few floors, sliding

down and jumping off bannisters. Murray was still clutching the blueprint he'd had all along, although after two landings, he attempted to destroy the evidence by cramming it into his mouth. However, the blueprint was much larger than Murray had anticipated. Instead of swallowing it, he ended up with half of it wadded up in his cheeks and the rest protruding comically from his lips, looking somewhat like a python trying to swallow a piñata.

The stairway led down to the great hall, and as we approached, descending one bannister after the other, we could hear that the night's fiesta was still underway. The air was alive with Latin dance music and the joyful murmur of happy partygoers.

I had nearly caught up to Murray as we reached the great balcony on the mezzanine level. The stairs led directly to it. Murray, knowing I was breathing down his neck, took the last bannister as fast as he could. When he reached the landing, he lost his balance and stumbled forward onto the balcony, where the exact same quintet of musicians who had performed at every event was now dressed as mariachis. Propelled by his momentum, Murray crashed into them, sending their maracas and castanets flying, then slammed into the railing and flipped over it. He dropped ten feet into the center of the buffet table, where he landed flat on his back in the guacamole. The force of his impact knocked the chewed-up blueprint from his mouth like a cork fired from a champagne bottle—and splattered everyone in a ten-foot radius with pulped avocado.

Between this and the music suddenly stopping, the fiesta immediately ground to a halt. A stunned silence fell over everyone—except for the passengers who'd been strafed with guacamole, who were shrieking in disgust.

The blueprint plopped into a bowl full of salsa. I leapt over the balcony railing to retrieve it, landing atop the buffet. This might have looked quite suave if I hadn't landed upon a stray carnitas tamale, which was as slippery as an overripe banana. I tumbled forward, catching the salsa bowl with my elbow and catapulting chopped tomato on the few people close by who had managed to not get hit by guacamole. The blueprint ended up in the middle of the dance floor. I scrambled through the crowd to recover it—and by the time I had, Murray was gone. There was only a massive platter of guacamole with a Murray-size crater left behind.

This caught me by surprise. Murray was already exhausted and certainly in pain after his fall. I hadn't counted on him still being able to run. Luckily, it wasn't hard to figure out where he'd gone: There was a trail of green splotches leading across the floor.

I crammed the soggy blueprint into my pocket and followed the guacamole. The path was so slimy, it was as though

I were following an enormous slug. It led past dozens of revelers and a troupe of salsa-spackled flamenco dancers into the main restaurant.

The restaurant was closed for the night, as the scheduled dining times were long over and there was plenty of food out at the fiesta. It was merely a big space filled with empty tables and chairs, so it was easy for me to spot Murray across the room, heading for the kitchen doors.

He was obviously in pain, probably in several places at once, and smeared from head to toe with guacamole. With his green pallor and shambling gait, he looked more like a zombie than a human being.

"You might as well just give up!" I yelled after him. "There's nowhere to run!"

"That's what *you* think!" Murray yelled back, then shoved through the doors.

So I followed him into the kitchen.

Which was the biggest kitchen I had ever seen in my life. It turned out, there was only one kitchen for all the restaurants on the ship. The food was prepared in this single place, then funneled to the various dining establishments through a series of conveyor belts and elevators. All the appliances were designed to cook food for thousands of people at once, and thus they were enormous; there were ovens the size of cars, fifty-foot-long griddles, and mixers with bowls big enough to bathe in. It was like being in King Kong's kitchen.

In the interest of hygiene, everything had been heavily sanitized. The stainless-steel appliances had been polished until they gleamed, and the floor was spotless—except for the slime trail Murray had left. Not that I needed to follow it anymore. I was now only a few feet behind him.

I sprinted the last steps and was about to tackle Murray when something caught the collar of my shirt and stopped me short like a dog on a leash. The next thing I knew, I was flying backward. I skidded across the freshly mopped floor and slammed painfully into a pastry oven.

Dane Brammage had arrived.

He was dressed in a tuxedo and now stood by Murray's side, amused by Murray's appearance. "You look like a giant snot," he giggled.

"No thanks to you!" Murray snapped. "Don't just stand there! Take care of Ben!"

"All right," Dane agreed, and lumbered toward me menacingly.

I was trapped in a dead end, surrounded on three sides by giant appliances, with nowhere to run.

Meanwhile, Murray hurried off through the kitchen, as though he was in a rush to be somewhere. "Don't take any chances with him this time!" he ordered. "No throwing him overboard and hoping for the best. Obviously, that didn't work. Kill him first and *then* throw him overboard!"

There was a menace in Murray's voice that I hadn't heard before. In our previous meetings, he had wanted me alive—usually for nefarious purposes, but still, that was preferable to the situation I now found myself in. This time, Murray clearly regarded me as a threat and wanted to get rid of me as quickly as possible.

And I was in little position to defend myself.

Although most of the kitchen was filled with items that I could have used as weapons—knives, cleavers, skewers, and assorted blunt instruments like pots and pans—I was in the one section that was devoid of anything useful. The only thing I could find was a whisk, which would have been handy if I were being attacked by some raw eggs, but was useless against a leviathan like Dane. Still, I tried to use it anyhow, throwing it at him in the vain hope that maybe it would poke him in the eye.

It harmlessly clonked off his skull.

Behind him, I could see Murray disappearing behind some enormous mixers.

Then Dane was upon me. I tried to scramble away, but there was nowhere to go. He caught me easily and clamped a hand around my neck.

"Nothing personal," he said. "It's just business."

And then he squeezed.

EVACUATION

Central Kitchen
The *Emperor of the Seas*
May 17
2345 hours

I felt like a tube of toothpaste as Dane Brammage throttled me. As though my head might come off and all my innards would be squeezed out through my neck. Stars twinkled in my vision, and I began to black out. I feared this really was the end.

And then I heard a loud clang.

The vise grip on my neck lessened, allowing oxygen to return to my lungs.

There was another clang. This time, Dane released me

entirely. I dropped to the floor, gasping for air.

My vision returned, allowing me to see what was happening.

Erica Hale stood behind Dane, wielding a large cast-iron pan with a dent shaped like Dane Brammage's skull in it. A whack like that would have leveled a normal human—and most elephants—but Dane shrugged it off as though it had been a mosquito bite. He wheeled around and attacked Erica.

So she hit him in the face with the pan. This staggered him slightly. He made another lunge for her, but she was too fast. She hit him again. And again.

And then Catherine Hale brained him with a soup tureen.

The cumulative effects of all those bonks finally got through Dane's thick skull. He wobbled precariously and then toppled like a sequoia.

Erica dropped her pan and came to my side, worried. "Are you all right?"

I thought about saying something cool and debonair like *I am now that you're here*. But I hurt too much to be glib about it. "Not really," I gasped.

Catherine kneeled beside me, looking very concerned. "I'm so sorry, Benjamin. We knew something was up when Dane left the casino abruptly."

"Murray must have radioed him for help," Erica

presumed. "So we tried to follow him, but he threw a roulette table at us."

"An entire table?" I groaned.

"Yes," Catherine said. "And in the ensuing havoc, he got away. We were able to track him back down, but not quite fast enough to protect you."

"Or to catch Murray," Erica said sullenly. "Any idea which way he went?"

I nodded, which turned out to be incredibly painful given the tender state of my neck. Then I pointed in the direction Murray had gone, which was also painful. My whole body ached. "He went that way. And he was really tired, so maybe he hasn't gone far. He was also covered in guacamole."

Erica gave me a curious look, then ran in the direction I had indicated. I got to my feet and followed. This was painful too, but then, so was sitting still—and I didn't want all that pain to be for no reason. I wanted to catch Murray.

Catherine quickly removed a syringe from her utility belt and injected something into Dane's prone body before joining us as we hustled through the kitchen.

"Was that a sedative?" I asked.

"No. I don't think normal sedatives will work on someone like Dane," Catherine replied. "That was rhino tranquilizer. I brought some just in case we ran into him."

"Look," Erica said suddenly. The trail of guacamole Murray

had left behind led to the doors of an enormous steel elevator. Erica pushed the button, and we waited for it to return.

I suddenly remembered the blueprint I had gone through so much trouble to recover and pulled it from my pocket. "Murray had this on him when I found him. He tried to destroy it while he was escaping."

"*Tried* to?" Erica gave the crumpled, chewed-up, and salsa-covered paper a skeptical glance. "Looks like he did a pretty good job."

"It's not *ruined*," I said defensively, then got my first good look at it as I unfolded it. "It's only *kind of* ruined." Sizeable portions of the blueprint were unreadable due to water or salsa damage. But they showed a boxlike object and a large key. The box looked vaguely familiar, but I couldn't recall where I had seen it before. There were also what appeared to be very detailed instructions for operating the object, but I couldn't read them, because much of the writing was smeared beyond comprehension. Plus, it was in Chinese.

The elevator arrived, and the great steel doors slid open with a pleasant *bing*. It was the largest elevator I had ever been inside, designed to move enormous amounts of food through the various levels of the ship. You could have parked a truck inside it.

The button for the first floor had a smear of guacamole

on it. So we pushed it and rode down. Slowly. The elevator was big and heavy and didn't move fast.

Erica and Catherine gathered around me to examine the remains of the blueprint as well.

"Looks like a radiation detector," Catherine observed.

Her saying this sparked a memory of where I had seen the device before. "Right! It was one of the five built into the housing around the nuclear reactor in the engine room."

"Why would they need five detectors?" Erica asked. "I know nuclear energy is dangerous, but still, it seems like three or four detectors would be sufficient."

"Maybe this one isn't really a radiation detector at all," I said. "Maybe it's just designed to look like one. Can either of you read what this says?" I pointed to the blurred and smeared Chinese words.

"No," Catherine said sadly. "Perhaps if it was less damaged . . ."

"Sorry," I said. "I did my best."

"I didn't mean that as a criticism," Catherine said, looking upset with herself. "Not of *you* at least. I've now failed you twice on this mission. If I had trusted your instincts better, we could have all caught Murray red-handed. This is on me, not you."

Erica took the blueprint and examined one section of writing closer. "I think I can make out some of this. Looks like it says, 'To set clock . . .' and then this part here says, 'enter code . . .' and this last part over here says 'rotate glorious cauliflower.'" She frowned. "It's possible I'm getting that last part wrong."

The elevator finally reached the lowest floor, and the doors slid open again.

We were now in a cavernous cargo room. It was the largest open space of the ship we had seen so far and filled with shipping containers. Some were open, revealing pallets of food inside, while others were closed and locked, presumably holding precious cargo. The room was dimly lit, with bare bulbs that dangled high above our heads, swinging from side to side as the ship rocked. It was as though we had entered an enormous maze.

We stepped out into it and tried to deduce which way to go.

"Great," Erica muttered. "It could take us *weeks* to find Murray in here."

Catherine gloomily scanned the floor. "And it looks like our trail is drying up. I don't see any more guacamole." She looked to me. "Any idea where he'd be heading?"

I thought back to my encounter with Murray in his room, right before he'd fled. "When he came into his room, he thought Bjorn was Dane and told him to pack his bags quickly. So he's probably planning to get off this ship somehow."

"In this storm?" Erica asked. We could feel the waves pounding against the keel around us and hear the ship groaning as it rocked. "He's not taking a helicopter unless he has a death wish."

"A lifeboat, then?" I suggested.

"Also treacherous in these conditions." Catherine suddenly cocked her head to the side. "Did you hear that? It sounded like voices."

I listened. Along with the groaning of the ship and the roar of waves, I could make out hushed voices.

Erica heard them too. And since she had the acoustic sense of a bat, she could pinpoint exactly what direction the voices were coming from. "This way," she said, and led us through the room.

We crept through the labyrinth of shipping containers. As we got closer to the exterior wall, I saw that there were great doors in the sides of the ship, big enough to move the containers in and out. They were supposed to be watertight, but the force of the waves was testing that. Seawater had leaked through and was oozing across the steel floor.

The noise of the storm swallowed up the sound of our footsteps, but still, we crept silently so as to not give ourselves away. The voices grew louder as we approached.

We spun around a corner, hoping to find Murray.

Instead, we found the worst living conditions on the ship yet.

The door to one of the shipping containers was open, revealing dozens of people inside. Most were asleep, huddled up in threadbare blankets, although four of them were playing cards in the feeble light of a single candle. Also inside the container were small suitcases and tins of food.

The card players froze in surprise upon seeing us, looking extremely worried.

Catherine held up her hands, palms out, to show that she meant no harm, and then began speaking to them in their native tongue; I didn't know it, but suspected it was Thai or Vietnamese. The card players relaxed—although not completely. They were obviously still wary of her. They spoke back and forth, and then all of them pointed in the same direction. Catherine nodded and thanked them profusely, then looked back to Erica and me.

"They say a man covered in guacamole passed this way a few minutes ago." She led us in the direction the cardplayers had pointed, running now. "There's an exit this way."

"What was going on there?" I asked, following her through the containers.

"They're immigrants. From all over Southeast Asia: Vietnam, Thailand, Cambodia . . . Heading for America. Or so they were told."

"This can't be legal," I said.

"It's not," Catherine said angrily. "But it's not their fault. They were conned. This sort of thing happens all the time. A huckster tells them he can get them to America, takes all their money, and the next thing they know, they're being treated like cargo. They stay hidden inside that container all day and only come out now, when the coast is clear."

"Still," Erica said, "that can't possibly work without someone on this ship knowing it's going on."

"You're right," Catherine agreed. "I'm sure plenty of people know about it, going right on up to the captain. And I'll bet every last one of them is taking a cut of the profits."

"Well, we all know that Captain Steinberg has to be crooked," Erica noted. "And all the officers. How else would they be allowing Murray to live in their quarters?"

"So there's human trafficking," I said, "stolen antiquities, whatever Murray's plotting . . ."

"And we noticed the dealers skimming profits in the casino," Erica added.

"Is there anyone on this ship who *isn't* breaking the law?" I asked.

We reached a set of doors at the end of the cargo bay and pushed through them. We found ourselves back at the point where we had first arrived on the boat the day before, the embarkation point for the passengers, where the shuttles docked.

From close by, we heard the roar of outboard motors.

It was coming from behind another door on the other side of the embarkation point. This was marked RESTRICTED ENTRY. We went through it anyhow.

It led to the boarding lounge for the elite passengers. This lounge was much more high-end than the one for the regular passengers, with comfortable couches, crystal chandeliers, and a bar. A patch of carpet around the exterior door was soaking wet, as though the door had just been open despite the storm.

A line of portholes dotted the wall. We each ran to a separate one and peered through it.

One of the fancy speedboat shuttles for the rich passengers was speeding away. It was getting batted about by the waves but still had the power to move quickly.

"Murray!" Erica pounded the wall in frustration, then turned to her mother. "There's another speedboat like that! We need to commandeer it and go after him!"

"In this weather?" Catherine asked, looking defeated. "At night? With that big of a head start on us? By the time we commandeer that other boat, Murray will be miles away. We'll never find him out on the ocean."

Erica pounded the wall again. "We were so close! I can't believe we lost him again!"

"But maybe not for good," I said, smiling despite the circumstances. "I know how to find out where he's heading."

INTERROGATION

Suite 1722

The *Emperor of the Seas*

May 18

0100 hours

"I order you to untie me!" Alexander demanded.
"Or your heads will roll once I have mutinied!"

"So," I said to Mike. "He's still looney?"

"Very much so." Mike stuffed the sock he'd been keeping in Alexander's mouth all night back into place. "He won't shut up unless I gag him."

Alexander writhed angrily on the bed, where he was still bound hand and foot, and did his best to shout for help, but the sock muffled his words.

Meanwhile, in the adjoining room of our suite, Erica and Catherine were having the opposite problem with Dane Brammage. While Mike and I couldn't get Alexander to keep quiet, they couldn't get Dane to speak. Not because Dane was refusing to talk out of loyalty to Murray. But because they couldn't wake him. He was sprawled out across all three of our beds, snoring loud enough to shake the room.

"You gave him too much tranquilizer," Erica observed.

"It *was* intended for rhinos," Catherine replied. "There weren't any instructions for how much to give a human. It appears I made a slight error in my calculations."

We figured that, when Dane *did* wake up, he would be angry and dangerous, so we had taken precautions. Our original plan had been to bind his wrists, but the zip ties Catherine and Erica carried in their utility belts were only designed for human beings of normal size and strength. Instead, we had bound Dane with plastic cling wrap. The ship's kitchen had industrial-size rolls of it several feet across, designed to preserve hundreds of pounds of leftovers at once, and we had swaddled Dane with it, wrapping him in thirty layers. His arms were pinned to his sides, and his legs were bound tightly together, so he now looked like a freshly swaddled mummy.

However, we couldn't interrogate him in the kitchen; sooner or later, an employee would stumble upon us. So we had dragged him back to our room, which had been a challenge. Not only was Dane heavy, but he was bulky. We couldn't even come close to getting our arms around him. So, once again, we had been forced to improvise. We had commandeered several gallons of discount olive oil (*A natural product of New Jersey*, according to the label), lubricated the floor with it, and then dragged Dane's prone body through. Thankfully, due to the late hour, most of our fellow passengers were asleep, although we did run into a few people, most of whom were initially startled to see us lugging along a shrink-wrapped behemoth who reeked of cheap olive oil.

Each time, Catherine simply said, "My husband had one too many margaritas."

And each time, the passengers' concerns immediately went away. It helped that many of them had consumed one too many margaritas themselves. Several said things along the lines of, "Been there. Done that." Or "If I pass out, can you drag me back to my place?"

Eventually, we made it back to the room. Since then, Catherine and Erica had tried rousing Dane with smelling salts and a variety of other noxious things, like Mike's dirty socks and Alexander's aftershave, but he remained stubbornly asleep.

"I have one more idea," Catherine said, "but it's probably a direct violation of prisoner rights. . . ."

"We're in international waters, so I don't think those laws apply out here," Erica told her.

"Fine," Catherine said, although she sounded slightly disappointed in herself for agreeing. Then she produced a bottle of hot sauce from her utility belt. "I pilfered this from the kitchen. I've never heard of this brand before, but it certainly appears to be potent."

The hot sauce was called Bring the Pain, and the label showed a cartoon man who had apparently consumed the product and now had flames coming out of every orifice on his body. It looked like the sort of warning that should have been on industrial waste, but for some reason, hot sauce aficionados must have found it appealing.

Catherine uncapped the bottle, releasing peppery fumes that made my eyes water even from ten feet away. Then she cautiously edged toward Dane and tipped the bottle into his open mouth.

For a few seconds, nothing happened. Then there was an ominous gurgle from deep inside Dane's body. His eyelids suddenly snapped open like window shades, and he let out a howl of pain. Sweat instantly beaded on his brow. I half expected to see steam venting from his ears. At first, he seemed confused by his location and the fact that he couldn't move his limbs. Then he quickly pieced together what had happened and grew upset. "Water!" he gasped. "I need water!"

Erica said, "Tell us where Murray Hill is going and you can have all the water you want."

Dane obviously needed a drink; his face had flushed as red as a beefsteak tomato. But he wasn't about to crack that easily. "I don't know what you're talking about."

Erica held up the bottle of hot sauce. "If you think this stuff is painful when you drink it, imagine what it'll be like when I rub it in your eyes."

"Erica," Catherine said sharply. "We do not torture witnesses in this family."

"He just tried to kill Ben!" Erica replied. "He deserves a lot more than hot sauce in his eyes."

Catherine said, "You are letting your emotions get the better of you. Studies have repeatedly shown that torture is not effective at eliciting accurate information. If anything, kindness is a much better way to do that." She filled a glass with water from our tiny sink and held it to Dane's lips.

Dane greedily guzzled it down.

"Mother," Erica said angrily. "You're undermining my authority here."

It looked like the two of them might start arguing, so I said quickly, "I know how to get Dane to talk." Then I turned to Dane and told him, "If you don't tell us where Murray Hill is going, you're going to die."

"Benjamin!" Catherine exclaimed. "What did I just say about coercing witnesses?"

"I'm *not* coercing him," I explained. "I'm merely telling him the facts. None of us are going to kill Dane. Murray Hill is."

Thanks to the water, Dane had recovered slightly from his infusion of hot sauce. But now he looked as though he'd had another gulp of Bring the Pain, growing red and sweaty once again.

"I know what Murray's plan is," I said. This was a bit of a bluff; I wasn't completely sure, but I had learned that faking confidence was pretty much the same thing as being confident. "He's not going to steal the nuclear reactor from this ship to use as a bomb. *The entire ship is a bomb.*"

Dane gulped, and I saw in his eyes that I was right.

This revelation was news to the others as well; there hadn't been time for me to explain my theory yet.

"What?" Mike exclaimed. "I thought there were all sorts of fail-safes to prevent that from happening."

"Murray seems to have devised a way around them," I said. "One of those radiation detectors we saw on the housing for the reactor wasn't really a radiation detector at all. That's what the blueprints Murray had were for. It's a detonator.

Back in his room tonight, Murray said the deed was done and they had thirteen hours to get very far away from here. I think he started the countdown. And now he's fleeing before this ship explodes."

"But what's the point of blowing up a cruise ship?" Mike asked. "All it's going to do is kill a couple thousand innocent people and maybe freak out some dolphins. We're way too far offshore to cause any real damage."

"Oh my," Catherine said. From the look on her face, I could tell she had figured out the next step in Murray's plan, just as I had.

So had Erica. "At noon tomorrow, this ship *isn't* going to be far offshore. It's going to be in the middle of the Panama Canal."

Dane sweated a bit more profusely, indicating that we were definitely on the right track.

"An explosion that large would destroy the canal and throw worldwide trade into chaos," Catherine said. "A third of the planet's goods pass through Panama. A severe disruption could send shock waves through the world economy."

"Why would Murray want to do that?" Mike asked.

"Because he's a jerk." I looked back to Dane, who was now sweating so profusely that he looked as though he'd just stepped out of the shower. "You knew this was the plan all along. But one thing has gone wrong: Instead of taking you with him, Murray left you behind. You came to his rescue when I was chasing him and helped him escape—and he repaid your loyalty by ditching you."

"No," Dane said weakly, like he was trying to convince himself this wasn't true. "Murray wouldn't do that to me. We are friends."

"Murray let me think he was *my* friend too," I said. "When I first met him. And then he double-crossed me. Since then, he has claimed to be my friend many other times. But obviously, he was never being honest. All Murray cares about is Murray. Face it: He abandoned you. And if we don't catch him, this ship is going to blow up with you on it."

Dane made a small whimper, which was unsettling coming from such an intimidating person. It was like hearing a hippopotamus squeak. "Maybe you only *think* he left. Maybe he's still on the ship somewhere, waiting for me."

"He's not," Erica said. "We saw him leave. He stole one of the speedboats and took off. He already has a big head start on us because it took forever to wake you up. So if you want to live, we have to move fast. We need to know where he's going. *Now.*"

Dane still didn't answer, but I could tell that he was worried. Between his fear of dying and his pained reaction to the hot sauce, he wasn't looking very good.

Mike came to his side. "I don't know why you're even

considering being loyal to that snake. If you think about it, Murray has *never* looked out for you. He left you for dead in Colorado. And Mexico. And Paris. Each time, you were in bad shape, and he just abandoned you. Real friends don't treat people like that. You don't owe him anything."

Dane still held out another ten seconds, quivering nervously as he pondered what to do—and then cracked like an egg. "You're right!" he exclaimed. "Murray has *never* been a good friend! He says he is, but he always sticks me with the dirty work. He never returns my calls unless he needs something from me. And he forgets my birthday every single year—even though it's the exact same day as his! Plus—"

Catherine interrupted him before he could go on. "I'm sure this epiphany you're having is very cathartic, but what we *really* need to know is: Where has Murray gone?"

"Oh," Dane said sheepishly. "Right. The plan was to head to a little town called Nueva Gorgona. There's a beach with a public pier to dock at and a small airport nearby. Murray has a jet waiting for us. Or, I guess it's really just for *him*. Seeing as he left me to die because he's the worst person ever."

"Er," I said uncomfortably. "You *did* try to kill me tonight."

"Only because Murray told me to!" Dane protested. "He's the real bad guy here! Not mmmmthmmptthh." He didn't quite get to finish his defense, as I crammed a sock in his mouth. As pathetic as he seemed at the moment, I didn't really feel bad for him after how he had treated me.

"Wait," Mike said. He stood over Dane and asked, "Is there any chance that *you* know how to defuse this bomb?"

Dane shook his head, then began desperately trying to speak, despite the sock in his mouth. I reluctantly removed it again.

"You can't even *try* to defuse this!" Dane explained. "Murray had the detonator custom made with all sorts of hair triggers. If you make the slightest mistake, we're all dead! Murray is the only one who knows how to shut it off! He didn't want anyone else to be able to do it. Because he's a big jerk who doesn't even know the meaning of the word 'loyalty.' Or 'friendship.' Or mmmthmmptthh." I shoved the sock right back into his mouth.

Now that we had the information we needed, there was no time to lose. Catherine and Erica began quickly packing their bags for an emergency mission.

"Looks like our only call is to go after Murray," Catherine said, "then drag him back here and force him to shut that bomb off. It's been approximately an hour and a half since he set the timer, which gives us eleven hours to do all that. It will be a close call, but it's still possible." She checked her watch, then added, "I *think*."

"We can do it," Erica said supportively. "Murray might

have a big lead on us, but now that we know where he's headed, perhaps we can make up the time."

Dane began writhing wildly on the bed and struggling against his bonds, although the thirty layers of industrial-strength plastic wrap were too strong for him to break. He also shouted desperately. We couldn't understand him, given the sock in his mouth, but the gist was clear; he really wanted to be set free.

"You're not going anywhere," Catherine told him. "You can wait right here until we get back. Use this time to think about the choices you have made in your life and how they have put you in this position."

Dane stopped shouting and looked rather ashamed.

"Hold on," I said. "Are we sure that we can even trust Murray to do this? He's not that competent where bombs are concerned. Back in school, he flunked bomb defusion. *Twice.* Maybe we ought to just tell the captain to steer this ship out to sea so that it won't blow up near land. And then evacuate all the passengers with the lifeboats."

Catherine shook her head sadly. "I had considered that, but it still wouldn't cancel out all the risks. A nuclear explosion of such size at sea might not damage the canal, but it would still affect people on land—as well as everyone in the lifeboats and anyone on another ship coming to their rescue. We simply can't let this explosion occur. We must go after Murray."

Erica finished packing her bag. "We'll need the other speedboat to do that," she observed. "Although it'll be a bit risky to steal it."

"I know just the person for that job," Mike said confidently, then turned to Alexander Hale and asked him, "How'd you like to have a little mutiny?"

APPREHENSION

Somewhere off the Pacific Coast of Panama

May 18

1000 hours

Once again, I ended up spending a night at sea in a tiny boat.

Alexander's mutiny went surprisingly well. He overwhelmed the guards protecting the second speedboat and commandeered it for our use with such skill and competence that he seemed like an entirely different person. Within minutes, we were zipping across the waves toward Nueva Gorgona.

"Maybe we ought to keep him on this medication all the time," Erica suggested.

The speedboat was far more luxurious than the life raft Mike and I had been in the previous night, with comfortable couches and a nice little kitchen, but the conditions at sea were far worse. The storm was still raging, and the sea was churning. The speedboat was tossed about like a bathtub toy in a Jacuzzi. The constant pitching and yawing quickly made all of us sick—except Alexander, whose medication not only counteracted it, but had also convinced him that he was a decent sailor. So we left him in charge of driving the boat while the rest of us balled up on the couches, clutching our nauseated stomachs and trying to get some sleep.

All in all, I would rather have been in my tiny room on the *Emperor of the Seas*.

I didn't end up sleeping much—and I threw up a lot. But in the end, our rough voyage paid off. By ten a.m. the next morning, we had the pier at Nueva Gorgona in sight—as well as Murray Hill. Which gave us two hours to apprehend Murray, get him back to the ship, and defuse the bomb.

The storm had finally abated, so the ocean was calm and the sun was shining bright and warm. We were able to come out onto the deck without getting drenched, and the fresh air was doing wonders for my nausea. (Although not having anything left in me to throw up also helped.) I could see the full length of the beach at Nueva Gorgona, a pristine, sweep-ing curve of white sand lined with small resorts and palm trees. The pier jutted out in the center of it like the center prong on a capital *E*. As we homed in on it, I could see the other speedboat from the *Emperor of the Seas* coming in at a slightly different angle, not far ahead of us. We had either made up time by barreling through the storm at top speed— or Murray had gotten slightly lost en route. Whatever the case, we were closing in fast.

However, we weren't alone out on the water. Several hundred tourists who had just spent a day of their vacation cooped up inside due to the storm were now making the most of the sunshine. Scuba boats were anchored along the fringes of the outer reef while snorkelers bobbed on the surface and divers swam below. In the bay, every conceivable form of resort watercraft was zipping about: Jet Skis, WaveRunners, sailboats, catamarans, kayaks, dinghies, sloops, and pontoon boats. Speedboats towed parasailers in the air and water-skiers on the surface. Traditional surfers worked the break at one end of the bay while windsurfers, paddleboarders, and kiteboarders traversed the flats. The beach was thronged with swimmers, waders, boogie-boarders, and body surfers, while scores of people bobbed about on inflatable rafts and tubes, many of which were designed to look like random animals such as flamingos, sea turtles, and unicorns. It appeared as though the population of an entire town had been swept out to sea and then decided to make the best of it.

The presence of all the people forced us to slow down considerably as we approached the pier, but then the other speedboat had to slow as well. It arrived at the pier only thirty seconds before we did.

There were many watercraft docked at the pier: scuba boats, motorboats and Jet Skis for rent, as well as sport fishing boats that stank of raw seafood and were thus attracting every pelican in Panama. This left little room to dock—and Murray wasn't an adept driver to begin with. Plus, he had certainly noticed us and was in a big hurry to park and run away. He aimed for a gap that was barely big enough for his boat, then missed it entirely and banged into a fishing trawler. There was a great rending of metal as the two craft scraped along one another, and then the speedboat rammed straight into a rental yacht, gouging a hole in it.

At this point, Murray gave up even trying to dock. He also didn't bother trying to moor his boat. He simply jumped out onto the pier, unconcerned that the speedboat would float away. After all, he didn't need it anymore.

To my surprise, he wasn't alone. Two more people disembarked behind him: Shayla and Jessica Shang.

Shayla was still in her heavily sequined fiesta outfit from the night before, with a sombrero as big around as a spare tire. From a distance, with her enormous hat, she looked like an extremely gaudy lamp. Jessica was wearing the exact same outfit I had last seen her in, which made sense, as she wouldn't have had time to change in the short period between when I had lost her at the roller rink and the speedboat had left. Shayla and Jessica appeared to be having a big argument, with Shayla trying to drag Jessica down the pier while Jessica dug her heels in.

Murray didn't bother waiting for them. He hustled down the pier as fast as he could go—which, given that he was out of shape, wasn't very fast at all.

Alexander expertly brought our boat in to the pier at a much closer spot to the beach, then deftly parked it between two motorboats for rent. Catherine, Erica, Mike, and I quickly sprang from the bow onto the dock, in a hurry to catch Murray, but also eager to be back on solid ground again. We all formed a line across the pier, cutting off Murray's route to the beach.

Unfortunately, a boat full of spear fishermen had just docked, and a crowd of them were disembarking right beside Murray. Murray snatched a speargun away from one fisherman, then aimed it our way. "Freeze or I'll shoot!" he ordered.

Although Murray's aim was terrible, he was so close that even he would have had a hard time missing at least one of us. We didn't know which one of us it would be, but still, no one wanted a spear through the brain.

So all of us froze and raised our hands. "We know what you're plotting," I told Murray. "Dane told us everything."

Murray was already upset that we were cutting off his escape, but now he grew dismayed. "That loser ratted on me? Whatever happened to loyalty?"

"You did leave him behind to die," Mike pointed out. "While he was saving you from Ben."

Murray waved this off, annoyed. "He swore an oath to protect me!"

Erica said, "He says you're the only one who can turn off the bomb. So you're coming back to the ship with us to do just that."

By now Jessica had noticed us. She appeared humiliated by the entire situation, the same way that a teenager might have looked upon seeing their parents show up at the prom. She stopped struggling against her mother and yelled to me, "Ben! I'm not part of this, I swear! My mother dragged me along against my will!"

"I'm not part of it either!" Shayla exclaimed, not too believably. "Murray dragged *me* along!"

"I did no such thing!" Murray protested. "I could never have made this plan work without your help!"

"That's ridiculous," Shayla scoffed. "Why would I want to blow up my own cruise ship?"

"For the insurance!" Murray accused.

We had now found ourselves in what was known in the spy business as a double down: an occasion where you caught two criminals at once, and they turned on each other in attempts to make themselves look better. It was a rare occurrence but one that our teachers spoke fondly of, because both parties often did all your work for you.

That was happening now. Murray and Shayla both tried to explain themselves to us while pointing the finger at each other.

"Shayla's husband got her into serious debt on this cruise ship thing," Murray explained. "Like a billion dollars' worth. He spent *way* too much money on that thing. The guy built a roller rink on a cruise ship, for Pete's sake! So Shayla came to me with a plan to blow it all up but make it look like a terrorist act."

"This was never about the insurance!" Shayla insisted. "Murray wanted to use my ship for a terrorist act all along! He forced me into it!"

"Ha!" Murray shouted. "This was all Shayla's idea! She's bankrupt and in desperate need of money. She told me there was a way to get around the fail-safes for the nuclear reactor so we could turn the whole thing into a bomb!"

"Well, I certainly didn't ask to blow it up in the middle of the Panama Canal!" Shayla exclaimed. "The whole idea of ruining world trade was Murray's plan from the start!"

While the two of them argued, a crowd was gathering: tour boat operators, fishermen, Jet Ski renters, scuba divers, snorkelers, and even a few curious pelicans. Catherine and Erica were trying to edge close enough to disarm Murray, but even in the midst of his argument, he hadn't dropped his guard. He kept the speargun aimed in our direction.

Meanwhile, Jessica was adding to the chaos by declaring her own innocence. "I didn't find out about *any* of this until last night, Ben. That's why I was chasing Murray with you! But after you left me behind, Mom came along and told me we had to leave the ship right away. She said it was because of an emergency, not because she was fleeing with Murray! I didn't find out the truth until I got onto the speedboat—and by then it was too late."

Shayla looked to her, hurt. "So now you're turning on me, the same way you turned on your father? What did I ever do to deserve this?"

"You plotted a huge crime!" Jessica screamed. "It was embarrassing enough when Dad tried to blow up Colorado! But now you had to be evil too?"

"Evil?" Shayla repeated, aghast. "Is that what you think of your own mother?"

"You're planning to turn a cruise ship into a nuclear bomb with thousands of innocent people on board," Jessica said. "What would you call that?"

Shayla now seemed to realize that this whole embarrass-ing exchange was taking place in front of a crowd, so she shifted into Chinese, hoping fewer of us would understand her. Jessica argued right back.

Erica and Catherine crept closer to Murray, cautiously watching his speargun.

Catherine said, "Murray, we are running out of time. One way or another, you are coming with us. So why don't you just spare us a few minutes and put that speargun down?"

"Do you need the Shangs to come too?" Murray asked. "Because that's going to make things awkward. But then, I guess it's always tricky to be in business with your fam-ily. Whether the business is crime—or fighting crime." He pointed toward the Hales with the speargun.

"There's nothing tricky about spying being the family business," Catherine said.

"Really?" Murray asked, flashing a sly smile. "You don't have any issues with Mike here dating Trixie?"

In the next few moments, a lot of things happened at once.

I immediately realized that I had been played—that Murray had been planning to drop this information all along. Behind him, Jessica grew mortified. Obviously, she had let the truth slip during their long speedboat ride, and now she was ashamed of it.

Erica and Catherine both turned toward Mike and me in astonishment, wondering if this could be true. This was Hosmer's Law of Inevitability in action: Even the very best agents could be distracted by the right piece of information. Catherine and Erica were as good as agents got, but Murray's revelation made them drop their guards.

Which was exactly what Murray was hoping for. In the split second of diversion, he leapt off the pier and onto our speedboat, where Alexander had also been stunned by the news about Mike and Trixie. Alexander hadn't moored the boat, nor had he cut the engines. Murray drove a shoulder into Alexander, knocking him overboard, then scrambled into the pilothouse and pushed the throttle forward.

By this point, Erica, Catherine, and Mike had recovered their wits enough to go after Murray—but not quite quickly enough to catch him. All of them sprang off the pier in pursuit—just as the speedboat roared away. Instead of landing on top of it, the three of them plunged into the bay.

Which allowed Murray Hill to speed away in the boat, taking our only chance of shutting off the nuclear bomb with him.

WATER SPORTS

Nueva Gorgona Bay, Panama
May 18
1015 hours

Not far from me, a tourist sat astride a WaveRunner by the pier. It was obviously a rental, as it had RENT ME AT PANAMA WATER SPORTS! painted on each side in bright pink letters. The tourist seemed to be a first-timer, as he was tentatively pulling away from the rental area at a speed that made continental drift look fast.

Without thinking, I sprang off the pier, landed on the back of the WaveRunner, and promptly shoved the tourist into the ocean. "Sorry!" I yelled—and I really did feel bad about it—but the fate of thousands of people hung in the balance. I had never been on a WaveRunner before, but it was quite easy to figure out. It was like a motorcycle designed for the water, with a set of handlebars to steer it, one of which was also the throttle. The key was in the ignition, and the machine was already running. I twisted the throttle as far as it would go, and the WaveRunner shot forward across the water.

It was a big, powerful model, and it took off so quickly that I nearly toppled off the back of it. But I clung to the handlebars tightly and set after Murray Hill.

Ahead of me, the speedboat was showing telltale signs that Murray was at the helm. It was weaving about erratically, as if being driven by someone who had never even seen a motorized vehicle before. If I hadn't known about Murray's horrendous driving skills, I would have thought he was *trying* to hit everything else on the water. Within the space of a few seconds, he nearly ran into a sailboat, a dinghy, and two Jet Skis. Three paddleboarders had to dive into the bay to avoid him.

As I took up the chase, I noticed something in the wake of Murray's boat, trailing behind him. It took me a few moments to figure out what—or actually *who*—it was: Erica Hale.

It appeared that she had grabbed one of the mooring lines before Murray could completely get away, and now she was being dragged behind the boat. Most human beings wouldn't have been able to hold on for long, or would have given up after the first few awful seconds, but Erica clung to the line tenaciously. Then, as I watched, she swung her body around so that her legs were in front of her and allowed the boat to pull her upright, so that suddenly she was water-skiing with only her feet. It was the kind of stunt that professional water-skiers probably trained for years to do, and yet, Erica had nailed it on her first try.

But staying on her feet wasn't *easy*, especially with Murray's spastic driving. I could see that Erica was struggling to keep her balance and guessed that she wouldn't be able to continue for very long.

So I steered into the wake of the speedboat and pulled up alongside her. "Need a lift?" I asked, in my most suave and debonair voice, only to realize that Erica probably couldn't hear me over the WaveRunner's engine. Between that and the roar of the speedboat's motor, I might as well have been inside a wind tunnel.

Still, she got the message. In one quick, graceful move, she hopped onto the back of the WaveRunner as easily as most people stepped onto the subway. Then she released the mooring line and cinched her arms around my waist.

Normally, I would have been thrilled to have Erica Hale clinging to me as we zipped across a gorgeous tropical bay on a WaveRunner, even though we were in pursuit of a notorious evildoer and Erica was as bedraggled as a cat that had been caught in a thunderstorm. But then Erica hissed in my ear, "How on earth did Mike meet my sister?" In that instant, I realized that she was livid at me. It wasn't only the tone of her voice; the way she was holding on to me seemed to have less to do with her safety and more to do with crushing my abdomen.

"You want to talk to me about this *now*?" I gasped. "We're in the middle of a chase!"

"How did they meet?" Erica demanded once again, then squeezed my abdomen even harder. It was already tender from my run-in with Dane Brammage the night before, so it didn't take much to make me wince.

"Trixie found *me*!" I exclaimed. "She followed your father to the hospital when I was there a few weeks ago. And then Mike showed up—whoa!"

The speedboat suddenly swerved in front of me. Murray had spotted us on his tail and was now driving even more senselessly in an attempt to ditch us. I didn't react fast enough and went soaring over the wake. We flew through the air for a few feet and then came down hard, forcing Erica to clutch my waist in earnest, sending a shock of pain through me.

Meanwhile, as a result of his evasive maneuver, Murray nearly lost control of his speedboat. It clanged off a buoy, dumping three sea lions that had been sleeping on it into the water.

I cut through a small flotilla of startled kayakers and resumed the chase.

"How did Murray know about all this?" Erica asked angrily, as though nothing else was going on.

"Jessica must have told him," I surmised. "They were together a long time on their getaway boat tonight. I guess she let it slip."

"And how did Jessica know?"

I hedged a bit, knowing Erica wasn't going to like the answer. But lying, even under the circumstances, seemed like it would only lead to more trouble later. "Er . . . she eavesdropped on the call I had with Mike earlier tonight. When I was getting the orders from you to investigate the officers' quarters on my own."

"You let a civilian eavesdrop on your call?" Erica asked heatedly.

"It was an accident! There was a lot going on at the time!"

"We can't afford accidents in our line of work. What if something really bad had happened, like Trixie finding out that the rest of us are spies?"

I grimaced. And then I tried to figure out what to say. I knew that, once again, lying would only cause more trouble later, but I also knew that telling Erica the truth now would still lead to plenty of problems for me—and probably also some pain. So I decided the best thing to do was to make a nice, noncommittal statement of fact. "That would be really, really bad," I said.

Erica groaned. "Oh no. You let her know that we're spies, didn't you?"

Her correct deduction caught me completely by surprise. "What? Why would you think that . . . ?"

"Because I heard you grimace before answering the question."

"You can *hear* a grimace?"

"I can hear and comprehend fifty-three separate facial expressions. But you also paused briefly before answering, as if you were trying to decide whether to tell me the truth or not . . ."

"I was trying to avoid a harbor seal!" I lied.

". . . and then you tried to fool me by going with a noncommittal statement of fact." Erica tightened her grip on my abdomen again. "I can't believe you let Trixie know the rest of us are spies! How could you screw up so badly?"

"She tricked me into it!" I exclaimed. "She's very sneaky!"

Ahead of us, Murray was still trying to give us the slip. He had veered toward the beach, where there were many more tourists, so I was now zigzagging through an obstacle course of banana boats, parasailers, and inflatable floating objects. A dozen people were using something I had never seen before: giant inflated plastic balls, which allowed them to roll on the surface of the water. Murray careened right through them, scattering them like billiard balls.

Two rolled into my way, and I had no choice but to carom off them, sending their poor inhabitants tumbling head over heels across the bay.

Meanwhile, Erica was so angry at me that I could actually feel her temperature rising. "Trixie and Jessica Shang are both civilians—and somehow, you have managed to let each of them know extremely classified information. If Murray gets away right now, it'll be because of your shoddy spying."

In all the time I had known Erica, she had never been angry at me. She had often been disappointed, disapproving, or downright disdainful of my abilities—but never angry. Her harsh words stung badly—and yet, rather than backing down, I responded in kind. "I'm not the only one who has screwed something up on this mission!" I snapped. "Murray only escaped just now because you and your mother dropped your guard back on the pier."

"Which wouldn't have happened if Murray hadn't caught us by surprise by revealing information that you had allowed to slip!"

"Well, we wouldn't even be in this position if either of you trusted my instincts to investigate the officers' quarters!

If you'd come with me then, we would have caught Murray back on the ship!"

"That's only because you let him get away in the first place!"

"I wouldn't have if Dane hadn't stopped me! And you were supposed to be watching Dane!"

"You're actually questioning *my* abilities?" Erica snapped. "I'm a better spy than just about anyone at the CIA, and I'm not even old enough to drive yet!"

"Maybe so, but you're not perfect!" I was surprised by the anger in my own words. But the last thing I needed at that moment was a dressing-down from Erica. I was struggling to follow the speedboat and avoid all the destruction Murray was leaving in his wake. In that very moment, he drove *straight through* a small sailboat, breaking it into two large pieces that I had to maneuver through the narrow gap between. (Thankfully, the sailors managed to leap into the water right before Murray destroyed their craft.) Plus, I was still aching after my various ordeals of the past few days, and each time the WaveRunner jounced on the choppy water—which it did almost constantly—it sent a shock of pain through my body. And on top of everything else, I was repeatedly getting splashed with salt water, so my eyes were stinging and my clothes were briny.

However, I had finally managed to catch up to the

speedboat—in part because it had been slowed greatly by plowing through the sailboat. As I pulled up alongside it, Erica said defiantly, "I never said I was perfect. I only *try* to be. Like *this*." With that, she stood on the seat of the WaveRunner and leapt onto the speedboat.

I had to admit, it was an amazing physical feat. The WaveRunner and the speedboat were both moving fast, bobbing wildly and slick with seawater. Jumping from one to the other required nerves of steel, incredible physical strength, and exquisite timing. Erica managed it—there was no other word for it—perfectly.

But then she slipped on a splotch of pelican poop and tumbled into the ocean.

I was stunned. Erica didn't usually fail at things; it happened about as often as a lunar eclipse.

My first instinct was to stop and help her—but I realized that was wrong. The priority was to catch Murray. Erica wouldn't have stopped to help me; in fact, Erica would have shoved me off the WaveRunner if she thought it would increase her chances of success. Stopping for her would give Murray a huge lead on me that I might not be able to make up again. My WaveRunner was starting to show strains from the chase. Being a rental, it wasn't in great shape to begin with; now the engine was groaning, and smoke was coming out of it.

So I left Erica behind and kept alongside Murray.

Only, I wasn't sure what to do next.

In theory, I could also attempt to leap from the WaveRunner to the speedboat and then apprehend Murray, but Erica had just proven how difficult that was, and my athletic skills weren't anywhere near as good as hers. If I failed, then Murray would surely get away.

Which meant I had to come up with another plan. Fast.

Murray suddenly veered into my path, trying to broadside me with the speedboat. I cut the throttle to avoid smashing into him, and the WaveRunner's engine promptly flooded and died, stranding me in the ocean.

But Murray's abrupt change of course forced him to temporarily slow down as well. As he did, the mooring line that Erica had been clinging to earlier popped to the surface in front of me.

I got an idea.

I had no clue if it would work, but I had no other options—and no time to waste.

So I dove off the WaveRunner and grabbed the line.

Then I swam downward as fast as I could, pulling the line taut behind the outboard motor of the speedboat.

Murray had brought us so close to the shoreline that the ocean floor wasn't far beneath me, an expanse of white sand strewn with a startling number of plastic bottles and lost snorkels. I touched down and pinioned the mooring line beneath me, hoping for the best.

As Murray regained speed, the line wrapped around the propeller shaft of his outboard motor, jamming it. The boat stopped dead in the water.

I swam to the surface, emerging by the speedboat's stern. A small ladder was affixed there, so I grabbed it and took a close look at the outboard propeller. Murray was still revving the engine, and the propeller was straining to turn, even though the line was now knotted around it. I cautiously wrapped the remaining line around the rudder, just to be safe.

After that, I climbed up the ladder and made my way across the boat to the pilothouse.

In the ocean around the boat, a great number of angry tourists were berating Murray in a variety of languages, upset at him for his reckless driving and his destruction of their watercraft.

Murray was ignoring them, focused on the control panel, unsure why everything had stopped and growing increasingly angry. He was pounding on the throttle with a wrench. "Come on, stupid boat!" he yelled. "Go forward!"

The speargun he had used to keep us at bay earlier was lying on a seat behind him.

I picked it up and pointed it at his back from a safe distance.

"Put your hands up," I ordered.

Murray wheeled around, gaped at me in shock, and then grew enraged. "Of course! Once again, you have to screw up everything for me!" He banged the wrench down on the throttle one last time.

In that instant, the propeller must have finally chewed through the mooring line, because the boat suddenly sprang to life, tossing Murray and me off our feet. But because I had wrapped up the rudder, the boat didn't rocket straight forward. Instead, it curved, heading for the beach.

Murray sprang back to his feet and grabbed the wheel, trying desperately to turn us away, but with the rudder jammed, he couldn't do it. "The steering's gone!" he yelped.

"Then cut the throttle!" I exclaimed.

"Oh! Right!" Murray tried to do this, only to discover that his attack with the wrench had rendered the throttle inoperable. So we were now racing at full speed right for the beach.

I quickly jumped into the captain's seat, buckled the seat belt, then blasted the air horn.

The beach was even more crowded than the water had been, mobbed with tourists building sandcastles, playing frisbee and paddleball, and staggering out of the surf after snorkeling. Four lines of beach chairs and umbrellas stretched along the sand, filled with people tanning and reading. Everyone scattered as the speedboat bore down on them.

We hit the sand at full speed and, powered by our inertia, shot right up the beach. As tourists fled out of the way, we smashed through the rows of chairs, leaving a deep gouge in the sand, then plowed through some tropical landscaping—and splashed into the swimming pool of a resort, startling the dozens of people there. Now that we were back in water, the boat picked up speed again. It shot across the pool, then crashed into a decorative waterfall and came to a sudden, final stop.

My seat belt kept me safely in place, but Murray sailed through the window of the pilothouse and cannonballed into a hot tub with such force that half the water sloshed out.

I unbuckled my seat belt, grabbed the spear gun again, and exited the pilothouse to survey the damage Murray had caused. The speedboat had left a great trail of destruction in its wake, although miraculously, no one appeared to have been hurt. Even Murray had somehow managed to escape without injury. He was clambering out of the hot tub, preparing to make a run for it.

I dashed across the bow of the speedboat and jumped down in his path, pointing the speargun at him.

He froze and glared at me with exasperation. "Just once, do you think you could go a day without thwarting my plans? What are you gonna do now? Throw me in jail again?"

"No. Right now I'm taking you back to the cruise ship."

Murray's anger turned to panic. "Are you crazy?! That ship's going to explode!"

"No, it won't. Because you're going to defuse the bomb."

"There's just one problem with that plan," Murray told me. "I don't know how to defuse the bomb."

EMERGENCY PLANNING

Somewhere on Highway 1
Near Nueva Gorgona, Panama
May 18
1045 hours

"How can you not have a way to turn off the detonator?" I asked Murray in exasperation.

He shrugged meekly. "I didn't think it would come up."

We were now in a courtesy van from the resort with the rest of my team and the Shangs. Alexander was at the wheel, and we were speeding down the highway, a two-lane strip of cracked asphalt that wound through the Panamanian countryside. Alexander's nausea medication had finally worn off, and he no longer believed that he was a pirate. He knew exactly who he was once again: a relatively incompetent spy.

Catherine, Alexander, and Mike had arrived at the resort shortly after Murray had wrecked the boat into it; it hadn't been hard for them to track our progress from the beach, given the trail of destruction. They had Shayla and Jessica Shang with them; Shayla was in custody, her wrists cinched with zip ties, while Jessica was still free. Erica had shown up a little bit later, having rowed to shore in a sea kayak she had commandeered from a hapless tourist. I was happy to see them all, in no small part because I was surrounded by angry tourists who were upset that Murray had nearly killed them and angry hotel employees who wanted us to pay for all the damage we had done. Catherine had calmed the situation by flashing her MI6 badge and pretending to take both Murray and me into custody for reckless endangerment, then demanded the use of their van. We had quickly fled the resort and were now attempting to get back to the *Emperor of the Seas* as fast as possible.

Although Murray's insistence that he couldn't actually defuse the bomb was putting a crimp in those plans.

"But Dane said you knew how to turn off the detonator," I told Murray. "In fact, he said you were the *only* one who could do it."

"Well, he's wrong," Murray said. "I never told him I

could do that. In fact, I ordered a detonator that *couldn't* be turned off."

I started to argue further but then realized there was no point. It was possible that Dane hadn't known the truth about the detonator. Or that he had been lying on purpose, trying to convince us that we had to go after Murray because he thought we'd bring him along.

"You didn't have a backup plan in case of emergencies?" Erica asked him.

"No!" Murray snapped. "Because my original plan was brilliant: start the countdown, then give myself plenty of time to get very far away before the explosion. But now all of you had to come along and mess everything up. If we die in the blast, it's all your fault."

"*Our* fault?" Mike echoed. "*You* started the countdown!"

"Let's not get into a whole argument about who started what," Murray said. "The point is, I can't shut this thing off. So the longer we stick around here, the better our chance of dying. Now, the jet I hired is at the airport. We still have time to get far away before the ship explodes."

"Sounds like a great plan," Shayla Shang said, then ordered Alexander, "Driver, take us to the airport as quickly as possible."

"I'm not the driver!" Alexander huffed, offended. "I'm a spy!"

"Then why weren't you with the others when they broke into my suite?" Shayla asked.

"I . . . er . . . had other important spy stuff to do at the time," Alexander replied.

"He was puking," Mike explained. "But he's the real deal."

Alexander turned red. "The point is, we're not getting on that jet."

"Actually, we are," Catherine told him.

"What?" Alexander asked. "Why?"

"Because it's the fastest way to travel," Catherine answered.

Murray gave a whoop of excitement. "Yes! Good call, Mrs. Hale! Finally, one of you is showing some intelligence. We can be halfway to Mexico by the time that ship blows!"

"We're not using the jet to get away from the ship," Catherine told him. "We're using it to go *to* the ship."

Murray's face fell. So did Shayla's.

"I take back the compliment I just gave you," Murray said to Catherine. "You're not intelligent at all. Going to the ship is suicide! I already told you that I don't know how to shut that bomb off!"

"You've told us plenty of other things over the past few years," I said. "And most of them turned out to be lies."

"Well, this one isn't!" Murray said. "It's the truth. If we return to that ship, we're going to die."

"That's a risk we'll have to take," Catherine said. "Because if we don't at least *try* to stop that bomb, then thousands of innocent people will perish. Maybe hundreds of thousands. If you happen to be among them, well . . . it serves you right for being evil."

"Um . . . ," Mike said uneasily. "I don't want to sound like a jerk here, but . . . *we* would also die in that scenario. And none of us really deserve it."

"I *had* thought of that," Catherine said. "And you're right. So . . . I'm not going to bring any of you children with us."

"What?" Erica exclaimed. "You can't do that!"

"Actually, I can," Catherine countered. "I'm your mother and you're only sixteen, so I certainly have the right to tell you what to do." Erica started to protest, but Catherine quickly cut her off. "Your father and I can deal with this. The rest of you are children, and it would be irresponsible of me to put you in such peril."

"But we've faced plenty of peril before . . . ," Erica began.

"When there was no other choice," Catherine said quickly. "This time, there is. I'm not placing you three in jeopardy unless I have to."

"*I'm* a child!" Murray pointed out. "Why are you putting *me* in jeopardy?!"

"Because you deserve it," Catherine told him. Then she

shifted her attention back to Erica. "I know you're not happy about this, but if things don't work out here, I don't want you anywhere near the explosion. I need you to look after Trixie."

At the mention of her sister's name, Erica shot me and Mike an angry look. Throughout the ride, there had been an undercurrent of agitation. Erica was obviously still upset with me for the mistakes I had made where Trixie was concerned— and I suspected she was also embarrassed to have failed at capturing Murray while I had been successful. To be honest, I was still upset with her, too, but there had been no time to confront any of those emotions given the emergency at hand.

Then Erica looked back to her mother, and her anger was replaced by sadness. Not because she was being told that she couldn't participate in the mission. But because she was grasping the gravity of what her mother was telling her. "Mom, I can help. This mission has a better chance of succeeding if I'm there than if I'm not."

"That's not a risk I'm willing to take," Catherine said.

"Me either," Alexander added. "You're a wonderful young spy, Erica. Far better than I could ever hope to be. I know I've made plenty of mistakes. I've fouled up missions. I've lost classified documents. . . ."

"You missed the turn for the airport," Catherine said.

"Yes," Alexander agreed. "I've missed plenty of turns in my time."

"No," Catherine said. "I mean you missed the turn just now." She pointed out the window. Sure enough, the clearly marked turnoff was now behind us.

"Oh crumbs!" Alexander exclaimed. He swerved off the highway, bumping across the grassy shoulder in an attempt to get back to the proper road. The van bounced roughly over the uneven terrain, banging all of us around.

"Why didn't you just go to the next exit and make a U-turn?" Shayla Shang demanded.

"There's no time for U-turns!" Alexander proclaimed. "Time is of the essence. . . . Uh-oh!"

A small farm sat by the side of the highway. The van crashed through its barbed-wire fence. Goats and sheep fled as we roared past.

"Now, what was I saying?" Alexander asked, his voice vibrating slightly as the van jounced along.

"That you make mistakes," Erica reminded him.

"Oh! Right! Yes, I make loads of them. Like, for example, how I'm driving through this farm right now." There was a crunch from outside the van as Alexander ran over a feeding trough. "But there's one thing I didn't make a mistake with, Erica. And that's you."

Erica didn't say anything, but I thought there might have been a tear in her eye.

There were *definitely* tears in Mike's eyes. He was very

moved by the whole scene taking place in front of him. "Oh boy," he sobbed, "here come the waterworks."

"You're going to do so many great things," Alexander continued, smashing through the fence on the far side of the farm and swerving back onto the airport road. "I know a lot of fathers *think* their daughters are going to change the world, but I *know* you're going to. You've already done it. Several times . . ."

There was a sudden bang as our rear tire blew out. Some of the barbed wire from the fence had become snagged on it. The van skidded wildly across the road while Alexander struggled to get it back under control. And he might have— if the other rear tire hadn't blown out as well. The van spun around, slid off the side of the road, and crashed into a tree.

The front end of the van crumpled, and the windshield shattered. The airbags deployed, filling the van with dust and the smell of slightly burnt popcorn. Thankfully, all of us were wearing our seat belts, but we were still shaken up quite a bit.

Shayla Shang lost what little cool she had remaining. "You are the worst driver of all time!" she exploded. "I lost some sequins off my dress! It's ruined! This is the worst day ever!"

"Uh, Mom," Jessica said, looking embarrassed by the outburst, "I'm pretty sure it'll be worse for all the people on the ship when it blows up."

Shayla didn't seem to notice this. "Look at my mani-cure!" she yelled, displaying her hand. One of her lacquered nails had a tiny chip in it. "I just had it done! This is terrible!"

"Also, I think I might have broken my leg," Catherine said. She was so quiet about it, she seemed practically apolo-getic, as though she was sorry for inconveniencing us all. Her reaction was the polar opposite of Shayla's when, if anything, it seemed that she *should* have been livid.

"Oh no!" Alexander cried. The front of the van was so smashed in that it was difficult for him to extricate himself from the driver's seat, but he managed it and then hovered over Catherine to see what he could do to help.

"It's not terribly bad," she said calmly. "I suspect it's only a fracture. It's not as though the bone is protruding from my leg or anything like that. But it *is* bloody painful."

Jessica fixed her mother with a hard stare. "Guess that chipped nail isn't so terrible now, is it?"

Shayla lowered her head in shame. "It was still an expen-sive manicure," she muttered under her breath, thinking no one would hear.

Erica leapt out of the van and wrenched the passenger door open so that she could get to her mother.

Murray immediately tried to make a run for it, but Erica simply stuck an arm out and clotheslined him, knocking him flat on his back in the mud.

"Where do you think you're going?" she asked.

"To find a doctor?" he offered meekly.

Erica placed her foot on Murray's neck, then pressed down just enough to make him gag. "This doesn't change anything. You're still going back to the ship."

"It does change *one* thing," Catherine said, sounding truly sorry. "Looks like I won't be able to defuse that bomb. You kids will have to do it after all."

25

VOLUNTEERING

Nueva Gorgona Airfield, Panama
May 18
1115 hours

Catherine desperately wanted to try to stop the
bomb instead of making us do it. But her leg was in worse
shape than she was letting on. She couldn't put any weight
on it at all. Which meant we then had to figure out who
would go to the ship and who would stay behind with
Catherine—and we had to do it quickly, as time was running out. There were only forty-five minutes left until the
bomb exploded. Thanks to my uncanny sense of time, I
was well aware of every second that ticked by.

The airstrip wasn't far from where Alexander had wrecked

the van. We could see it down the road: a long strip of tarmac with a few weather-beaten hangars alongside it. Alexander hoisted Catherine out of the van and carried her while Erica, Mike, and I forced Murray and Shayla Shang on ahead of us. Jessica followed at a slight distance, making it clear that she was extremely upset with her mother.

Even though we were close to the beach, the ocean breeze didn't make it that far inland, so the heat was sultry and humid.

"I'll go," Alexander announced. He might not have been the most competent spy, but he was certainly brave. "In fact, I'll do it alone."

"No dice, Dad," Erica said. "We can't trust you to do this by yourself. You nearly killed us just now, and all you had to do was take the correct exit off the highway."

Alexander sighed and gave in. "You're right. I really can't do this alone. But I'm still going."

"I am too," I said.

Erica gave me a look that I couldn't quite read. "No. Dad and I can handle this. You stay here and look after Mom."

"I think I can help," I insisted.

Erica started to argue, but before she could, Catherine cut her off. "First of all, I don't need anyone to look after me. I can take care of myself."

"But your leg is broken . . . ," Erica began.

"I once made it three days through hostile territory in Afghanistan with a dislocated shoulder and a ruptured spleen. I can handle this just fine. More importantly, Ben is right. He should go with you, Erica. He's been invaluable on several missions so far—and his strengths complement yours. The fact is, the two of you make a very good team."

I couldn't help but look at Erica as Catherine said this. She looked at me, too, then averted her eyes.

Catherine then said, "Benjamin, I hate to ask this of you. And if you hadn't volunteered, I wouldn't have, but . . . there are many, many lives at stake here, and I don't know what else to do."

I could tell she felt horrible merely saying those words, so I gave her a smile to let her know everything was all right. Although, in truth, I didn't feel like smiling at all. I felt like throwing up. The idea of heading back to a ship that was about to explode was terrifying. And yet, I knew that fleeing to safety wouldn't make me feel any better. I would still be nervous to the point of nausea, fearing the worst—and I would be overwhelmed with guilt, knowing I had allowed Erica to go without my help. If Erica succeeded in saving the day, that guilt would never go away—and if she failed, then I would feel even worse.

Mike must have been thinking the same thing, because he said, "I'm going too."

"No," I told him.

He held up an open hand, signaling me to keep my mouth shut. "You think I'm going to run away while you guys get all the glory? That's not happening."

"Well, it sounds like you've got a full crew there," Murray said. "So I'll be happy to volunteer *not* to go. You guys have fun on your suicide mission." He waved good-bye and tried to walk away.

Erica caught his arm and wrenched it so that he yelped in pain. "You're definitely coming with us, dipwad."

"I keep telling you I don't know how to turn the bomb off!" Murray howled. "I'll literally be deadweight!"

Erica said, "I honestly don't know if you're lying or not. But I *do* know how to find out. Once you're facing that bomb, you'll either defuse it—or you won't."

"You're willing to risk your life on whether or not I know something?" Murray asked. "That's a terrible bet. I'm not that smart. In fact, I'm kind of an idiot."

"You're still coming," Erica informed him. "Even if you don't know how to shut this thing off, you started it, which means that you know more about the system than any of us do."

Murray made a show of pouting, like a toddler who had just been informed that he had been given a time-out.

We arrived at the airstrip. It was a bare-bones operation,

used by small aircraft, like sightseeing planes and private jets. There was no waiting room for passengers, only a small control tower that looked as well constructed as the treehouse Mike and I had built in fourth grade. The air traffic controller was seated in a rickety folding chair in the shade of it, napping soundly. At the time, there was one plane ready to fly, a large private jet that idled by one of the old hangars.

"I assume that's our ride?" Mike asked.

"Er . . . no," Murray said, clearly lying. "Looks like our jet isn't even here. We must have missed it. Oh well. I guess we can't go on our suicide mission after all."

He tried to slip away once again, but Erica kept her hand latched firmly around his arm. Then she looked to her parents. "I guess we better get going."

"Right," Catherine said, obviously struggling to keep her emotions in check. She looked like she was on the verge of breaking into tears. Alexander gingerly set her down, although she only placed her uninjured leg on the ground, leaning against him for support. "We're proud of you," she told Erica, and then opened her arms for a hug.

Until recently, I had thought Erica wasn't the type of person who would have ever hugged anyone unless she was being forced to at gunpoint. But either Erica had changed— or I had been wrong all along. She shoved Murray toward Mike, then hugged her mother tightly. Alexander clamped his arms around both of them. Even though we were pressed for time, they all stayed like that for quite a while.

Jessica Shang came up alongside me, looking awkward and sheepish. "I *really* didn't know that my mother was involved in any illegal activity," she said.

"I believe you," I told her.

Jessica heaved a sigh of relief. "It's just so embarrassing, having parents who are criminals. I don't want you to think that everyone in my family is corrupt. I have plenty of aunts and uncles and cousins who haven't ever plotted anything evil."

"I'm sure," I said.

"I don't know what's going to happen now, with Mom getting arrested and everything, but I hope that we can still be friends after all this . . . if you don't get blown up today."

"That'd be great," I told her, and I really meant it. Not only did I trust Jessica, but I felt bad for her. I often found my parents embarrassing, and they were completely normal parents; discovering that they were actually villains in front of my friends would have been mortifying.

Jessica smiled, then gave me a hug and a quick peck on the cheek. "Good luck," she said.

I could feel the blood rush to my face. Not far away, Mike gave me a thumbs-up and a wink. And Erica, who had finally stopped hugging her own parents, was glaring at me.

"Thanks," I told Jessica. "I gotta go."

Catherine told Erica, "I have something important to give you before you go." Then she withdrew a gun from her belt and handed it to her daughter.

It was only a flare gun, but still, Erica seemed touched. As though her mother had just given her a precious family heirloom.

"Where did you get this?" she asked.

"I stole it from the speedboat," Catherine explained. "It's not much, but I figure it might come in handy. Along with *this*." She pressed something much smaller into Erica's hands.

Erica considered it, then nodded and said, "I'll use it well."

"I know you will," Catherine said. "Now get going. We're running out of time."

Erica quickly dragged Murray to the private jet, while I woke the air traffic controller and then explained to him in Spanish that he needed to phone the police. He proffered his chair to Catherine so she could rest her injured leg, while Shayla and Jessica Shang sat on the ground in the shade.

Catherine gave Alexander a hug good-bye as well. "Keep an eye on our girl," she ordered him.

"I'll do my best," Alexander said.

Then he, Mike, and I headed for the jet. Despite Murray's claims to the contrary, it was, in fact, the very plane he had hired to flee the country, although Erica had already explained to the pilot that there was a change of plans, and that instead of escaping to the United States, we would be heading toward the Panama Canal.

I had only been on a private jet once before, one that had been owned by the CIA. That one had been old and run-down. This one was high-end, the sort of plane that extremely rich people used. It had leather seats, wood paneling, a business center with a computer, a small bedroom, a fully stocked kitchenette, and two stewards.

It was ready to go. So we buckled ourselves into our seats, and within minutes, we were in the air, flying toward the largest bomb that had ever been built and desperately hoping that we would be able to defuse it in time.

EXPLANATION

Somewhere above Panama

En route to the Panama Canal

May 18

1130 hours

"I bet you're wondering what my plot *really* was with this bomb," Murray said.

He was seated across the aisle from me, devouring a bag of Doritos that one of the stewards had found for him in the kitchenette. His lips were already coated with neon-orange Dorito dust.

I asked, "Didn't you tell me that you weren't going to share your plots with me anymore?"

"That's when I thought I was going to live another day,"

Murray replied. "Now that we're all going to die, you might as well know how brilliant my scheme was. There was way more to it than just blowing up a cruise ship for the insurance money."

"I don't really care about your scheme," I said, although it was a lie. I really did want to know about Murray's plans. But there was no better way of getting under Murray's skin than acting like you didn't want to listen to him.

Sure enough, he grew sulky, but he didn't shut up. "Well, I'm gonna tell you anyway. Because you've forced me to come along with you against my will. So you're all stuck with me." He signaled for the attention of the stewards and asked, "Is there any meal service on this flight? I'd like a sandwich. With as much bacon as possible."

One of the stewards shrugged. "I'm sorry, Mr. Hill. We don't have any bacon on this plane."

Murray looked almost as horrified as he had when he'd learned he was being taken back to the cruise ship. "No bacon?! Fine. Then take everything you can find that's not healthy and put it between two slices of bread."

The steward looked at him curiously. "Everything?"

"Everything," Murray repeated. "Chips, chocolate, aerosol cheese. Whatever you've got. I might not have much time left, so I'm going to enjoy every last second I can."

While the stewards went to work, I looked out the window at the land below me. Nueva Gorgona wasn't very far from the Panama Canal, so even though we hadn't been in the air long, I could already see it ahead of us. The canal wasn't a simple cut directly through Panama. Instead, it had been designed to take advantage of Lake Gatun, a large body of water in the center of the country, which required less construction. Thus, in a way, it was really two separate canals. Ships went through one, crossed Lake Gatun, then went through the other. This was located at the narrowest point in Panama, where the country arched like a horseshoe on its way between North and South America, so bizarrely, the canal really ran north to south rather than east to west. We were closer to the Pacific terminus, and I could see dozens of container and cruise ships queued up to enter the waterway.

I scanned them all, hoping that perhaps the *Emperor of the Seas* was among them, still stuck in traffic rather than in the center of the canal. Unfortunately, I didn't see it.

Erica was doing the same thing in the seat ahead of me, while Mike was taking advantage of the plane's free Wi-Fi and computer terminal to check his messages. Alexander was simply fidgeting nervously.

Erica hadn't spoken to me the entire flight. Even though there was an empty seat next to her, it had been clear that she didn't want me sitting in it. I was still upset with her, too, but unsure how to fix things. Certainly, this wasn't an opportune time for a heart-to-heart discussion.

"Anyhow," Murray said, "here's the deal: I'm not only working with Shayla Shang here. I met Shayla when I free-lanced with her husband for Operation Golden Fist last winter, and one night, Leo told me that the *Emperor of the Seas* was costing billions more than it was supposed to. So I got the idea that maybe the Shangs would be interested in having someone help them destroy the ship and make it look like a terrorist act. But then I thought: What's the point of making a fake terrorist act . . . when you could have a real one?"

I turned to him from the window, unable to control my interest. "Who would want to destroy a cruise ship?" I asked.

"No one," Murray replied. "Except for the Shangs. But there are *lots* of people who'd like to destroy the Panama Canal: truck and train companies that want to hurt the shipping industry, South American ports that will get much more traffic if ships have to go all the way around their continent instead of skipping it altogether, construction companies that want the contracts to rebuild the canal, concrete companies, steel companies, companies that make earth-boring equipment, Nicaraguans who want to build a rival canal through their country, people who just hate Panama . . . I found dozens of shady organizations that were each willing to pay me separately to do this!"

Erica said, "And I'm guessing you didn't tell any of them about each other."

"Nope!" Murray exclaimed. "I charged each one for the full price of my services!"

"How long have you been plotting all this?" I asked.

"Since I first started working with Leo, right after you blew up SPYDER's evil spy school. Of course, I didn't let SPYDER know I was freelancing—which might have been one of the reasons they tried to kill me back in Mexico. But I was done with them anyhow. The Croatoan had already asked me to help bring SPYDER down, so I manipulated you guys into helping me do that and got the Croatoan to pay me for it! Brilliant, right?"

"No," I said, even though I was secretly kind of impressed. I just didn't want to give Murray the respect he was craving.

Murray frowned, but only for a second. He was too intent on laying out all his plans. "So, anyhow, while SPYDER and the Croatoan both thought I was working for them, I was setting up my own evil empire the whole time: SMASH!"

"SMASH?" Erica asked.

"Yes! Because a smash is a big hit. And also, I destroy a lot of stuff. So it works on two levels. Pretty cool, huh?"

"It's okay," I said, knowing this would annoy Murray.

Which was exactly what happened. He immediately grew defensive. "Oh, come on! It's a cool name. Way cooler than the Croatoan. Or SPYDER."

"No, SPYDER was much cooler," Erica said. "SMASH sounds like the name of a toy company."

"Shows what you know," Murray said petulantly. "The name is trending very well in the evil community."

The steward brought Murray his sandwich. As Murray had requested, it was loaded with everything unhealthy from the kitchenette. The steward was carrying it at arm's length, as though it were radioactive. "Here's the meal you requested, sir."

"Fantastic!" Murray grabbed it and took a bite, then rolled his eyes in ecstasy. "Ooh! There's gummy worms in it! Nice touch!"

"Hey, Ben!" Mike called suddenly. "Zoe wants to talk to you."

"Zoe?" I asked, surprised. "How'd she even know . . . ?"

"I was answering all my messages," Mike said. "And Zoe saw I was online, so she started writing to me, and now she wants to talk to you, too."

I hesitated, wondering if this was a good idea, but then realized this might be the last time I ever got to communicate with Zoe. I glanced out the window again to see how much time we had left. The Panama Canal was coming up fast. "All right." I unbuckled my seat belt and started toward the computer center.

"Wait!" Murray said, his mouth now crammed with

sandwich. So many gummy worms dangled from his lips, he looked like a bait box. "Don't you want to hear the rest of my plot?"

"No, I get it," I said. "You suckered a bunch of bad people into paying you to do something horrible so you could get rich while causing worldwide chaos and killing a bunch of innocent people. Not cool, Murray."

Mike evacuated the seat in front of the computer, and I slipped into it. "Trixie says hi," he whispered to me, then headed back to his own seat.

A second later, I got a request to video-chat with Zoe. I agreed and a window popped open, showing her face. Since we were on a plane, the connection wasn't great. The image was grainy and stuttered a bit. But I could still see Zoe clearly enough to recognize that she was in her dormitory at school and that she was doing her best not to look jealous.

"Hey," she said. "Mike says you're on your way to defuse a nuclear bomb?"

"Actually, this time, it's really more of a nuclear reactor rigged to detonate. But yeah, same concept."

Zoe frowned. "You always get to have all the excitement. I *never* get to defuse nuclear bombs."

"It's not as much fun as it sounds. In fact, it's not fun at all. It's really scary."

"You're only saying that to make me feel better."

"I'm not! I'm really terrified! This mission has been extremely difficult. Dane Brammage nearly killed me twice!"

"You've had multiple attempts on your life?" Zoe exclaimed enviously. "How many action sequences have there been?"

"A couple," I admitted, feeling strangely bad about this. "In fact, I just had to chase Murray down on a speedboat."

"I *knew* there would be a chase like that," Zoe said sadly. "Remember? Right before you left? Were you on a Jet Ski?"

"A WaveRunner," I admitted.

"Oh, man! That is so cool! I'll never get to chase anyone on a WaveRunner working for DADD."

"I'm sure you will someday," I said supportively.

"I doubt it. All I've been doing for them is filling out forms. Agent Taco told me that the worst injury she ever suffered on the job was a paper cut."

"Ben!" Erica called to me. "We're getting close. You need to get back to your seat."

"All right," I said. Although I didn't go back to my seat right away, because I wasn't ready to say good-bye to Zoe quite yet.

I turned back to the computer monitor. "Zoe, I know you're upset about all this, but what I'm about to do here really is dangerous. So if you don't hear back from me, could you let my parents know that—"

"I'm going to hear back from you," Zoe said. Something in her voice had changed. She was no longer jealous. She was confident, letting me know that she believed in me. Despite the grainy image, I could see the faith in her eyes. This wasn't an act, just to make me feel better. "You're going to succeed. I know it. If anyone can handle this, it's you and Erica and Mike."

"Thanks," I said.

"But just in case you need it, I'm sending you something that Mike asked me for." The computer pinged, indicating that a message had just arrived.

"What is it?" I asked.

"Schematics for the nuclear reactor on the *Emperor of the Seas*. They weren't that hard to find."

"Ben," Erica said, more firmly than before. "Get ready."

"Okay," I said, then looked to Zoe one last time. "I've gotta go."

"Go save the day," Zoe told me, then thought to add, "again."

I clicked off the video chat, then opened the file Zoe had sent. Sure enough, the blueprints for the nuclear reactor and its housing came up. I went to print it but then noticed . . .

"There's no printer on this plane?" I asked the stewards.

"No," one answered. "However, we do have a large selection of beverages if you'd like one before we land."

"This plane has a screening room, but no printer," I muttered. Then, without any other choice, I focused on the schematics and did my best to commit them to memory.

"Ben," Erica said one more time.

"Give me a moment," I told her, staring at the screen.

The jet shuddered slightly as the landing gear deployed.

I glanced out the window. We were coming down alongside the canal, which cut through the land between the Pacific Ocean and Lake Gatun like a giant scar. Although there was a good amount of protected forest terrain close by, the area on both sides of the canal was heavily industrial. I could easily see the *Emperor of the Seas*, as it was the largest object for miles. It was in the process of moving through the Miraflores Locks.

Since Lake Gatun was a hundred feet above sea level, ships had to go uphill to get to it. This involved an intricate series of locks, which were kind of like hydraulic elevators. A ship would pull into the lock at sea level; then the lock would be closed off and flooded to lift the ship up to the next level. At this point, the ship would be released into the higher section of canal and move on. This was a relatively slow process, which is why it took eight to ten hours to get through the canal—although that was still several weeks shorter than it would take to go all the way around South America.

The canal was less than two hundred feet wide, so from

the air, it was a surprisingly thin line across the landscape. The *Emperor of the Seas* almost filled it completely. (I would learn later that the width of the ship had actually been dictated by the size of the Panama Canal, which was the case for almost every ship on earth. There was little point in building anything too wide to use the world's most famous maritime shortcut.) From my vantage point, it looked as though there was virtually no room at all between the ship and the sides of the locks; it fit into the gap as perfectly as a Lego piece.

There was no airstrip near the locks. The pilot was bringing the jet down on a road that paralleled the canal. It appeared to be in a restricted maintenance area, rather than for the public, so there weren't any cars on it at the moment.

"Are we allowed to land here?" Mike asked.

"Probably not," Alexander said. "But this is an emergency situation. We need to get as close to that ship as possible."

"Ben!" Erica exclaimed sharply.

"Right." I took one final look at the plans that Zoe had sent, then scrambled back to my seat and buckled in as the plane came down for its landing.

We passed close to the *Emperor of the Seas*. Large crowds of passengers were gathered along the railings, watching the lock fill up around the ship.

The tires screeched as the jet touched down. We jolted once, then braked. The jet hadn't even come to a full stop before Erica had unbuckled her seat belt. She grabbed Murray's arm and said, "Let's go."

"I haven't finished my sandwich yet!" Murray protested. Although he had made surprising progress; only a few bites were left. The front of Murray's shirt was spattered with chocolate sauce, potato chip crumbs, and tiny flecks of Spam.

Erica yanked him out of his seat. Murray desperately crammed the remainder of his sandwich into his mouth as he was dragged down the aisle.

Alexander, Mike, and I were right behind them. As the jet came to a stop, Erica punched the button that controlled the door. It opened automatically, extending a small flight of stairs down to the road.

Erica led the way out, pulling Murray along with her, and the rest of us followed. We were immediately walloped by a wave of heat. It was late spring near the equator, so the sun was blazing and the road was baking.

As the whine of the jet's engines shut down, it became quiet enough for us to hear something else: police sirens.

A black sedan was barreling down the road toward us, lights flashing.

Erica kept on going, hurrying toward the canal with Murray in tow. Murray was doing his best to drag his feet, like a petulant child who was being forced to go shopping with his parents, so I gave Erica a hand, grabbing Murray's other arm and pulling him along.

"I guess the police are upset at us for landing in the road like this?" I asked.

"That's not the police." Erica was studying the car that was racing toward us with concern. "That vehicle is from the Drug Enforcement Administration."

"Why would the DEA be interested in us?" I asked.

"Maybe because we came here on a drug dealer's jet," Murray said. "I borrowed it from a friend of mine in Costa Rica. A guy named El Diablo."

"El Diablo?" Mike repeated. "We know him too! He's a great guy!"

I wasn't nearly so excited, as I realized what was going on. "So the DEA thinks we're involved with a drug dealer?"

"It sure seems that way," Murray said.

The black sedan screeched to a stop between us and the *Emperor of the Seas*, blocking our access to it. Two agents leapt out, aiming guns at us.

"Hands in the air!" they yelled. "You're under arrest!"

27

MUTINY

The Miraflores Locks
Panama Canal
May 18
1140 hours

Murray said, "If we run, we can probably make it back to the jet before the DEA can shoot us. Then we can escape and still get pretty far away from here before the ship explodes." The expectant look on his face signaled that he'd been hoping for an opportunity like this to back out of the mission. Which was probably why he hadn't bothered to mention that he had borrowed the jet from El Diablo until then.

And for a moment, I actually considered it. Because our situation looked awfully bleak.

However, Erica didn't seem the slightest bit fazed. "I know how to handle this," she said, then turned to her father. "Dad, I'm going to need you to act like you have no idea what's going on."

"What?" Alexander asked, confused. "I don't understand."

"Perfect," Erica said. "Keep acting just like that."

"But I'm not acting . . . ," Alexander told her.

Meanwhile, the DEA agents appeared to be perplexed by our presence. Even though we were in Panama, they were American. I knew from my Law Enforcement Organization seminar at school that United States DEA officers operated throughout Central and South America, and the Panama Canal was one of their major points of focus, as it was a good place to stop illegal items from moving north. Obviously, upon seeing El Diablo's jet, they had expected to find hardened criminals. Instead, they were confronting four bedraggled teenagers (Erica, Murray, and I hadn't been able to clean up after our boat chase) and a befuddled adult. We looked like a family whose vacation had gone horribly wrong.

Erica capitalized on this confusion by completely changing her personality. She stopped being calm and collected and started sobbing at the top of her lungs. "Don't shoot us!" she bawled. "We're innocent! We're just lost! We didn't mean to land on your nice road here. But we can't seem to find the Dallas airport. Do you know where that is?"

The two DEA agents looked at each other, unsure what to make of this. Finally, one with bushy eyebrows who seemed to be in charge spoke up. "Er . . . it's like a thousand miles north of here."

"A thousand miles?!" Erica shrieked. "Where are we?"

"Panama," Agent Eyebrows said.

"Panama?!" Erica echoed, then wheeled on Alexander. "I *told* you this didn't look like Texas, Daddy! That stupid discount pilot you hired screwed everything up!"

"Oh," Alexander said, looking completely stymied. "Well . . . I . . . uh . . ."

Erica returned her attention to the DEA again. "I'm so sorry we landed here! It was an emergency! We couldn't find the airport, and I really have to go to the bathroom! The one on the jet isn't working and I had way too much iced tea!"

The DEA agents looked at each other again.

Agent Eyebrows asked, "How is it that you ended up on that plane?"

"Can I tell you in five minutes?" Erica hopped back and forth from one foot to the other like she had ants in her pants. "I have to pee sooooo bad! I feel like I'm gonna explode! Is there a bathroom anywhere around here?"

The DEA agents lowered their guns. We were now in a

situation that the CIA referred to as an age-induced reduction of expectations. If an adult had acted the way that Erica was acting, it would have been suspicious. But teenagers acted bizarrely all the time, and adults rarely seemed to know how to handle them. It was one of the great advantages we had as young agents. The DEA no longer seemed to think we were involved in any drug smuggling business—and they certainly didn't think we were spies.

The second DEA agent said, "I think there's a bathroom over by the lock control building."

"Oh!" Erica exclaimed. "That's amazing! You're the best! Thank you so much!" The lock control building was past the DEA agents, so Erica waddled toward them in the way that someone with a full bladder might. Just as she came beside them, she turned back to the rest of us and asked, "Do any of you guys need to go too?"

Both DEA agents turned their attention back to us, which was a natural response when you were waiting for someone to answer a question.

That was when Erica attacked them. All she needed was a single moment for the agents to drop their guard to get the jump on them. She was a blur of motion, disarming both of them and laying them out flat on the ground within seconds.

It occurred so quickly, neither agent seemed to be able to

comprehend what had happened. They just gaped at Erica in amazement as she aimed both of their guns at them.

"I'm not going to hurt you as long as you don't do anything stupid," she said, back to her normal calm and collected self. "But I'm afraid I do need to cuff you." She beckoned to the rest of us.

We hurried over, took the cuffs from the DEA agents, cinched their arms behind them, then hurried onward toward the ship. Only, as we ran, we heard more sirens.

Four more DEA sedans were racing down the road.

"Nuts," Mike said. "Backup's on the way."

I cased the area around us. There was nowhere to run. We were in a great, wide-open area between the road and the canal lock, which the *Emperor of the Seas* was resting in. Ideally, we should have been getting inside the ship itself, but all the access points were tightly sealed while it was in the lock, making it as impenetrable as a steel wall.

"Why didn't you just tell them that we're CIA?" I asked Erica.

"You think they would have believed that?" Erica asked. "Or that this ship has been turned into a floating bomb by this guy?" She pointed disdainfully at Murray as we dragged him along. "He looks like he'd have trouble figuring his way out of a cardboard box, let alone planning something like this."

"Hey!" Murray said, sounding offended. "I don't look that dumb!"

"You have a gummy worm stuck to your cheek," I told him.

"Oh." Murray seemed momentarily disappointed in himself, but then he pulled the gummy worm off, popped it in his mouth, and exclaimed, "Ooh! It still has some chocolate on it!"

We were getting close to the canal now. The edges of it were lined with railroad tracks, which specially designed locomotives ran along. These would stabilize the ships as they passed through to keep them from slamming into the canal walls. They were known as mules, because originally, actual mules had towed boats through the canal. Just beyond the tracks, the *Emperor of the Seas* loomed like a skyscraper. The lock was about half full of water, so we were facing the fourth story of the ship.

Just above it was the Promenade Deck. Tourists were crowded along the railings there to watch the passage of the ship through the locks—although many of them were far more interested in watching us. Which made sense, as watching a canal lock in action was about as exciting as watching a bathtub fill with water. Many tourists waved excitedly to us, as though we were actors performing for their amusement.

The railing of the Promenade Deck would have been a great place to attach a grappling hook, and then we could have climbed the rope to get inside the ship. I didn't have a grappling hook on me at the moment—although if anyone would have come prepared for something like this, it was Erica.

So I turned to her as we ran. "You aren't, by any chance, carrying a grappling hook, are you?"

"No," she replied. "I have something better."

"What's better than a grappling hook?" Mike asked.

"This." Erica took out the flare gun that her mother had given her before we got on the plane. "I need you both to handle the dummy," she said, letting go of Murray.

Mike and I each seized an arm of his and dragged him onward.

Erica then took out the other object her mother had given her. This was a small plastic vial. Whatever was inside, I couldn't make it out.

"What's that?" I asked.

"Remember the RDX explosive the Croatoan was going to use on our last mission? I took a little bit of it."

"You did?" Alexander asked, sounding shocked. "Whatever for?"

"Times like this," Erica replied.

I remembered the RDX quite well, as I had spent a considerable amount of time trying not to be blown up by it. It was incredibly powerful—and very reactive. All it needed to detonate was a good-size impact. Like whacking it with a hammer. Or dropping it from a tall height. Or impacting the wall of a cruise ship at great speed.

"Hey!" Murray said. "I'm the one who sold the Croatoan that RDX in the first place! It's *really* dangerous! If you're not careful with it, you'll blow us to the moon!"

"Relax. I'm always careful," Erica said, then upended the vial and dumped the RDX into the barrel of the flare gun as we ran.

"Hey, guys!" a cheerful voice shouted. "Up here!"

We looked up to see Kit Karoo at the railing of the Promenade Deck, along with several sullen teens. It appeared the Koolnezz outing of the day was a trip to watch the locks at work, although no one appeared to be enjoying it except Kit—and given Kit's behavior in the crew quarters, I could only assume that her good cheer was an act.

Even though we were running for our lives and trying to drag Murray between us, Mike still waved back, nice and friendly. "Hey, Kit! How's it going?"

"What are you doing down there?" Kit asked, concerned. "No passengers are supposed to be off the ship at this time!"

"Really?" Mike asked. "Whoops! We'll come right back on board!"

"How?" Kit asked.

"Give us a moment," Mike replied. "And, uh, maybe plug your ears."

Kit and everyone else on the deck looked at Mike curiously, wondering if he was joking. But then Erica told us, "Get down." We dropped and took cover amongst the railroad tracks, at which point everyone on the ship realized we were serious.

Erica fired the flare gun directly at the side of the ship, then dropped and took cover beside me. We curled into balls, wrapping our arms over our heads.

There was a very large explosion, followed by a wave of heat. When I looked up again, there was a hole in the side of the ship big enough to drive a truck through. Tiny bits of metal were raining down around us.

The DEA sedans screeched to a stop on the road not far behind us, so we got back to our feet and ran for the ship.

All the tourists were now peering over the railing to see what we had done. Many of them appeared to be extremely upset that we had blown a hole in the ship, seeing as ships with holes in them tended to sink. Kit was doing her best to shift the blame from herself. "Those children are not under my supervision!" she announced to the crowd. "Koolnezz does not authorize the use of explosives!"

As it was, the *Emperor of the Seas* wouldn't have sunk with the hole Erica had blasted in it. Not in the canal, at least. The hole was high above the waterline.

It was directly in front of us, and since the ship filled the lock so tightly, the gap between the edge of the canal and the hole was only a few inches. We easily leapt across and found ourselves in the great hall.

The guests inside the boat, who'd had no warning that a hole was about to be blown in the side, were in a far more agitated state than the guests who'd witnessed the event from the Promenade Deck. Another theme party appeared to be underway, this one to celebrate crossing through the canal. One side of the room was decorated with an Asian theme while the other side was European, complete with buffet tables laden with stereotypically representative cuisines: Chinese food, Korean barbecue, and sushi on the Asian side; crepes, pasta, and knockwurst on the European. For perhaps the first time in cruise ship history, there were no lines at the buffet tables: The guests were hiding behind them, or under them, or had fled from the room altogether.

As we entered the great hall, one frightened woman pointed at us and screamed, "Pirates!"

Which actually made a certain amount of sense, seeing as we had just blown a hole in the ship and leapt aboard.

Ship security arrived on the scene and seemed to think we might be pirates as well. They were only armed with long-range Tasers, but still, we didn't want to get hit with one. "Freeze!" one of them ordered.

We didn't. Instead, we fled through the room, heading toward the stern.

Security came after us. Erica upended the European buffet in their path, although Murray—showing a dexterity and speed I had never seen in him—managed to snatch two chocolate éclairs off it before she could. An enormous tureen full of fettuccine Alfredo sloshed across the floor, and several guards slipped in it at once.

The DEA now rushed through the hole in the side of the ship.

Mike muttered, "Do you think, just once, we could encounter some security who *doesn't* aim a weapon at us? Half the people on this ship are committing crimes, and everyone's acting like *we're* the bad guys!"

This time, we circled around the restaurant and kitchen complex, sticking to the corridors along the sides of the ship.

"The fastest way to the engine room is probably still through the theater," Erica said. "The other entrances will have security systems."

"It won't be easy to get through that hatch with all these guys after us," I pointed out.

"I'll divert them!" Alexander announced, although he sounded slightly queasy. I glanced at him and noticed he was turning greenish again.

"Are you feeling all right?" I asked.

"Er . . . no. My seasickness medication wore off some time ago."

"You're feeling nauseous *now*?" Mike asked, stunned. "We're not even at sea! The boat's in a canal!"

"It's still on the water," Alexander said. "I'm afraid I wouldn't be able to make it to the engine room anyhow. So I'll handle the diversion."

We arrived at one of the vertical integration points. While Erica, Mike, Murray, and I went down the stairs, Alexander went up—although it was obviously a struggle for him in his condition. However, that worked to our advantage. I could hear him gagging, retching, and ultimately vomiting from two floors away.

Thus, the distraction kind of worked. The various agents pursuing us split into two groups. Most went after Alexander, but two DEA agents and a fettuccine-spattered ship security agent came down the stairs, just in case we had tried to pull a fast one on them.

They caught a glimpse of us as we got off at the next landing and took up the chase.

Our only route now led directly through the ship's casino. We raced through the glitzy entry foyer into an extremely large room filled with card tables, roulette wheels, and thousands of clanging slot machines. Hundreds of guests were busily winning and losing money. Mostly losing.

It occurred to me that Murray had stopped forcing us to drag him along. Now he was running along with us, although he was trying to eat his éclairs at the same time, which had resulted in him having cream filling and chocolate icing smeared all over his face.

"You're hurrying *toward* this bomb," I observed.

"What's your point?" he asked, bowling over a tourist couple on their way to the blackjack tables.

"Does that mean you actually know how to defuse it?"

Murray wavered for a moment, then admitted, "I might have an idea or two."

"So you lied to us about that?" Mike exclaimed.

"What was I supposed to do, tell you the truth? Then you would have dragged me along against my will for sure! But now, since you wouldn't fly away from danger like sensible people, I'm gonna die unless I do something. So I might as well do it. Although, I don't know how much more I can run. My stomach's killing me. I feel like I'm gonna puke."

"Then why are you still eating an éclair?" I asked.

"Because I don't know if I can defuse this thing for sure. And if I'm gonna die, I intend to enjoy my last minutes. I'm not gonna eat a *salad*." Murray squeezed his last éclair like a tube of toothpaste, firing the remains of the cream filling into his open mouth.

I was having some issues running myself. We'd been going flat out for a while, and I was already achy and tired.

But we had limited time to defuse the bomb, and security agents were pursuing us. Even Mike, who was in better shape than me, seemed to be flagging. Only Erica showed no signs of exhaustion.

"I think I can get these jerks off our tail," Mike said.

We were passing a man who had hit a jackpot on the slots. He had a large bucket full of coins, and he was rubbing his good fortune in all the other gamblers' faces. "Look who made the big time, suckers!" he crowed, shaking his bucket.

Mike smacked it out of his hands as we ran past. The bucket clattered on the floor, spilling coins everywhere. "Free money!" Mike shouted.

Dozens of gamblers pounced on the coins, like pigeons descending on bread crumbs in the park. They dropped to the floor with such speed, it was as though a wall had instantly formed between us and the pursuing agents, allowing us to leave them behind in the casino.

As we raced down an aisle of pirate-themed slot machines, I came alongside Erica. She gave me an icy stare, like she was still upset with me. Which was exactly why I wanted to talk to her. I didn't think we should be angry with one another when the time came to defuse the bomb.

I told her, "I'm sorry about the things I said before."

"Okay," she replied.

A few seconds passed. "Um . . . ," I said awkwardly. "Usually, when one person apologizes, then the other person apologizes in return."

"Only when the other person did something they need to apologize for."

"B-but . . . ," I stammered. "You *did* do something! You said some really nasty things!"

"Which you needed to hear."

"And *you* needed to hear what I had to say too! But I still feel sorry for the way I said it! Don't you feel that way?"

"No," Erica said flatly.

Something occurred to me. "Erica, have you ever apologized for anything before?"

"People apologize when they make mistakes. I don't make mistakes."

I thought about pointing out to Erica that she *had* made mistakes before but realized that would only escalate things. As it was, my plan to try to fix the bad blood between us hadn't worked; in fact, I was more upset with her now than I had been a minute before. So I took a deep breath and tried to calm myself. We were in the midst of a serious crisis, and I needed to be serene and focused, not angry and agitated.

Unfortunately, it didn't work. Or maybe I needed some more time to cool down—but time was a luxury we didn't have.

We barged through the doors at the end of the casino and found ourselves in front of the ship's theater.

According to my mental clock, we had ten minutes left until the bomb went off.

I was really hoping that my bet would pay off—and that Murray could stop the detonator—or else these were going to be the last ten minutes of my life.

COOL UNDER PRESSURE

Engine Room

The *Emperor of the Seas*

May 18

1150 hours

Thankfully, the theater was empty. There were no shows or elaborate rehearsals taking place. So there was no one to interfere with our progress. Now that we knew where the emergency hatch was and how to open it, it only took us a minute to locate it, get through it, and find ourselves back atop the housing for the nuclear reactor.

The hard part was getting Murray to defuse the bomb.

It wasn't that Murray didn't *want* to defuse the bomb.

Murray didn't want to die. But it turned out, he couldn't function under pressure at all.

Murray had spent his entire time at spy school slacking off. And he had spent his entire time as a double agent rigging weapons of mass destruction and chaos—as opposed to turning them off. Defusing a bomb was an extremely stressful ordeal that required a very special sort of person to succeed—and Murray was not that sort of person.

"Oh boy," he said, staring at the nuclear reactor. "I'm feeling kind of faint here. And I've lost sensation in my hands. I think I'm having a panic attack. Or a heart attack. Definitely some kind of attack. And it's not good."

"You know what won't be good?" Erica said angrily. "You not stopping this bomb. In eight minutes and thirty seconds, we all are going to be reduced to steaming piles of radiated mush."

"That's not helping," I told her.

Which was the truth. Murray began hyperventilating.

I grabbed him by the shoulders and looked into his eyes. "Calm down, Murray. We have some time left. I need you to focus. Let's start with the easy stuff. Which of the radiation detectors on this housing is the fake one that controls the bomb?"

Murray's eyes flickered to each one quickly. "I don't remember," he said meekly.

"How do you not remember?" Erica snapped. "You used it to set the timer going last night!"

"I had the blueprints last night!" Murray retorted. "And then Ben made me ruin them."

"If you don't figure this out, I'm gonna ruin your face." Erica started toward him menacingly, but Mike blocked her path.

"Let's see if we can find you something more productive to do," Mike said.

There was some angry shouting in Chinese from the other end of the engine room.

"Sounds like the engineers have heard us," Erica said. "They're coming to chase us off again. I could go beat them up."

"Sure," Mike said. "That's a good use of your pent-up anger."

Erica grabbed a crowbar and started through the engine room.

"Wait!" I yelled. "Maybe you could try talking to them first? You know, explain the situation and see if that works?"

Erica paused and considered this thoughtfully. "And if it doesn't, then can I beat them up?"

"Sure," I said. "Have fun." And then, as Erica headed off, an idea came to me. I looked back at the housing for the nuclear reactor. "Hold on. I was just looking at the plans for this. The ones that Zoe sent me. So I think I can remember which is the fake." I considered the reactor for a while, comparing it to the one in my memory. Then I pointed to the detector on the top right-hand side. "This is the fake," I said, taking a step toward it.

"Wait!" Murray exclaimed. "Are you completely sure?"

"Why?" I asked.

"Because all the real ones are rigged to explode if you try to open them," Murray said.

"What?" Mike cried. "Why would you even design something like that?"

"It sounded like a fun option at the time," Murray said. "Another deterrent to defusing this thing. If I'd known that *I* would be the one defusing it, I probably wouldn't have paid for it."

I considered the reactor one more time, aware precious seconds were slipping by.

In the distance, I heard the engineers yelling angrily at Erica, followed by Erica speaking sharply to them in Chinese. The engineers stopped yelling and listened.

I made my decision, pointing to the same radiation detector I had pointed to before. "It's definitely this one." In truth, I wasn't 100 percent certain, but I was running out of time. "What now?"

"There's a switch at the top," Murray said. "Flip it."

The detector was the size of a toaster oven, with all sorts of gauges and dials on the front. I flipped the switch.

It did not blow up.

Instead, the front dropped down, revealing a keyboard, while the top popped up, revealing a small computer screen.

The screen displayed the timer, which now had slightly less than four minutes.

There were two boxes on the screen below the time, one for user ID and one for password. Just like every other password-protected device on earth.

I pointed Murray toward it.

He shook his head. "My fingers are numb. I'm losing circulation. You need to type for me."

"Okay," I said. "What's your user ID?"

Murray hesitated a moment, as if considering dying was better than revealing his ID. Then he reluctantly said, "MurrayLovesZoe. All one word."

Mike burst into laughter. "You've got a crush on Zoe?"

"No!" Murray said in a way that was so overly defensive that it was clear he was lying. "That user ID is ironic. I don't like Zoe at all. So therefore, no one would ever guess that MurrayLovesZoe is my user ID. See? It makes perfect sense." He paused a moment, then asked, "Do you think Zoe likes me?"

"She *hates* you," Mike said. "You're evil."

"I thought maybe she was just playing hard to get," Murray said.

At the far end of the room, the engineers all started screaming in terror in response to something that Erica had said. I heard them running for the door.

I entered the user ID. There were two and a half minutes left. "What's the password?"

"Er . . . I forget," Murray said weakly.

I wheeled on him, doing my best not to freak out. "You forget?!"

"Kind of," Murray admitted. "I had it written on the blueprints so that I wouldn't forget it—and you made me destroy them. So really, this is *your* fault."

Mike was trying his best not to panic either. "Do you remember anything about it?"

"Kind of." Murray was starting to freak out again. "It was something mean about Ben. BenRipleySucks. Or BenRipleyStinks. Or maybe BenRipleySmells. And there were three exclamation points after it. Or maybe four. Or five. Aaah! Why did I make it so complicated?" Murray started hyperventilating again.

Mike looked to me, appearing close to hysteria himself. "You think maybe there's another way to shut this thing off? Like hitting it really hard with a wrench? My dad does that to stuff when he gets angry. Sometimes it works."

"No!" Murray wailed. "If you hit it, that triggers the countdown to end right away!"

Mike frowned. "Another bonus option?"

"It sounded cool at the time," Murray said dolefully.

However, even though things seemed dismal, I had an idea. I had learned something important from Erica, shortly after I had met her, when we were on our first mission together: There was nothing that made a boy focus so much as a girl.

"Murray," I said, "Mike was wrong before. Zoe really does like you."

Murray stopped hyperventilating. His eyes went wide. He seemed to forget about everything else. "Really? How do you know?"

"She told me," I said. "But she's really embarrassed about it, seeing as you're evil and all. . . ."

"I can change!" Murray exclaimed.

"The thing is, I can't set the two of you up if we're dead," I said. "So I need the . . ."

"BenRipleyStinks. Four exclamation points," Murray said, without the slightest bit of doubt in his mind. "Oh! And there's one of those weird star doohickeys at the end."

"An asterisk?" I asked.

"Right! One of those!"

I entered *BenRipleyStinks!!!!** into the password spot.

It worked. The computer screen changed and asked *Do You Want to Cancel the Detonation?* There were yes and no buttons.

I looked back at Murray. "Any more tricks I should know about? Like if I click the wrong button, we all blow up?"

"No," Murray said. "That one's the real deal. So what did Zoe say about me?"

There were thirteen seconds left on the timer.

I clicked the yes button.

The timer stopped counting down.

I heaved a huge sigh of relief. So did Mike.

Erica came running back through the engine room, looking worried—until she saw the time frozen. Then she stopped and broke into a smile. "Nice job," she said.

"I see you didn't have to fight off the engineers," I replied.

"You were right. Talking worked."

Mike asked, "You told them the nuclear reactor was about to blow up?"

"More or less. I told them it was about to emit a kind of radiation that would make their private parts fall off. I think that scared them more than the prospect of death." She looked to me. "How'd you get Murray to function properly?"

"I told him Zoe had a crush on him."

Erica gave a short laugh. "And he believed it?"

"Completely."

Murray's face fell. He looked so upset, I almost felt bad for him. Almost. But not quite. "That was a lie?"

"Yes," I said. "Mike was telling the truth. Zoe hates you."

"Why would you lie to me like that?" Murray yelled.

"Uh . . . to save all our lives," Mike reminded him. "If Ben hadn't figured out how to make your dumb brain work again, we'd all be dead."

This didn't make Murray feel better at all. He glared hatefully at me. "You're the worst, Ben Ripley!" he shouted. "It's not bad enough that you had to thwart my scheme? You also had to toy with my emotions?"

There was a loud clang from above us as the emergency hatch was pulled open. Several members of cruise ship security dropped through it. They all looked extremely peeved.

"You kids get away from there!" one of the security guards yelled. "It's a nuclear reactor! Do you have any idea what would happen if that went off?"

"Yes," Erica replied. "As a matter of fact, we have a very good idea."

"Put your hands up!" another guard told us. "You're all in a lot of trouble."

The four of us followed his orders. "Just so you know," Mike said, "we're not the bad guys here. Except for *him*." He pointed to Murray. "He's as bad as they come."

Murray didn't notice. He was still venting at me. "No

matter what I do, no matter how hard I work, you destroy it all! What did I ever do to you to deserve this?"

"Besides the multiple attempts on my life?" I asked. "You've also tried to bomb the spy school and frame me for it, assassinate the president, steal nuclear launch codes, blow up Colorado . . ."

"That was only business," Murray snapped. "But you've made it personal. So now, in return for all the trouble you've caused me, I'm going to destroy you, Ben Ripley."

"Ha!" Mike laughed. "I'd like to see you try!"

"*I* wouldn't," I said quickly. "This isn't personal at all, Murray. If you wanted to have a normal job, like a dog-walking business, I would have been happy to let you be."

Murray glowered at me angrily. "I'll bet."

The security guards came down and surrounded us. Mike, Erica, and I didn't try to fight them off, because we figured everything would eventually get sorted out and our innocence would be proven. This sort of thing had happened to us a lot. I wasn't too worried about it.

But I *was* worried about Murray. Even though we'd had plenty of nasty encounters in the past, he had always remained surprisingly good-natured toward me. As though we were merely friends who had ended up on rival soccer teams, rather than opposing sides in a battle between good and evil. But this time, there was a malice to his tone that unsettled me.

"You will rue the day you ever met me," he warned as ship security handcuffed us all—and suddenly broke into a smile as he noticed a familiar hulking shape coming through the engine room. "Starting right now." He called out to the approaching figure. "It's about time you got here, Dane!"

Now I was *really* worried. It appeared that Dane had managed to escape our cling-wrap cocoon and come down to get revenge.

But it wasn't Dane Brammage who emerged from the maze of machinery. It was Bjorn Turok.

Murray immediately soured upon recognizing him.

Bjorn addressed the other security guards. "Nice work, men. I'll take things from here."

The other guards hesitated, unsure of what to do. It was evident that Bjorn outranked them, but they didn't seem to want to give up their criminals so easily. "There's four of them," one said. "Are you sure you can handle them by yourself?"

Bjorn flexed a bicep the size of a watermelon. "Yeah, I think I can. C'mon, kids." He clamped a meaty hand on Murray's shoulder and steered him through the engine room, toward the normal door. Erica, Mike, and I dropped in behind him.

The other security guards followed us. "You're sure you don't need any help?" one asked.

"I think he has things under control," Erica told them. "Although, if you all wanted to be useful, those shrink-wrapped items by the wall are terra-cotta warriors that have been stolen from China. And half the dealers in the casino are skimming profits. Oh, and there appears to be some sort of human-trafficking operation in the cargo hold."

"Er . . . what now?" one of the security guards asked, sounding flummoxed.

"The terra-cotta warriors are right over there," Mike said, pointing them out. "Although personally, I'd make the human trafficking a priority."

The guards headed over to inspect the stolen artifacts.

Bjorn led us out of earshot, then spoke in a low voice. "Jessica called and told me what was going on. Sorry about those bozos."

"You're Bjorn, right?" Murray asked. "Dane's cousin? He had very nice things to say about you. Any chance you'd like to make a quick ten thousand dollars? All you have to do is kill these guys and help me escape. . . ."

Bjorn calmly bopped Murray on the top of the head, knocking him unconscious. Murray gave a grunt and collapsed on the floor.

"That's for sedating me earlier," Bjorn told him, then hoisted Murray's limp body onto his shoulder and led us out of the engine room.

The crew areas were incredibly cramped for a man of Bjorn's size. He could barely fit through the narrow halls. So we had to tail behind him, rather than walking alongside him.

"Thanks for saving the ship," Bjorn told us. "And everyone on board. I owe you one."

"It's funny you should say that," Erica told him. "Because I need a favor."

"Name it," Bjorn said.

Erica whispered something to him. Bjorn glanced back at me, looking surprised, then said, "Sure."

"What's going on?" I asked.

"You'll find out soon enough," Erica replied. "There's one last thing you and I need to take care of on this mission."

WRAP-UP

Emperor Suite

The *Emperor of the Seas*

Lake Gatun, Panama

May 18

2000 hours

Preventing a nuclear explosion is exhausting.

The past few days had been physically strenuous and mentally draining, and I hadn't gotten much sleep. So I had been hoping for a little downtime. A nap would have been great, although I would have settled for a few minutes to sit and have a snack. But that didn't happen.

Erica's comment had been an understatement; there were actually *hundreds* of things we needed to take care of.

Alexander was being held in custody by the DEA. (He had only managed to lead them a few flights up on the ship before succumbing to his nausea and getting captured.) Catherine was still stranded at the airstrip in Nueva Gorgona, waiting for medical care while keeping Shayla Shang from escaping. The proper authorities had to be made aware of the various international crimes taking place on board the *Emperor of the Seas*. And Murray Hill and Dane Brammage had to be placed in federal custody. (For the meantime, there was actually a small jail on the *Emperor of the Seas*, and the two of them had been locked up there.) The CIA had operatives stationed in Panama, but it took them two hours to get to the ship and, in the meantime, a lot of the work fell on our shoulders, even though we were kids.

Meanwhile, there were plenty of issues with the cruise ship itself. Even though it had a hole blown in the side of it, it couldn't stay in the middle of the lock, because that would jam traffic on the Panama Canal, resulting in delays for the shipping and cruise companies, which would have serious economic effects. Therefore, emergency procedures were enacted. Since the hole was above the waterline, the ship could still float—although it couldn't go back to sea; another storm like the one we had encountered the night before would sink it. So the *Emperor* was moved out of the lock and into Lake Gatun by a flotilla of tugboats, then surrounded by a protective ring of inflatable pontoons; it was as though the entire ship had been given an enormous life preserver. A tarp was then placed over the hole to prevent any birds or crocodiles from getting inside.

Many questions remained about how to conduct repairs—and what should be done with all the guests and crew in the meantime. Unfortunately, the very people who should have been answering those questions were busy trying to flee from justice. Captain Steinberg and most of his subordinates had abandoned the bridge, fearing charges on crimes ranging from harboring criminals to allowing the kitchens to serve meat that was ten weeks past the sell-by date. (This crime was news to us; there were so many criminal offenses taking place aboard the *Emperor of the Seas* that it would take weeks to sort through them all.) Captain Steinberg had made a desperate escape attempt, swiping a costume from the production of *Symphony at Sea* and attempting to swim to shore disguised as a giant mackerel—but this had failed miserably when the costume became waterlogged and he nearly drowned. Bjorn Turok had rescued him—and then tossed him into the ship's jail as well. In the absence of any leadership, a skeleton crew of rookie cadets was left in charge of the *Emperor of the Seas*. They had managed to move it into Lake Gatun without capsizing it but were at a loss as to how to handle everything else.

In theory, the passengers should have been getting off the ship, but there wasn't really anywhere for them to go. The Lake Gatun region didn't have nearly the hotel space to manage a sudden influx of thousands of tourists and crew members. And there weren't enough flights available out of Panama to get everyone home. So for the time being, everyone was still on board. There was enough food in the hold to last for seven days of all-you-can-eat buffets, which was probably fourteen days of normal eating. Ideally, someone would come up with a way to repair the ship or get everyone off it by then.

In the meantime, the ship's crew was gamely trying to keep the passengers entertained. All the facilities remained open, and the East Meets West party was still in full swing. The fireworks display that was intended to celebrate reaching the Caribbean Sea remained scheduled for that night as well.

I figured I would sleep through it. It had been an exceptionally long day.

But when I finally managed to return to our suite after hours of trying to help straighten things out with ship security, the DEA, and the CIA, I found that all of my stuff was missing. Instead, there was only an envelope with my name on it.

Inside was a key to the Emperor Suite.

As exhausted as I was, this seemed like a good turn of events.

I took the elevator up, using my key to access the Premier

level. This was the first time I had arrived there normally, rather than rappelling down from the top deck or being rendered unconscious and then lugged in. The normal way was much nicer.

Mike and Alexander were in the main room when I entered, engaged in a heated game of foosball. Alexander had finally been given a medication that did away with his nausea and left him coherent. A private buffet of lobster and king crab was spread out on the dining room table.

"Congratulations!" Mike proclaimed as I entered. "We've been upgraded!"

"The Shangs gave us their suite?" I asked.

"Not exactly." Mike took his hands off the controls to grab a crab leg, then went right back to the game. "Bjorn agreed to let us move in here. At Erica's request."

"That's the favor she asked him for earlier?"

"Yes. Although, I figure, it's not that big a deal. The Shangs aren't using this place at the moment. So why should we stay down in our crummy little suite? Especially after we kept this ship from exploding. We deserve a little luxury. Score!" Mike whooped triumphantly as he knocked the ball into the goal.

I looked to Alexander. "And you're okay with us accepting this?"

"Certainly." Alexander retrieved the foosball and put it

back in play. "Technically, this isn't accepting a gift from a *presumed* criminal, because we've already busted them. So there's no ethical issue with it." He paused a moment, then added, "Although we probably shouldn't tell Catherine that we did this."

"How's she doing?"

"She's fine," Alexander reported. "I just talked to her. She had her leg set at the hospital in Nueva Gorgona and is recuperating well. Luckily, it was only a small fracture. I'll go see her the moment anyone can figure out how to get us off this ship."

I helped myself to a lobster tail from the buffet. "And the Shangs?"

"Our compatriots from the Panama City office have Shayla in custody. As for Jessica, she's in a bit of a spot, seeing as both of her parents are now felons. For the time being, she's staying at the hospital with Catherine."

I had plenty of other questions, but before I could ask them, the sliding glass door to the balcony slid open. "Ben?" Erica said. "Can you come out here?"

"Sure," I replied—although a bit more guardedly than I had intended. "Give me a minute."

With everything that had happened, Erica and I hadn't had a chance to talk since our last argument, right before defusing the bomb. So now, I didn't expect that our conversation would be a pleasant one. I stalled as long as I could, taking my time to put together a plate of expensive shellfish at the buffet before heading out to join her.

"Crab puff?" I asked, holding one out as a peace offering.

"No thanks. I'm not hungry." Erica slid the door closed behind us.

It was a soundproof door, cutting off the noise of the foosball game entirely. That meant Mike and Alexander wouldn't be able to hear us, but even so, Erica led me down the long balcony to the port side of the ship.

The sun was setting over Lake Gatun. The *Emperor of the Seas* was parked out of the sea-lane, where it wouldn't be in the way, so we were far from the other ships that were passing through. The shoreline was surprisingly pristine, with thick jungle and a healthy mangrove swamp. Brightly colored birds roosted in the trees, and I thought I could even see a distant troop of monkeys.

The gaping hole we had blown in the side of the ship was below us and toward the stern. Several boats were clustered around it. It looked like various contractors were inspecting the hole to figure out how repairs might be done.

Erica said, "As I mentioned earlier, there's one last thing we have to take care of."

"Does it involve me getting chewed out?" I asked. "Because if it does, I'm fine waiting until morning."

Erica regarded me curiously, then gave a short, amused laugh. "No. It doesn't involve that at all."

I heaved a sigh of relief. "I'm really sorry about all the things I did wrong on this mission. I was careless, and I made some serious mistakes. . . ."

"You're not the only one," Erica said.

I was so busy apologizing, I got several words further along before I realized what she said. ". . . and I know that letting Trixie find out about your family business was a huge error on my part, and I will do whatever it takes to . . . Wait. What did you say?"

"You're not the only one who has made mistakes." Erica paused for a long time before continuing, as though it was going to be painful. "I did too."

"Oh," I said, surprised. "Well, in your defense, *anyone* probably would have screwed up some of the things you attempted. Like jumping from the WaveRunner to Murray's boat. That was almost impossible. . . ."

"I'm not talking about that. Although, if it hadn't been for that dang pelican poop, I would have pulled it off." Erica turned away from me and looked toward the horizon. "The mistakes I made were bigger. Maybe even bigger than what I accused *you* of doing wrong. Like, when I let Dane Brammage throw you off the ship the other day."

"Well, I let my guard down then too. . . ."

"Don't make excuses for me, Ben!" Erica snapped. "I *knew* you were bait. You didn't. You almost died because of my screwup!"

I shrank back from her, surprised by the sharpness of her tone. Erica caught herself and grew embarrassed.

"Sorry," she said. "I'm new at this apologizing thing. I haven't done it very often."

"Because you don't make many mistakes?"

"Because I *thought* I didn't make them. But I have. Like today, when my first instinct was to beat up the guys in the engineering room, and you pointed out that just talking to them might work better. Or when I thought that friends were liabilities, but you proved to me that they were strengths. And then, there's the biggest one of all. . . ." Erica trailed off, looking uncomfortable.

"Which was what?" I asked.

"When I told you that having a relationship in the spy business was a bad idea . . . I might have been wrong."

I was so startled by this comment, I accidentally dropped my seafood platter over the railing. It clanked off the side of the ship and plopped into the lake far below, where a dozen seagulls instantly went after the shellfish. "So you think that relationships are okay?"

"I'm still not sure, really. I was basing things on my parents, whose relationship was a mess because of their jobs. But maybe part of that was because they didn't really know the truth about each other. And if Mike is dating Trixie, that could be messy too." Erica paused, then asked, "*Are* they dating?"

"They're really only texting. But they seem to like each other a lot. She calls him SnuggleBunny."

Erica looked like she was going to throw up. "Just so you know, if you ever call me *anything* like that, I'll kill you."

Despite the threat, I couldn't stop smiling. My heart was beating wildly. "Are you saying that you'd like to go out with me?"

"I'm saying that I'm *thinking* about it." Suddenly, Erica's usual steely reserve was gone, and I saw something in her eyes that had never been there before. She looked vulnerable. "You might be the worst fighter I've ever met, but you're insanely smart, and if it wasn't for you, all the bad guys we've faced would have won several times over."

"Well . . . I couldn't have defeated them without you."

"Right. We make a good team."

Fireworks started going off. For a brief moment, I thought I was imagining them, because hearing Erica say these things made me feel like a sparkler on the Fourth of July. But then I realized that the cruise ship staff was setting them off. We hadn't quite made it to the Caribbean Sea, but we hadn't all sunk or died in a nuclear explosion, so that was worth celebrating.

"You really think so?" I asked.

Erica smiled in response.

Over the past two days, I had been used as bait, thrown overboard, insulted, berated, pummeled, strangled, threatened, almost drowned, and nearly incinerated. I was exhausted, and every part of my body ached. But still, it was the best vacation of my life.

Because Erica Hale kissed me.

To: My Evil Friends around the World
From: Murray Hill

If you are receiving this email, then things have gone horribly wrong with my most recent evil plan. I set up my account to automatically send this message to all of you today unless I stopped it from transmitting. And since I haven't stopped it, that means we have a problem.

Yes, I said "we" there. Not just me. *All of us* have a problem.

His name is Benjamin Ripley.

I know Ripley is only a teenager, but he has already helped thwart many of your brilliant evil plans—and if he hasn't thwarted yours, then you certainly know someone whose plans he has thwarted. Frankly, I'm sick of it.

If it wasn't for Ripley, a lot of us would be very, very rich. But now, we're not. And to make matters worse, other bad things have befallen us. Some of us have been captured. Some have lost body parts. Some have nearly died multiple times.

This has to stop. I have talked to all of you about Project X before. The time has come to initiate it.

If you are reading this email, consider yourselves activated.

May the best person win.

Your friend,

Murray Hill

P.S. Ben Ripley sucks!!!!!

acknowledgments

It's probably not going to be a shock to anyone that this book was inspired by a cruise.

It was a Disney cruise—although I am going to point out right away that the *Emperor of the Seas* is not based on the Disney Cruise Line in any way. That ship, its myriad problems and number of crimes, is entirely fictional. In truth, my cruise made me realize that a mission at sea could be a great deal of fun—and the Disney Cruise staff was exceptionally generous in answering my questions. While I couldn't get tours of the bridge or the engine room, I was allowed to speak to several officers about the intricacies of running a cruise ship, and was even allowed to visit some of the areas that are generally off-limits to guests, such as the kitchens. So I am very thankful to everyone at Disney Cruise Line for their help.

I also talked at length with Alan Zachary, a writer and lyricist for many of the musicals that have been performed aboard Disney cruises, and am very thankful to him for his help—and his description of what might go wrong with a show during bad weather. Alan is the brother of one of my dearest friends, Marc Zachary, who—by coincidence—also happens to be very close friends with Gibson Frasier, the narrator of my audiobooks. Therefore, I had met Gib twenty years before he was selected to be my reader. Which reminds me that I am woefully delinquent in thanking Gib for all the fine work he has done on this series over the years. If you ever enjoyed a Spy School, FunJungle, or Moon Base Alpha book on audio, that has a huge amount to do with Gib's wonderful readings.

After the cruise, there was still plenty of research to do for this book, so thanks to my summer intern, Caroline Curran, for all her help with that. It was a bummer that the 2020 pandemic prevented us from ever being able to actually meet in person, but she did an amazing job remotely. And thanks, once again, to Mingo Reynolds, RJ Bernocco, and everyone at the Kelly Writers House at the University of Pennsylvania for finding me such great interns every year.

Then there's my incredible team at Simon & Schuster, starting with my editor, Krista Vitola, who spearheaded the fast-tracking of this book, and also Justin Chanda, Lucy Cummins, Kendra Levin, Dainese Santos, Catherine Laudone, Anne Zafian, Milena Giunco, Audrey Gibbons, Lisa Moraleda, Jenica Nasworthy, Chrissy Noh, Anna Jarzab, Brian Murray, Devin MacDonald, Christina Pecorale, Victor Iannone, Emily Hutton, Emily Ritter, and Theresa Pang. And massive thanks to my incredible agent, Jennifer Joel, for making all this possible.

Thanks to my amazing fellow writers (and support group) James Ponti, Sarah Mlynowski, Julie Buxbaum, Christina Soontornvat, Karina Yan Glaser, Max Brallier, Gordon Korman, Julia Devillers, Leslie Margolis, Elizabeth Eulberg, and Rose Brock.

Thanks to all the school librarians and parent associations who have arranged for me to visit, all the bookstore owners and employees who have shilled my books, and all the amazingly tireless festival organizers and volunteers who have invited me to participate.

Thanks to the home team: Ronald and Jane Gibbs; Suz, Darragh, and Ciara Howard; Megan Vicente; and Georgia Simon.

Finally, thanks to my fellow cruise mates, Barry and Carole Patmore, Alan Patmore and Sarah Cradeur—and, of course, my favorite research assistants, Dashiell and Violet, who helped me explore as much of the cruise ship as possible. D and V, you are excellent travelers, idea generators, sounding boards, and junior editors. I love you both more than words can say.

A Reading Group Guide to
Spy School at Sea
by Stuart Gibbs

About the Book

In the ninth and latest addition to the *New York Times* bestselling Spy School series, Ben Ripley faces his nemesis, Murray Hill, on the high seas. Thanks to the evidence Ben uncovered in his investigation of the Croatoan, the CIA has tracked Murray Hill to Central America, where they believe he is boarding the world's biggest cruise ship, the *Emperor of the Seas*, on its maiden voyage around the world. His mission: pose as part of a family—with Alexander and Catherine Hale as his parents, Erica as his sister, and his best friend, Mike, as his brother—to find out what Murray is plotting. At first, having a mission on the most glamorous ocean liner on earth sounds exciting; however, as usual, nothing goes according to plan. There is action, danger, and plenty of surprises as Ben and his team quickly find themselves in hot water.

Discussion Questions

The following questions may be utilized throughout the study of *Spy School at Sea* as reflective writing prompts, or they can be used as targeted questions for group discussion and reflection.

1. Though the Croatoan was defeated, the latest classified document reveals that Murray Hill is once again up to his nefarious ways. Despite his blunders, what makes Murray someone to be taken very seriously?

2. In *Spy School at Sea*, Ben and his team are assigned to Operation Deadly Manatee aboard the *Emperor of the Seas* cruise ship. Are there ways in which this mission is more challenging than their earlier assignments? If so, what might those be?

3. The CIA Deputy Director of Operations tells Ben's principal that the "'Director has been very impressed with the performance of these agents-in-training.'" Though he is seemingly pleased, can you think of reasons why the principal may not be particularly excited by this praise? Why has the principal's relationship with Ben and his peers been such a tumultuous one?

4. CIA Deputy Director Indira Kapoor offers, "'You have all handled yourselves capably and acted with ingenuity and skill, which is obviously a testament to the education you have received at this institution.'" Why does seeing her principal take credit for the successes of their team upset Erica so?

5. After learning that their mission will be carried out on the *Emperor of the Seas*, Mike exclaims, "'Awesome! It's supposed to be the most amazing ship ever built! There's a bunch of swimming pools and miniature golf and a ropes course and a rock wall and a water park!'" Why does Deputy Kapoor seem irritated by Mike's enthusiasm for this mission? Is Mike's approach to remind Deputy Kapoor that they should look like "normal tourists" a wise one? Explain your answer.

6. Catherine addresses Ben, Mike, and Erica, saying, "'I know that you children have served your country well and faced considerable danger on several other missions. But you're still . . . well, children.'" What do you think of Catherine's argument? Do you think the CIA is taking advantage of these young agents? If so, in what ways?

7. Deputy Kapoor tells Ben, "'Agent Ripley, you probably understand Murray Hill better than anyone else at this agency.'" Do you think his previous experiences facing Murray Hill give Ben an advantage? Explain your answer.

8. Zoe tells the group, "'This stinks. Why aren't they sending me on this mission, too? I've been a student here way longer than Mike has. And I contributed just as much to our missions as Mike did in Mexico and London.'" In what ways is Zoe's work as a junior agent at DADD keeping her from being assigned to assist?

9. Though Ben would typically be delighted to get to spend a great deal of time with Erica on a mission, he is fearful that this one will be a disaster because of what was revealed to her sister, Trixie. Is his reaction and fear warranted? How do you predict Erica will react when she learns the truth?

10. Readers discover that Erica is "extremely protective of Trixie," so much so that she doesn't reveal to Ben that she has a sister. Why would the Hale family go to such great lengths to keep this secret from one of their own? Do you agree or disagree with their choice?

11. Ben tells Mike, "'Erica is like a human lie detector. She always finds out the truth.'" Consider what you've discovered about Erica from *Spy School at Sea* as well as from earlier missions. Do you believe this to be an accurate description of her?

12. Ben points out all the ways this assignment could end poorly, reminding Mike of how close they'd come to dying on their last mission to the tropics. Mike replies, "'But we didn't. Not only did we stay alive, but we also saved the day and thwarted the bad guys. Face it, Ben, we're pretty good at this spy thing.'" Compare Ben's and Mike's attitudes toward this new mission. Which of them do you believe has the more appropriate approach and why?

13. Ben had been excited to see Nicaragua, the starting point of the journey; however, he's disappointed by the lack of opportunity due to the cruise ship experience. The passengers are immediately put on tour buses and shuttled to the cruise ship terminal to wait in long lines and are treated like kindergarteners. Have you ever had a similar experience where a trip hasn't gone the way you expected? If so, where was it and what happened?

14. When Ben shares his suspicions that Murray's taken the "cushy route" by staying in expensive accommodations aboard the cruise ship, Catherine tells the group they can't stay in first class because "'espionage may be extremely important, but most operations still have shoestring budgets.'" Do you find this news surprising? Think of all that's involved in a CIA operation like this. What kinds of things need to be paid for?

15. Though Koolnezz, the teen club on board the ship, ffers dance parties, arcade games, Ping-Pong, karaoke, and trivia, Ben and his friends have to feign interest in visiting and participating. Why aren't they more excited? Would you enjoy spending time in a place like that?

16. After accidentally trespassing on a well-known drug trafficker's private property, Ben and Mike discover that El Diablo is a complicated, complex individual. What do you learn while reading about El Diablo that supports that statement?

17. Consider Ben's reaction to discovering that Jessica Shang and her mother are owners of the *Emperor of the Seas*. How does Shayla Shang's behavior complicate matters for his relationship with Jessica?

18. After being captured by Murray and Dane, Ben attempts to learn about the evil plans that are underway. Murray, unwilling to share, tells Ben, "'You're the one being devious here, Ben. Very cunning of you. With your mind and my schemes, we would have made a great team.'" What do you think of Murray's statement? Do you believe his assessment of Ben is correct? If so, in what ways?

19. How does almost drowning in the ocean and being saved by Mike help Ben better appreciate his friend? What are some of the specific ways Mike shows his fortitude?

20. What are your earliest impressions of Bjorn Turok? Given what is learned about him throughout the course of the novel, do you believe him to be truly different from his cousin, Dane Brammage? Explain your answers.

21. After discovering that the ship contains stolen national treasures from China, the team realizes that the *Emperor of the Seas* is being used for a number of criminal endeavors. In what ways does learning this complicate their mission?

22. Thinking about the events of *Spy School at Sea* and the Spy School series in general, what's been your favorite mission that Ben and his team have undertaken so far? Explain your answer using examples from the books.

23. After Ben manipulates Murray into believing Zoe reciprocates his feelings to get him to assist them in defusing a bomb he'd set, Murray tells Ben, "'You've made it personal.

So now, in return for all the trouble you've caused me, I'm going to destroy you, Ben Ripley.'" Do you think Ben has anything to worry about? What do you predict will happen when the two next face off?

Extension Activities

1. In *Spy School at Sea*, readers learn that the *Emperor of the Seas* is run on nuclear power. Working with a partner, learn more about how nuclear power is harnessed and used to run ships and a variety of other things by researching the following:

- What is nuclear power?
- How is it created and used?
- In what ways is it useful as a source of energy?
- What makes it dangerous?
- Besides ships, what else uses nuclear power and energy?
- What are other interesting facts you've uncovered?

After completing your investigation, share your discoveries with others.

2. In *Spy School at Sea*, the grand scale of the fictional *Emperor of the Seas* is considered at length, but what goes into designing and building a real cruise ship? Discover more by first watching "Sail Away! New Technology in Cruise Ship Design" here: https://www.youtube.com/watch?v=drA7Dc-osCo. After viewing, participate in a group discussion about the ways author Stuart Gibbs's ship is similar to or different from what you learned. Then create a wish list of what you'd want included if you were part of a ship design team.

3. In *Spy School at Sea*, the team discovers that their cruise ship is being used to transport priceless, stolen clay Chinese soldiers from the Terra Cotta Army. Using this article, "Terra Cotta Soldiers on the March" from *Smithsonian* magazine (https://www.smithsonianmag.com/history/terra-cotta-soldiers-on-the-march-30942673/), learn more about these antiquities. Be sure to discover:

- Where were these warriors originally found, and by whom?
- What made this archeological find so important?
- How many clay statues were uncovered?
- What do these pits of soldiers help us understand about the leader who commissioned their creations?
- Why are pieces like this so valuable and vulnerable?

After reading, join a small group for a focused discussion about the article and how it relates to what you learned while reading *Spy School at Sea*.

4. *In Spy School at Sea*, readers learn that the children's education continues onboard the *Emperor of the Seas*. Using library and internet resources, research more about schools on cruise ships, being sure to discover the following:

- What types of schools at sea exist?
- What are the age ranges of most students?
- What are reasons young people go to school on boats or cruise ships?
- Are there any specific benefits for a young person in doing so?

After completing your research, share the three most interesting things you learned with your peers.

5. After Mike rescues Ben from the ocean, their perilous journey ends in northern Costa Rica where they marvel over witnessing sea turtles coming ashore to lay their eggs. Begin your focused learning by visiting the National Ocean Service's site here: https://oceanservice.noaa.gov/facts/turtle -hatch.html. After building a basic understanding of how sea turtles hatch, use other resources to learn more about sea turtles and their conservation, focusing on the following:

- Besides the National Ocean Service, which is run by the

U.S. Department of Commerce, what other conservation groups focus on sea turtles?

- Beyond predators, what are the greatest dangers to sea turtles and their eggs/hatchlings?
- What are some specific things that young people can do to help?

After completing your research, share your new knowledge with others.

This guide was created by Dr. Rose Brock, an associate professor in Library Science Department in the College of Education at Sam Houston State University. Dr. Brock holds a Ph.D. in Library Science, specializing in children's and young adult literature.

This guide has been provided by Simon & Schuster for classroom, library, and reading group use. It may be reproduced in its entirety or excerpted for these purposes. For more Simon & Schuster guides, please visit simonandschuster.net or thebookpantry.net.

Turn the page for a
sneak peek of
spy school
project X!

SELF-PRESERVATION

Lyman Gymnasium

The CIA's Academy of Espionage

Washington, DC

June 11

1200 hours

I had an emergency meeting with the principal.

As if finals at spy school weren't stressful enough.

I used to go to a normal middle school, so I'm aware that exam weeks everywhere are difficult, but ours was brutal. Not just mentally—but often physically as well.

For example, an algebra exam in regular middle school might have a few questions on working out parabolas—while an algebra exam at spy school entailed having live grenades lobbed at you. The grenades were loaded with paint instead of explosives, so they would merely color you blue, rather than blow your limbs off, but still, the test was so traumatic, it frequently left students gibbering in fear. I'm lucky enough to be gifted in mathematics, and yet, there's a very big difference between doing a complex equation in a nice, quiet classroom as opposed to a muddy foxhole with paint-filled explosives raining down on you.

And that was one of the easier exams.

The most difficult was in Advanced Self-Preservation. It also happened to be the most painful.

Well, it wasn't painful if you were *good* at self-preservation. In that case, the exam could be rather hazardous for your instructor. But I wasn't good at self-preservation at all.

Everyone has their strengths. Mine happen to be more cerebral. I'm quite skilled at deducing what bad guys are plotting and then figuring out how to defeat them. This wasn't only in a classroom setting: I had faced *actual* bad guys a surprising number of times, given that I was only in my second year of spy school. Due to some extraordinary circumstances, I had managed to prevent evil organizations from dismantling the planet's electrical grid, destroying the Panama Canal, assassinating the president of the United States, and melting Antarctica. And that was just in the spring semester.

Unfortunately, at spy school, we didn't get good grades for successful missions. In fact, we still had to make up the homework we missed while we were away.

To be honest, I've gotten much better at self-preservation since coming to spy school. I could probably defeat the average person in a fight. But when you're a spy, you don't get attacked by *average* people. You have trained killers come after you. And so, to properly prepare us for the field, the exams in Advanced Self-Preservation were extremely difficult.

The final involved a little-known Tibetan style of martial arts known as Nook-Bhan-San, which loosely translates as "Wow, That *Really* Hurts." Each student had to fight one of the academy's many martial arts instructors. If we could defeat them, we would get an A. Personally, I felt that was highly unlikely. The best I could hope for was a D, which involved losing the fight, but not getting sent to the school infirmary.

I would have been nervous enough about the self-preservation exam on a normal day, but the impending meeting with the principal made everything worse. The principal had two basic personalities, angry and incompetent, and he tended to swing back and forth between them without any warning at all, so being with him was never a pleasant experience. He also had said that my life depended on this meeting, which made me even more anxious.

Then, to top things off, Professor Crandall had been late for the exam. Crandall was an elderly and doddering instructor with a big secret; in truth, he was very aware and capable, but only pretended to be in decline to throw off his enemies. (I was one of the few people who knew this, having learned of it during my first mission, and had sworn not to tell anyone.) Crandall was exceptionally good at the doddering act, and his lectures were famous for being incredibly boring and only vaguely coherent. In his final class of the semester, he had rambled on for a half hour about how to protect yourself against Vikings, even though the last time they had been a threat was 1000 AD.

The exam took place in the school gymnasium. Two students at a time were paired with instructors to fight. Crandall sat in the stands, ostensibly watching the proceedings, although he seemed to keep nodding off. (Like I said, he was a very good actor.) Normally, I would have been in no rush to get my butt kicked, but I was hoping to go early so that I could still make my meeting with the principal.

Instead, I was placed in the final pairing.

By then, I knew there was very little chance that I would get to the meeting on time, which would certainly incur the wrath of the principal. I never enjoyed incurring wrath, but the only way to be punctual would be to throw my exam. That would be extremely painful, and I enjoyed pain even less than wrath. Also, I didn't want to get an F in self-preservation and have to take the course over again the next semester.

So I tried my best.

The student who was selected to compete at the same time as me was Zoe Zibbell.

For much of my time at spy school, Zoe had been my closest friend, although we had recently hit a bumpy patch. Zoe had thought that one of our fellow students had switched to working for the bad guys and had gone behind my back to try to have them arrested. Her intentions were good—although she was wrong about the other student—but I had felt betrayed. Zoe had apologized profusely, and I knew she meant it. Yet things were still awkward between us.

Zoe didn't look impressive physically, being small and slight of build, but she was a formidable fighter. Plus, her size sometimes worked to her advantage. Her opponent, a wiry, muscular instructor, had certainly been told not to underestimate her—and then he did it anyhow. In under a minute, Zoe had him pinned to the mat and howling in pain, an A-plus performance for sure.

My own exam didn't go nearly as well. I was matched against a young woman with muscles so taut, they looked like iron bands. I started out decently well, employing a Nook-Bhan-San move called "Fast as Lightning." This wasn't really an attack. Instead, I just darted about quickly in an unpredictable pattern, hoping that my opponent might grow tired of chasing me around before she got the chance to hurt me. It wasn't the sort of technique that earned you an A, but then, it was a lot less painful than staying put and getting punched in the nose.

Unfortunately, my opponent responded with a move called "Even Faster Than Lightning" where she simply moved quicker than I did, then locked her hand around my wrist with the Grip of Extreme Stickiness and unleashed the Ordeal of a Thousand Smacks to the Face. I managed to slip free of her grasp with the Greased Snow Monkey, although my attempt to counterattack with the Fist of Annihilation failed miserably when she executed a perfect Evasive Yeti Maneuver and all I ended up punching was air.

But then, to my surprise, my opponent made a mistake. She shifted into the unmistakable stance of Pangolin Death Strike, for which the proper response was to drop to the floor and implement a Golden Jackal Leg Sweep. So I did it. In fact, it was the finest Golden Jackal Leg Sweep I had ever performed. There were sixteen separate movements, and I made each one of them perfectly.

Only, it didn't work. My opponent didn't perform the Pangolin Death Strike at all. Instead, she nimbly leapt out of the way of my leg sweep and dropped on top of me, driving her elbow into my solar plexus.

One moment, I thought I was about to win the match—and the next, I was pinned.

Professor Crandall came down from the stands, clucking his tongue in disappointment. "Oh, Benjamin, you walked right into that one. In dropping to the floor, you left yourself wide open for the lethal Here Comes the Avalanche move."

"But you never taught us about the Here Comes the Avalanche move!" I protested. "That's not fair!"

"When you're on a mission, the bad guys are rarely going to play fair," Crandall informed me. "You need to be prepared for *anything*. I'm afraid I'll have to give you a D minus for that performance."

"But . . . ," I spluttered, peeling myself off the floor. "That was my best Golden Jackal Leg Sweep ever!"

"Perhaps so, but this is Advanced Self-Preservation, not Interpretive Dance. In a real-life fight, you don't get points for style. And if you lose, you end up dead. Oh goodness, there appears to be a slice of cheese in my pocket." Crandall removed what was, in fact, a slice of cheese from his fleece vest and looked at it in wonderment, as if its presence was one of the great mysteries of the universe.

At this moment, I began to question how much of Professor Crandall's doddering act was an act and how much was actual doddering.

I really wanted to stay and argue that I deserved a better

grade than a D minus, but I reluctantly had to admit that Professor Crandall had made a valid argument about what real-life fights were like—and I was now late for my meeting with the principal.

"I have to go," I said.

"Have a nice summer!" Crandall told me cheerfully, then nibbled the cheese he'd discovered and exclaimed, "Ooh! It's Havarti! My favorite!"

I grabbed my backpack and headed for the door, moving a little slower than I'd intended, as I was still aching from the Here Comes the Avalanche.

Zoe dropped in beside me, doing her best to act like her extremely supportive pre-betrayal self. "That was really uncool of Crandall just now. You performed one of the best Golden Jackal Leg Sweeps I've seen all semester!"

"Maybe, but Crandall's right about what it's like in the field."

"Yeah. I guess you would know." There was a great deal of jealousy in Zoe's voice. She had recently managed to land an internship with the Double Agent Detection Division, which hadn't turned out to be nearly as exciting as she'd hoped. "While I was stuck working for DADD, you got to go to Central America and prevent a cruise ship from exploding."

"I nearly got killed on that mission," I reminded her. "Multiple times."

"I know. You're so lucky." This statement wasn't said with the slightest bit of sarcasm. Zoe really meant it. "Was this your last exam?"

"Yeah."

"Mine too. Are you heading back to the dorm to pack for spy camp?"

Normally, that's what I *would* have been doing. We were scheduled to begin our summer of wilderness training in a few days. However, I couldn't tell Zoe about my meeting with the principal, as it was classified. All I could say was, "In a bit. But I have to do something else first."

"Like what?" Zoe asked suspiciously.

We exited the gymnasium into Hammond Quadrangle. It was a glorious late spring day. The sun was shining, and yet, there wasn't a trace of the usual wilting humidity that Washington, DC, was famous for. The lawn of the quad was lush and green and fringed with flowers. Many of our fellow students were reveling in being done with their exams—playing frisbee, kicking soccer balls, or basking in the sun.

"Just a meeting," I said. "With an adviser."

Zoe gave me a doubtful look. "What is it really? A top secret conference? Are you being sent on *another* mission?"

"No! I swear."

"I bet. You're probably going to get air-dropped onto

Mount Everest to defuse a nuclear bomb or something amazing like that."

"Defusing nuclear bombs isn't amazing. It's terrifying."

"Well, I wouldn't know, would I? I haven't ever gotten to do it. But you have. Like four times."

"Only two of the bombs I defused were nuclear."

"Do you even hear yourself? Do you realize how fortunate you are? Most students don't get to defuse a bomb until their sixth year here—and those are just pretend ones for class. On your last mission, you got to disarm a real nuke, go undercover in exotic locations, *and* chase a speedboat on a WaveRunner! That's awesome! All I ever get to do at DADD is staple expense reports together."

I was about to counter Zoe's argument, but didn't for two reasons.

First, that WaveRunner chase had actually been pretty cool.

Second, the principal was coming across the quad toward me.

It was easy to see him approaching, as all the other students were giving him a wide berth. He looked even angrier than usual, so everyone was behaving as though he was radioactive, hurrying out of his path.

In addition, he hadn't bothered to put his toupee on properly. Even on good days, his hairpiece looked like a mangy badger camped out on his head, but today it seemed he'd forgotten it even existed, so it was completely askew, leaving a good portion of his bald, sweaty brow gleaming in the sunlight.

"You!" he exclaimed upon seeing me, and then pointed a thick, meaty finger my way. "You have a lot of nerve, Ripley!"

All around the quad, I noticed my fellow students experiencing dual emotions: genuine concern for my well-being—and relief that the principal wasn't angry at *them*.

While I had feared the principal would be upset at me for being late to the meeting, the level of fury in his eyes was far greater than I had expected. Still, I did my best to explain as he approached. "Sir, I'm very sorry that I kept you waiting. My exam in self-preservation went long . . ."

"That's true!" Zoe added, even though she knew this was risking the anger of the principal. "You can ask Professor Crandall yourself! He's right over there!" She pointed back to the gymnasium. Crandall had just exited the building, although he seemed preoccupied, clutching a kosher pickle with bemusement. I suspected he had recently discovered it in another one of his pockets.

"What are you even talking about?" the principal snapped at me. "I'm not angry about you being late! I'm angry about *this*!" He thrust a handwritten note in my face.

It read:

> To the principal,
> You are a jerk, a buffoon, a
> numbskull, a dolt, and a fathead.
> Also, you smell like a diseased
> pustule on the butt of a wildebeest.
> I'll be in the quad if you'd like to
> discuss this further.
> Sincerely,
> Ben Ripley

Many things were strange about this letter, but the most startling to me was that it was in my own handwriting. If I hadn't known better, I would have believed that I had actually written it.

"This was wrapped around a rock and thrown into my office five minutes ago!" the principal proclaimed.

It usually would have been quite difficult to throw a rock into the principal's office, as it was on the top floor of the Nathan Hale Building, five stories above the quad. However, the exterior wall of the office was currently missing, having been demolished the previous September by an errant mortar round. (I was the one who had fired it, although it wasn't really my fault; still, the principal remained annoyed at me for it, which was compounded by the fact that red tape had prevented any repairs from getting done, leaving a gaping hole in the building for the entire school year.) But while this made it *possible* for someone to throw a rock into his office, it still wouldn't have been easy; if I had tried to do it, I probably would have missed the fifth floor entirely and put a rock through one of the lower-level windows instead.

"I checked our handwriting database!" the principal continued indignantly. "This is your handwriting, isn't it?"

"Er . . . yes," I admitted. "But someone must have forged it! Why would I write something like that?"

"Because you're an insolent little pip-squeak!" the principal shouted. "I have half a mind to boot you out of this school!"

"You only have half a mind, period," Zoe muttered under her breath, too low for him to hear.

"This doesn't make any sense," I said to the principal. "I was coming to see *you* for our meeting. So I wouldn't have—"

"What meeting?" the principal demanded. "I didn't schedule any meeting with you today!"

I took a step back, confused. "You didn't send me a message about it yesterday?"

"Absolutely not! And if I *was* going to meet with you, it certainly wouldn't be in my office!"

"Why not?"

"Because you destroyed my office!"

"That wasn't Ben's fault . . . ," Zoe began.

The principal ignored her and kept glaring at me. "Because of you, I have spent the last eight months working at a desk made of two sawhorses and a piece of plywood! But I was finally able to requisition a *real* desk. It was delivered yesterday, and it's beautiful. It's big, expensive, and expertly crafted—and I'm not letting you anywhere near it, Ripley. You're a menace! If you got anywhere near that desk, I'm sure it would catch fire or explode or get eaten by a shark!"

"I think that's all highly unlikely," I said.

"*I* don't," the principal declared. "Not only are you insubordinate, you're also a walking disaster area."

"That's not true," I insisted.

At which point, the principal's office exploded.